The Last
Time
She Saw
Him

ALSO BY KATE WHITE

FICTION

If Looks Could Kill

A Body to Die For

Till Death Do Us Part • *Over Her Dead Body*

Lethally Blond

Hush • *The Sixes*

So Pretty It Hurts

Eyes on You • *The Wrong Man*

The Secrets You Keep

Even If It Kills Her

Such a Perfect Wife

Have You Seen Me? • *The Fiancée*

The Second Husband

Between Two Strangers

NONFICTION

Why Good Girls Don't Get Ahead but Gutsy Girls Do

I Shouldn't Be Telling You This: How to Ask for the Money, Snag the Promotion, and Create the Career You Deserve

The Gutsy Girl Handbook: Your Manifesto for Success

The Last Time She Saw Him

A Novel

Kate White

HARPER LARGE PRINT

An Imprint of HarperCollinsPublishers

HarperCollins books may be purchased for educational, business, or sales promotional use. For information, please e-mail the Special Markets Department at SPsales@harpercollins.com.

FIRST HARPER LARGE PRINT EDITION

ISBN: 978-0-06-338655-6

Library of Congress Cataloging-in-Publication Data is available upon request.

24 25 26 27 28 LBC 5 4 3 2 1

HB 03.25.2024 0216

The Last
Time
She Saw
Him

Prologue

You're really pretty," he told her. "You know that, don't you?"

Though it was dark out, enough moonlight shone for her to see the sly grin that fanned across his face.

She smiled back. He was nice, courteous—chivalrous really. And, of course, good-looking, just as she'd always thought. But over the past few minutes, a dull throb of unease had begun to form in the pit of her stomach. At moments he seemed . . . *too* courteous, and always an inch closer to her than he needed to be.

Besides that, her head was spinning from the booze, not only the vodka he'd brought in a flask but the beer she'd drunk earlier. She'd sampled a few kinds from the microbrewery stands while she waited for him to show up.

She flicked her eyes to the right and squinted, trying to see through the thick cluster of trees they were standing in. There were bursts of colored lights, and she could still hear the noise from the fairgrounds—music, clanging, the roar and rattle of the roller coaster, and the muted screams of riders. But somehow, everything seemed farther away than even a few minutes ago.

The two of them had clearly drifted as they'd been talking, like twigs bobbing in a stream. She remembered him motioning ahead a couple of times, wanting to show her a constellation through the tree branches.

She breathed deeply, trying to force her thoughts to make sense of things.

"I should get back," she said, the words sounding a little slurred to her ears.

"Really?" he asked. "Why the rush?"

For the first time she noticed the smell of alcohol on his breath, and she had to fight the urge to gag.

"It's, you know, getting late."

"It's not that late. Besides, I like having a chance to talk to you alone, without a ton of people around. I've wanted to get to know you for a while."

That was nice to hear, but this didn't seem like the best way for them to find out more about each other. "Maybe . . . maybe we could do something together one night."

"Aren't we doing something together now?"

"Yeah, I was just thinking we could have dinner. Or, like, see a movie."

She heard him snicker under his breath. "You girls never like freebies, do you?"

"What do you mean?" she said, feeling her brow crease.

"Women are always looking for a *date* date, aren't they? But what's wrong with having the woods to ourselves, not having to be part of any scene?"

"I just—" The throb of worry was back. She darted her gaze toward the right again, peering through the trees. Everything seemed so distant.

"No, no, I get it," he said. "And you're right, we should go. Time to call it a night."

He stepped back a little, crunching a few twigs under his shoes and giving her some breathing room. She felt the tension drain from her shoulders. It was going to be okay.

She put one foot ahead of her and tried to see into the darkness. The only problem was that she had no idea how to find her way back to the gap in the fence that they'd slipped through to get to the woods.

"Not that way, though," he said, pressing a hand lightly to her arm. "There's a faster way to reach the parking lot. That's where your car is, right?"

"Yeah."

"I'll make sure you get to it."

"Thanks."

He shifted his hand to her elbow, guiding her. She stumbled, almost falling flat on her face, but he caught her just in time.

"You okay?" he asked. "Do you want to hold on to me?"

"No, I'm all right."

A piney scent rushed to her nostrils. They were snaking through trees now, a denser patch than where they'd been before, and the bursts of light were no longer visible. When she stretched her arm in front of her, she could barely see her hand.

"You're doing great," he told her from behind. "It's not much farther."

"But I don't see the parking lot."

"We just keep bearing to the right and then it's straight in front of us. You can't quite tell from here because the lights are lower there."

Her thoughts seemed to swim in her head, struggling to stay above water.

"Okay. But—"

"But, but, but."

There was an edge to his tone, and her heart froze.

"Sorry," she said, trying to sound agreeable. "I was just wondering."

"You should wonder less, you know that?"

That edge again, but stronger this time. Fear foamed through every inch of her. She had to do something, but *what*?

"Yeah, I know," she said, struggling to keep her voice light.

She slowed her pace a tiny bit and strained to hear through the darkness. There was no more music, no clang of the rides, no engines starting.

Her fear mushroomed into full-blown panic. They were lost or headed the wrong way. She needed to get back to the gap in the fence.

Go, she told herself. *Go now.*

And then she was off, stumbling over rocks and branches and tree roots, blood pounding in her ears. *Don't stop running*, she ordered herself.

But fast as a bang from a firecracker, his arm shot from behind and jerked her backward. His hand fumbled roughly around her face and then, before she could cry out, it clamped down hard against her mouth. Seconds later she was shoved forward until her body hit the ground, face forward, knocking the breath out of her.

1

I shouldn't have come to the party tonight. I had some misgivings as soon as I accepted the invitation, and they only grew today as I drove from Manhattan and checked into the inn. Now, as I stand on the front stoop of my friend Ava's house, the qualms are suddenly strong enough to make my stomach twist. It's too soon for me to be here. It will be excruciatingly awkward. People will start buzzing the moment they spot me.

But there are reasons I had for coming, and since I've driven all this way, I'm going to have to suck it up and make the best of things.

It's Ava who answers my knock, and she graciously ushers me into the foyer of her charming eighteenth-century house.

"Oh, *Kiki*," she says, embracing me warmly. "I'm thrilled to see you, dear."

"The feeling's mutual," I exclaim, hugging her back. "It's so great to be here."

And in one sense, I'm totally sincere. I love this house, with its low, wood-beamed ceilings and endless warren of floral-scented rooms. More importantly I've really missed Ava, my former boss and mentor—and savior, too—who's since become a good friend. I just have to tamp down the part of myself that wants to turn on my heel and flee.

"Tonight should be fun," she says, beaming. "We've had a great turnout."

"Oh, that's wonderful. Vic must be so pleased."

From the hum in the rooms behind us, I estimate that there are already twenty-five to thirty people here. I steal a glance through the door into the cream-colored parlor. Though it's early August, most of the men are sporting navy blazers; the women are in flowy Eileen Fisher–style dresses or silky blouses over pants.

Have I overdone it, I wonder, in my short black cocktail dress? Not if I use Ava as a measure. She's super elegant in cropped turquoise pants and a matching silk tunic that looks beautiful against her caramel-colored skin. Though there are crow's-feet in the corners of her deep brown eyes, it's hard to believe that she's in her midfifties.

"The bar is in the study, per usual," she says, "and I think that's where Vic is holding court at the moment. He's dying to see you, Kiki."

Victor Davenport, a highly regarded historian and Ava's husband of five years, is tonight's guest of honor. His new book, a fresh look at the Salem witch trials, has just been published, and Ava decided to host a celebratory dinner party here at their home in Litchfield County, Connecticut.

"I'll go find him and say hello."

"Good, and I'll look for you later. Daphne's already here, by the way, and she's very eager to meet you."

"Thank you," I say, giving an inner sigh of relief. Daphne is the other reason I talked myself into coming—and I'd be kicking myself if she hadn't shown up for some reason.

"And Jamie," I ask, lowering my voice, "is he here yet?"

"Yes," Ava says, keeping her own voice close to a whisper. "The last time I saw him, he was with a group in the solarium."

My breath hitches a little as I picture him only a few yards away from where I'm standing. Though he and I have spoken on the phone, it's been more than four months since I've laid eyes on him, and it was a tense encounter to say the least.

"You okay about this?" she asks.

"Yes, I'm fine, thanks."

"Good," she says with an empathetic nod. "And just so you're aware, there's a woman with him."

"Yup, he told me he was bringing someone. That's okay, too."

The doorbell rings and Ava gives my arm a comforting squeeze before turning to greet her next guests. I inhale deeply, then make my way through the parlor to the study. Candles are burning everywhere, creating the amber glow I so associate with this house at nighttime. Though I've always found that glow enchanting, there's an odd, melancholy cast this evening. At least to me.

The pewter-gray, bookshelf-lined study is even more crowded with guests than the parlor. Knowing I'll have a glass of wine with dinner, I ask the bartender for a sparkling water. As I fish out the lemon slice he's dropped in the drink, I let my eye roam the room discreetly. From what Ava had told me, the crowd tonight is a mix of local friends and people from the book world, some of whom have driven out from the city for the occasion, and others who live in the area either full-time or on weekends.

I didn't see Vic when I first entered the room, but I spot him now against the far wall of bookshelves, talking intently to a bespectacled fortyish man with a closely cropped beard and mustache, who I'm pretty sure is his agent, Dan. Probably best not to interrupt right this second. Unlike most of his male guests, Vic has opted for jeans along with a white linen shirt. He's a rule breaker of sorts, something Ava seems to find beguiling. In so many ways, they are an improbable pair—him a sixtysomething, sometimes edgy, somewhat pretentious, twice-divorced author/lecturer/retired professor, and her a warm, inclusive, even-tempered former head of HR for a midsize media company, who'd never married before.

And there's also the fact that Vic is white, and Ava is Black. But after meeting five and a half years ago at another dinner party, they discovered that, despite how different their backgrounds are, they have a chemistry most people would kill for.

With a start I notice that Jamie's best friend, Sam, is in the room, but there's no sign of Jamie yet. Perhaps he's still in the solarium. I take another long, deep breath, trying to steady my nerves. How's it going to feel, I wonder for the hundredth time this week, to run into the man I almost married in June—and to see him with another woman, no less?

When the invitation for the party appeared in my inbox, I knew Jamie must have been invited, too. He'd been renting a small weekend cottage in the area for years—it's where he'd spent summers with his parents as a kid—and he and Vic, despite their age gap, had eventually become tennis buddies. Then I entered Jamie's life a couple of years ago and started spending weekends here, too. It was pure luck that Vic's wife happened to be a good friend of mine, and it meant that I could spend more time with Ava, something that had been tough to do since she retired early to take up residence with Vic here in the countryside, leaving New York behind.

Though I hated having to send my regrets for the party, I decided it was best, but when I called Ava to RSVP, she explained Jamie had a business trip scheduled for the week of the party—he runs a small money management company specializing in socially responsible investing—and wouldn't be coming. "Then count me in," I'd told her, delighted. Days later she emailed to say that Jamie's business trip had been canceled and he was coming after all. She would understand if I changed my mind.

But by then, I was invested in coming, in the chance to be back, if only for a little while, in that magical world that Ava had created with Vic. Besides, she'd since promised to introduce me to a literary agent friend who was spending the summer in the area and would be attending the party. I'd confided in Ava that I'd been hammering out a proposal for a nonfiction book based on my work as a career coach, and she thought this agent might be interested in it.

And since there was a good chance I'd eventually run into Jamie in New York anyway, I convinced myself it would be smart to rip off the Band-Aid sooner rather than later.

"Kiki."

I spin around and find myself face-to-face with Tori Larsson, the wife of Jamie's first cousin Liam, and not someone I'd expected to encounter. She's wearing an attractive beige shift, but the only makeup on her face is a brownish-pink lipstick, and her long, wheat-colored hair is tucked simply behind her ears. Tori, who like her husband is close to fifty, isn't one to fuss with her appearance.

"Tori, hello, this—"

"I know, you're probably surprised to see me here," she interrupts and then, a few beats later, smiles wanly. Tori's always had what I think of as a *delayed* smile, as if it takes her brain a few seconds to remind her face to do it. "Ava joined the library board, and since I've been helping her out with the fundraiser, we've gotten to know each other a little."

"How nice that you two have the chance to work together," I tell Tori sincerely. "By the way, thanks again for your email. It meant a lot to me."

She'd sent me a note after Jamie and I broke up, saying she was sorry to hear the news and wishing me well. It was more than what most people had done— and more than I'd expected from Tori. Though we've always gotten on well enough, she's generally pretty reserved and plays her cards close to the vest.

"Well, I'm sure it wasn't an easy time for you," she says. "Are you doing okay?"

"Pretty well. I've been busy with work, so that helps."

"It doesn't slow down for you during the summer?"

"The corporate training assignments do because people are on vacation, but not the private coaching. By midyear people start to worry that they're not where they'd hoped to be, and they want to hit the ground running in the fall."

"Why aren't they where they'd hoped to be?" she asks, her dark eyes narrowed.

"Ah, good question. Generally, because they either got complacent or kept waiting for the perfect moment instead of making that moment happen. Speaking of work, are you still enjoying yours at the library?"

She's a library assistant, a job she started just a year or so ago after being out of the workforce for a while.

Jamie told me that she'd once been in real estate but had quit several years ago, saying she needed a break. Had the reason been more complicated than that? I'd wondered. Sometimes I've sensed that Tori's reserve masks a deep disappointment over the way things turned out for her. That perhaps *she* isn't where she hoped to be at this point in her life.

"It's a job," she replies with a shrug. "And as you said, it's nice working with Ava."

"How's Liam? And Taylor? He's living in Fort Myers, right?"

I've met her son, Taylor—who must be about twenty-seven or twenty-eight by now—just once, at a family reunion, and I know that after dropping out of college, he struggled to find a career path.

"Well, actually—that's where he lived for the first three years, but he moved closer to Miami last summer. He's teaching at a really nice sailing school there."

I can almost feel the relief in her words.

"Wow, that's great. Didn't he used to teach sailing around here during the summers?"

Tori nods. "As for Liam, he's actually here tonight, too," she adds. "He's not generally a fan of parties, but he knew I wanted to come." She raises the glass of red wine she's holding. "Which reminds me, I promised to bring him a drink before he goes outside for a cigarette."

"I hope I have a chance to say hi to him later." Though I wasn't any closer to Liam than I was to Tori, things were always cordial between us.

"I'm sure you will. By the way," she adds, lowering her voice, "you know Jamie's here, right?"

"Yes. The two of us cleared it with each other, don't worry."

As she moves away, I follow her with my eyes until I see her join Liam in the hallway outside the study. Unlike Jamie, who was raised in Boston and spent weekends and a big part of the summer here with his parents as a kid, Liam grew up in the area. He joined the army for a few years instead of attending college and now runs a local plywood distribution company. Though Liam is reserved like his wife and a straight-arrow kind of guy, Jamie is fond of him. They both lost their fathers within the past ten years—Liam's of cancer and Jamie's in a car crash—and they share a special bond with their fathers' surviving brother, Drew, an artist who lives in Litchfield County, too.

Tori touches Liam's elbow and I see him mouth *thank you* as he accepts the wine. When he and Jamie are standing side by side, it's easy to accept that they're cousins. Not by their physiques—where Jamie's tall and slim, Liam's only about five nine, and super compact—but they've got the same deep blue eyes and dark blond hair.

I'm just turning back to the bar, ready for another sparkling water, when I hear Jamie's voice behind me. I actually gulp at the sound.

"Sure," he's saying. "I could play Saturday, but also any weekday. I'm actually here for most of August."

He seems to be scheduling a tennis game, and though my back is to him, I can see him clearly in my mind's eye—the pale eyebrows, strong nose, high cheekbones, and those lovely eyes. He was by far the handsomest man I'd ever dated. I picture his body, too, probably very tanned by this point in the summer.

We've had only two brief conversations since our split in March. The first one, in May, was when he'd called me to say his fourteen-year-old golden retriever, Cody, had died, and he thought I'd want to know. I'd loved that dog and had been grateful to Jamie for reaching out. The call had also struck me as a possible olive branch.

I was the one who made the first move the next time, explaining that I'd been invited to Vic's party and asking if he'd mind if I attended. He assured me it was fine. "Besides," he'd said. "You've known Ava even longer than I've known Vic."

I twist my head the tiniest bit, doing my best not to seem obvious. He's talking to a local professor pal of Vic's. His best friend, Sam, is nearby, chatting with

Tori, who's come back into the room. And there's a woman hovering not far from Jamie, dressed in a low-cut royal blue cocktail dress. His date, I assume. She's hazel-eyed like me, with blond hair, too, though not as light as mine, and she's probably in her early thirties, which means she's five or six years younger than I am. Her features are sharp, angular, and her face seems to be frozen in a pout, like she's not pleased with how the night's progressing.

"Glad to hear you're giving yourself some time up here this summer," the professor says. "Surely your clients won't hold that against you."

"Oh, there'll be a fair number of Zooms, I'm sure," I hear Jamie reply. "But I intend to take plenty of afternoons off."

"What will you do when you're not playing tennis with old farts like me?" the professor asks with a chuckle.

Jamie chuckles, too. "Mostly, I want to read a lot, bike a lot, perfect my pomodoro sauce, and learn more about the Norwegian side of my family, which my dad always swore is descended from Vikings."

"Are you thinking of going to Norway one day?"

"Yeah, maybe in February, so I can get a look at the northern lights. I also . . ."

Two guests, chatting loudly, squeeze in next to me

to reach the bar, and I don't hear what Jamie says next. But I've learned all I need to know. Jamie's making plans, staying busy. He's moved on.

The crowd shifts slightly again, reconfiguring like pieces at the end of a kaleidoscope. And then suddenly Jamie and I are face-to-face. He pulls in his breath, perhaps more unnerved than he anticipated at the sight of me.

"Hello, Jamie," I say.

"Hi," he says. He smiles pleasantly but there's a distinct coolness to his tone. His hair, I notice, is shorter than when I saw him in March.

"How's your summer going?" I ask.

"Pretty well. Yours?"

"Okay. I've been in the city mostly, hanging out on the roof garden when I can."

"It's nice your building has that," he says flatly.

What's he really thinking? That if we were still together, I'd be spending every weekend here with him and taking advantage of the summer weather, rather than baking on the tar beach of a midrise apartment building on the Upper East Side of Manhattan?

"How's your grandmother these days?" I ask.

That's another reason Jamie feels committed to Litchfield County. His grandmother on his father's side, an awe-inspiring retired pediatrician, is in assisted living not far from here and suffering from advancing Alzheimer's.

"I just saw her today as a matter of fact," he says. "Her short-term memory is even worse, but if you get her talking about the distant past, she can still engage."

"I'm glad you've found a way to connect with her."

I notice his date again, edging a little closer to us, but he makes no move to introduce us. With a start, I realize that she's not the only one who is watching us. So are some of the other guests in the room. They've probably heard about the breakup and, just as I expected, are eager to see if we'll behave ourselves.

And then it occurs to me. Some of them probably assume I'm the jilted party, left at the altar by a catch like Jamie Larsson. They wouldn't necessarily know that I'm the one who called off the wedding.

"If you'll excuse me," Jamie says. "I promised Vic I'd help open the wine before dinner so it can have a few minutes to breathe."

"Of course," I say. As he strides off, his friend Sam shoots me a withering glance.

I slip out of the study through the door near the bar and end up wandering the house for a few minutes, trying to get a handle on my emotions. The encounter was stilted, unnerving for me on one level, especially the rubbernecking from the other people in the room, but Jamie seems to be doing pretty well. Though it's hard to imagine us ever being the kind of friends who grab a beer after work, at least I didn't see open loathing on his face.

After passing the entrance to the solarium, an addition built a few years ago, I find myself in the small mudroom at the rear of the house, where the door to the backyard is wide open. The pegs along the walls hold barn jackets, slickers, scarves, and well-worn cardigans.

What I need, I realize, is a short break outside. I give the screened door a push and step onto the flagstone patio, where I'm greeted by a cacophony of crickets and katydids. I tip my head back and stare up at the sparkly night sky, and almost instantly the tension in my shoulders begins to subside.

I'm just about to go back in for dinner when I hear a voice coming from the mudroom.

"You doing all right?" I'm pretty sure the speaker is Jamie's friend Sam.

"Yeah, hanging in there." He's talking to Jamie, I realize. The two of them must be right on the other side of the door, only inches away. "Feels like a fucked-up situation for me but it would have been rude to Vic not to come."

A voice in my head tells me to move away, that I

won't like where the conversation is going, but curiosity gets the better of me.

"So, she just showed up?"

"Yeah, even though she knew I didn't want her here."

My stomach tightens. Jamie had assured me it would be fine.

"Anything you can do about it?" Sam asks.

A pause.

"Ignore her, I guess," Jamie says. "And try to learn from my mistake. She's a complete and total fraud, not at all who she pretended to be—but I've got no one to blame but myself."

2

The words sting so much that I flinch. Is that what Jamie really thinks, that I'm a fraud? That I conned him or something?

I get that he's angry and upset. My decision to end our engagement tipped his world off its axis. But would he have preferred I go ahead with the marriage out of decorum, knowing that eventually my true feelings were bound to catch up with us as a couple? Though I loved Jamie, admired him fiercely—he's not only smart and charming, but also steady as a rock—and we got along really well, I'd begun to understand that I wasn't *in* love with him in that delirious way you should be with the person you marry. I'd allowed things to progress, I came to realize, because I liked how secure the relationship made me feel. It was a mistake I'd also made once in my professional life—by sticking with a "safe" job in HR for half a decade, even though I knew it wasn't right for me.

Would Jamie have wanted to exchange vows with a woman who'd been drawn to him in large part because he was a sheltered harbor, a woman who couldn't reciprocate his passion, a woman whose head was more and more filled with thoughts of another man?

It's not as if what I did was easy for me. For weeks I was heartsick about upending his world—and mine as well. It meant being single again, and at thirty-seven. In recent weeks, my best friend, Megan, has been urging me to at least set up a profile on a dating app or two, even if I don't take immediate action, but right now I have zero interest in romance again.

With my pulse racing, I edge as quietly as possible away from the door, praying they don't decide to take their conversation outside.

"I better go in," I hear Jamie tell Sam. "I need to manage this situation, so it doesn't turn ugly."

"I'm going to have to take off early, by the way."

"Okay, let's catch up later this weekend. There's something I want to circle back to you about."

Jamie's voice grows fainter, indicating that the two are retreating from the mudroom. Still, I don't want to reenter the house through the back door in case they spot me coming in and realize I'd heard them. Instead, I make my way along the strip of land between the house and the driveway, so I can go in from the front.

My heart is still thumping as I walk. *Not at all who she pretended to be.* I can't believe Jamie thinks that about me—though there's no doubt I'm a different person today than I was on our first date, two and a half years ago. When Jamie and I met, I was at the tail end of my recovery from the major career disaster I'd experienced in my midtwenties, a disaster that had stripped away most of my nerve and initially sent me into the field of human resources with my tail between my legs. I'd already started my career counseling business at the time of our meeting—thanks in large part to tons of encouragement from Ava—but I was still struggling at times to gain all my confidence back.

I creep along the side of the stone house, passing my rental car in the process. Though the invitation for the party had instructed guests to park in the field behind the barn, Ava suggested that I leave my car behind theirs in the driveway in case I felt uncomfortable and wanted to make a quick exit. For a moment I feel the urge to do just that, to head back to the inn and curl up with a book. But my friend has put too much effort into tonight for me to just bolt.

Finally, I reach the front of the house and climb the

stoop for the second time tonight. Behind me is the near-deafening roar of crickets and katydids, but as soon as I step inside and close the front door, I discover how quiet the house is. And then I realize why: Ava is toasting Vic, both of them standing in front of the hearth in the parlor. I slip inside as unobtrusively as possible and position myself at the end of the room.

"It's five hundred and twenty pages long, but I guarantee you will *devour* this book," Ava is saying. "It's a fascinating, provocative look at not only the trials, but also mass hysteria, paranoia, mean girls, and religious extremism." She chuckles. "Sound familiar? This book offers wonderful insight into Salem, as well as many of the issues we are being forced to wrestle with today." She raises her glass. "To my brilliant, amazing husband, Victor. Bravo on an extraordinary achievement. . . . And now dinner is served."

The crowd breaks apart and I follow a group into the dining room. The meal is buffet style, and after filling a plate with poached salmon, couscous, and green salad, I return to the study to get a glass of wine. There I spot Vic, talking with two middle-aged men I don't know, and though I hate the idea of interrupting, I don't want to go any longer without greeting him.

"Vic, *congratulations*," I say, approaching. "I downloaded the book as soon as it came out on Tuesday, and

Ava's right, if I didn't have to work and sleep, I'd never put it down."

"Oh, Kiki, how lovely of you to say that—and how great to see you." He cocks his head—with its lion's mane of silver hair—toward a card table set up in a corner. "We were just about to commandeer that spot for dinner. Won't you join us?"

I graciously accept the invitation and, after securing a glass of white wine, take a seat. Vic announces to the men that I'm a career coach, and they immediately pepper me with questions, but our dinner conversation soon returns to Vic's book. As he regales us with insights from his research, his deep, full voice carries over the sound of nearby chatter and clinking glasses, and his almost violet-colored eyes pin us one by one at moments. Even though I find Vic very charismatic, I've always been a tiny bit intimidated by him.

From time to time, I sneak a peek around the room. Through the doorway, I see that Jamie is at a table for eight that's been set up at the far end of the parlor. With him are Sam, Vic's agent, Dan, a woman I think is Dan's wife, and Jamie's date. Oddly, she's sitting at the opposite end of the table from him.

Our plates are eventually cleared by a waiter, who reappears soon after to pass around a platter of brownies and lemon bars. I'm about to rise from the table, worried that I'm hogging Vic's attention, when Ava heads in our direction. She kisses Vic on the top of his head and announces she needs to steal me away.

"Time to meet your future agent," she whispers with a smile. Guiding me by the elbow, she leads me into the solarium, where she introduces me to her friend Daphne Kudlow, who's sitting on the sofa with a glass of wine. She's wearing an attractive printed wrap dress, revealing a substantial amount of tanned cleavage. Her shoulder-length ash-blond hair is flipped up a little at the ends in a kind of retro sixties style.

Instead of rising, she pats the spot next to her on the damask sofa. "Join me," she says, "and we can talk for a bit."

She has a Waspy air and a clipped way of speaking, but she's smiling, and her light brown eyes seem friendly enough. My immediate takeaway: she's happy to chat as long as I don't waste her time.

"So, you and Ava worked together?" she asks once I'm seated.

"Yes, for almost five years. She was my boss in the HR department of New Horizon Media. From there, thanks to everything I learned from Ava, I took a job at a boutique coaching company and then started my own coaching business just over three years ago."

Daphne takes a long sip of wine and sets the glass on a small antique wood table next to the couch.

"What made you make the switch from recruiting to coaching?"

I chuckle. "I'd begun to realize that I spent half my time in interviews with job candidates wishing I could give them advice instead of asking questions. Tell them to smile more and make eye contact and not be afraid to show they're hungry for the job."

This is not the moment to tell her the full story, but if she signs me, perhaps I will one day. HR was never a field I'd set my sights on. I'd nailed a job right after college at another media company, a more cutting-edge one, and within two years I'd already been promoted to creating content, earning a generous salary for my age. I loved every minute of it—until my boss's boss, a hard-charging guy in his early forties, pushed me against an office wall one night when we were both working late and rammed his tongue down my throat and his hand down my pants. It took everything I had to fight him off, and I fled the building, completely shaken.

This was a few years before Me Too, and though I considered reporting the incident, I eventually decided against it, fearful my actions would backfire on me. During the next two months nothing else happened, and I was able to avoid the predator—a guy I called only R in my mind—convinced it had been smart not to rock the boat. But then out of nowhere, I was fired, not even by my boss but by someone in HR. I knew R had to be behind it.

I tried to find another job creating content, but I kept coming up against brick walls and I sensed that someone from my old company had spread rumors about my work. I was living off my savings by then and desperate for a paycheck. Through an alum of my college who I connected with on LinkedIn, I learned about a junior HR position at New Horizon and said yes without hesitation when it was offered. It felt like I'd managed to heave myself onto a life raft. I prayed I'd find my way back into content creation, but I soon realized that I associated that work too much with what had happened. In time, with Ava's guidance, I began to recognize that I'd love to transition into career coaching. Though I've stumbled along my own professional path, I've developed good objective sense about other people's careers—the mistakes they're making and the strategies they need for success.

"So, tell me about your book idea," Daphne says.

"It's about five key risks women need to take at various points in their careers—in order to end up where they want to be."

"Such as?"

"Instead of biding your time for a promotion opportunity to materialize, you need to design a brand-new role for yourself in your department or company that makes so much sense your boss *has* to say yes when you pitch it. Too often women wait around to be picked."

"Do you have a proposal already?"

"Yes—I've drafted an outline, three sample chapters, and a section called Why This Book."

She smiles. "Terrific. What about a title?"

"I have a great one in mind," I say. "I'll include it with the proposal—if I can send it over?"

"Of course, I'd love to see it," she says, and smiles, seeming to appreciate that I'm holding the title back for now.

As I finish typing her email address into my phone, I notice a man across the room catch her eye, and she lifts her chin in acknowledgment.

"My husband is signaling that he's ready to go," she says, "but it's been nice speaking to you, Kiki. I'll keep an eye out for your proposal."

We both rise from the couch, and I thank Daphne enthusiastically. After she's left, I need a moment to take it all in. If I end up writing and publishing a book, I'll surely be able to attract additional clients, and also secure more talks at conferences and company events, something I not only enjoy doing but that also pays exceptionally well. Beyond that, I simply love the idea of sharing what I've learned with as many women as possible.

And yet as good as I feel, there's been a hum of anxiety running through me since hearing Jamie's conversation with Sam.

As I leave the solarium, I notice the crowd has thinned and that people are bunched in the hall, preparing to depart. From the open front door comes the distant sound of cars pulling out of the field on the other side of the barn. It's time for me to go as well, though first I need to thank my hosts.

I wander through the rooms and eventually spot Ava through the doorway into the kitchen, but she appears to be talking to the caterer. There's no sign of Vic, or either Jamie or the woman he came with, which is a relief. They must have left for the night.

I eventually end up back in the solarium, a room that is now empty except for one person, whom I realize too late is Jamie. He's staring out at the darkness through the floor-to-ceiling glass windows, and his expression is close to grim. For a second, my heart forgets to beat.

"I thought you'd gone," I say.

He turns and looks at me, his face blank.

"Nope, still here," he says, coolly. "Tori grabbed me at the last minute to discuss birthday gift ideas for my uncle."

"What about your date?" I can't believe I'm asking him that, but part of me just wants to know that things are okay for him.

"If you could call her that," he says dismissively. "She's long gone by now."

I wonder if she bolted because he was ignoring her, something that seemed out of character for someone as considerate as Jamie.

"And speaking of going, I need to head out as well," he adds. "Are you staying here at the house?"

"No, I'm at the Salisbury Inn." I take a deep breath, summoning my nerve. "Jamie, I'm sorry about tonight. I hope my being here didn't upset you. When Ava first invited me, she said you'd be out of town and—"

"Don't worry about it, Kiki. We were bound to run into each other at some point."

And yet he'd told Sam he didn't want me here tonight, and that I should have been aware of that fact.

"Do—do you think you'll ever be able to forgive me?"

He shrugs. "Of course. People fall out of love. I don't hold that against you."

"You mean that?"

"I'm sure you could see it hurt like hell when you broke the news, but I'm over the worst of it. Life goes on." He tugs his mouth to the side in the smallest of half smiles. "I even got a rebound haircut."

It's clear he's not going to confess how he really feels about me, and I'm hardly going to admit what I overheard.

"It's a nice haircut," I say feebly. "It suits you."

"Good. . . . I've already said goodbye to Ava and Vic, so I think I'll slip out the door here. My car's out behind the barn."

"Good night then."

"Good night, Kiki. Take care."

He starts to turn, then hesitates, as if he has more to say, but a second later he's crossing the flagstone floor, pushing open a glass door, and stepping into the darkness. I picture him driving through the night and returning to an empty house, without Cody there to greet him. During our last phone call, he'd mentioned that he'd recently changed to a different rental, making me wonder if he felt uncomfortable living in a place we'd shared.

Suddenly I'm almost swamped by a wave of remorse. Not over the split—which I know was the right thing to do—but for coming tonight, too selfish to turn down the invitation. I should have waited until the fall to meet Daphne, when she was back working in her New York office. I'm sure Ava could have orchestrated a meeting for us there.

When I return to the front of the house, I'm relieved

to see I'm not the very last to leave. Vic's agent and his wife are still here. But then I remember Ava telling me on the phone that Dan would be staying at the house this weekend.

"Oh goodness," I say to Ava. "I've somehow overstayed my welcome."

"You haven't at all," she insists. "A few of us are going to have a nightcap and do a postmortem on the party. Would you like to join us?"

"That's so nice of you, but I should head back to the inn. Thank you for a wonderful party, Ava. Can you wish Vic good night for me?"

"Of course. And if you're up for it, stop by for coffee tomorrow on your way back to New York."

As I'm telling her I'd love that, Tori appears behind me and touches my arm. "Kiki, any chance you can give me a lift?" she asks. "Liam went home a while ago, and I figured I could bum a ride from you to Salisbury."

"Sure," I say, happy to oblige. Tori and Liam live only a short drive from the inn.

After I wish the two houseguests good night, Ava walks Tori and me into the foyer. A departing guest has left the door ajar, and a light breeze enters the space, rustling the edges of the curtain on the hall window. The insect chorus has quieted just a little from earlier.

"What great music to fall asleep to on a summer night," I say.

"It is," Ava concurs. "It's part of why I love August here so much."

And then comes something different: a sharp popping sound—from somewhere to the right, and not that far away.

I could swear it's the crack of gunfire.

3

I freeze. It can't be a gun. It must have been a car backfiring, the sound carrying from the road at the end of the long driveway.

"Hmm," Ava murmurs, looking perplexed. "Someone might be setting off fireworks."

Dan's wife, a pretty redhead, emerges from the parlor. "Was that anything to be alarmed about?" she asks.

"I was just saying that it could be fireworks," Ava tells her. "Kids setting—"

And then another sound pierces the night. A car alarm, or no, a car *horn*, coming from the road as well, it seems, and not letting up. It's the kind of response you get from hotheaded New Yorkers stuck in traffic—

except we're not in New York. Tori raises her arms and presses her hands to her ears.

"Well, *that's* not fireworks," Dan's wife says.

Ava turns and faces the rear of the house. "*Vic?*" she calls out down the hall, doing her best to be heard above the noise.

"Dan thought he might be upstairs in his office," Dan's wife says. "He went to look for him."

Ava walks to the base of the stairwell and calls out again, this time directing her voice up the steps. There's no response. The horn sound keeps on, relentless, and I'm tempted to cover my own ears.

"*Vic,*" Ava calls once again. She flips over her hands in dismay and then glances at the rest of us. "Goodness, where is he?"

Suddenly Vic appears at the far end of the downstairs hallway and hurries toward us.

"Sorry, I was making sure the caterers had turned everything off. Who in god's name is blowing their horn like that?"

"We have no idea," Ava says. "There was some kind of bang, like a firecracker, and then *this.*"

Vic approaches the open doorway and ventures out onto the stoop, cocking his head to one side and then the other. "Someone must be having car trouble out on the road—or else they're signaling for help. I should probably see what's going on."

"Darling, why don't we call 911?" Ava suggests, a trace of nervousness in her voice.

"It'll take forever to get them here. And it's just a car horn."

He steps back inside, swings open the small closet in the foyer, and grabs a flashlight from a wicker basket on the top shelf. "Don't worry, I'll be careful," he tells Ava.

At the same moment, Dan comes scurrying down the stairs. "Oh, there you are, Vic," he calls. "I went up to your office to look for you."

"I came down the back stairs and then stopped in the kitchen. But I'm headed out now to see what in hell is going on."

"Why don't I go with you?" Dan says, pushing his horn-rimmed glasses on top of his head.

As the rest of us hang back, Vic and Dan exit the house. They hesitate briefly in the front yard, exchange a few words that we can't hear, and then take off to the right.

"Why aren't they going toward the road?" I ask no one in particular. Tori, I notice, still has her hands pressed tightly to her ears.

Ava shakes her head, clearly as clueless as I am. She

takes a few steps out onto the stoop, and I follow behind her. She cocks her head just as Vic did. "I think because the noise is actually coming from behind the barn," she says after a minute. "That's where most people parked tonight."

"*Jamie*," I say at the same moment his name bursts into my head. "His car was out there."

"But he's been gone for a while now," Ava says.

"No, I just spoke to him in the solarium," I say. "Then he left through that door."

My heart has started to skitter. If Jamie's having car trouble, why wouldn't he come back in the house instead of blowing his horn so obnoxiously? And what was the first sound we'd heard?

Without even thinking, I hurry down the steps and set out in the same direction Vic and Dan went.

"Kiki, wait," Ava calls.

"I just want to make sure Jamie's okay," I call back to her.

The sound of the horn is even worse out here, of course, a deafening blare that could make you lose your mind. There's enough illumination from the house that I spot the two men at the very end of the yard, the beam of the flashlight bouncing in front of them. With Vic a few steps ahead of Dan, they approach the weathered barn. As I trail behind, the three-inch heels of my slingbacks keep sinking into the dirt, but I don't dare go barefoot out here.

It's obvious now that the noise is coming from the field. I watch as Vic and Dan reach the barn, hurry along the side of it, and round the far corner. Before I can catch up with them, though, the blare stops as quickly as it started, leaving behind the faint chorus of insect mating calls. A second later, a howl cuts through the night. It's coming from one of the men, Vic maybe—as if he's crying out in anguish.

Fear fizzes through my body. I start to run, feeling the manicured lawn give way to bristly field grass. As soon as I round the far corner of the barn myself, I stop in my tracks.

There's a single car parked in the field, about ten yards away from me, and though there's a security light shining from the top of the barn, it's too dark for me to tell the make of the car, to know if it's Jamie's. What I *can* see is that the door on the driver's side is open, and Vic is leaning into the car a little, with Dan stopped a few steps behind him. The car's interior light is on, but I'm not close enough to see inside—even if Vic weren't blocking my view.

Dan steps forward and peers over Vic's shoulder.

"Jesus," I hear him exclaim.

"*What?*" I cry out, advancing again. Something bad has clearly happened. "What's going on?"

Vic spins around and spots me across the field.

"Go back to the house," he yells.

"Is it Jamie?" I plead.

"Go back, Kiki, please. We'll be there in a minute."

I don't want to defy him, so I turn around and stumble back to the house, my panic spiking with every step. As I near the stoop, I see that Ava's still standing there, waiting, while Tori and Dan's wife are hanging back in the foyer.

"Kiki, what is it?" she yells.

"I don't know, they won't tell me. But I don't think it's good."

I've barely climbed the steps before I hear panting and turn to see Vic hurrying in our direction. Dan is a short distance behind him, speaking rapidly into his cell phone.

"Is it Jamie?" I demand again. As I race back down the steps to meet him, I notice that the front of Vic's white linen shirt is smeared wet with something dark. "Vic, please tell me."

Vic reaches me and folds me into an embrace. "Oh, Kiki," he says. "Jamie—Jamie's dead."

My knees buckle, and I let out a moan of despair. "*Dead?* No, no."

"Dear god," Ava exclaims.

This can't be real, it can't be. I was speaking to Jamie only minutes ago.

"I'm so sorry," Vic says, choking back the words. I finally register the wetness on his shirt against my bare arm and realize that it's blood. Jamie's blood.

"*How?*" I beg. "I don't understand."

"I don't either. Dan is calling 911 and we need to wait for help."

"But we can't just leave him out there," I exclaim. "We have to do something."

"It's too late," Vic says mournfully. "I took his pulse, and—it's clear there's no hope."

"Let me see for myself." I break free from Vic's embrace and take a few steps away.

"Kiki, please don't," he says. "It's too awful for you to see. Jamie—Jamie's been shot."

4

The ground seems to crater beneath my feet, and I feel myself sway.

"*What?*" I say in shock. "But—who would do that?"

Ava hurries down from the top of the stoop and wraps an arm around my shoulder. I can feel her trembling through the silk of her tunic.

"I don't know," Vic answers. "But we need to get into the house right now."

I realize suddenly what he's implying. Whoever shot Jamie might still be on the property. As Vic ushers Ava and me toward the steps, Dan comes up behind us.

"The police are on their way," he says. "Everyone needs to get inside."

The second we're in the house, Dan breaks the news to the others. His wife gasps in shock, and Tori slumps against the wall of the foyer, her hand pressed to her mouth. Vic announces that he's going to lock the other doors to the house and suggests we all have a seat until the police arrive.

Ava grabs my arm, leads me slowly into the parlor, and eases me onto the sofa. After wrapping a throw blanket around my shoulders, she tells me she wants to check on Tori for a minute, but she'll be back.

The lightheadedness I experienced in the yard dissipates, and it feels now as if someone's dropped a weight on my chest, squeezing the air from my lungs. I lean forward, trying to catch a breath, but reality keeps overpowering me. Jamie's *gone*. He's never going to see thirty-nine, dazzle any more clients with his insights, discover his Nordic roots, read another book, hit another tennis ball. Someone's killed him.

But *why*? He certainly didn't have any enemies. In two and a half years, I heard him raise his voice only a few times—mostly at bad drivers—and I don't think I ever saw him seriously angry at anyone.

Could it have been a robbery? What if someone knew there was a party and waited in the field with a gun? Has someone snuffed out Jamie's life simply to get their hands on his wallet?

I slowly lift my head and see Ava speaking to a shell-shocked Tori by the fireplace, trying to comfort her.

Dan and his wife are at the other end of the room, where they sit with stick-straight posture, clearly stunned. Vic appears in the doorway to the room and Ava goes to him. They huddle briefly, their expressions stricken and their voices too low for me to overhear—almost as if they don't *want* to be overheard. Is there more going on than I realize?

The two of them then disappear down the hall toward the kitchen. *Please come back, Ava,* I pray to myself. I can't bear being here on my own. As if reading my mind, Tori lowers herself next to me on the sofa. Her face is as white as candle wax, as if someone has drained the blood from her body.

"Tori," I say, the word choked in my throat. "I don't understand any of this."

"I know," she mutters. "It's horrible."

"Have you called Liam yet?"

"I texted him and said I needed him to come pick me up, that I couldn't find a ride. I knew if I told him, he might crash into a tree on his way. I—I'm going to wait by the door for him so I can break the news in private."

Tori gets up again and drifts into the hall, and seconds later Ava reappears with a tray of glasses and a liter of sparkling water, setting it on a wooden butler's table. After pouring drinks for everyone, she joins me on the couch.

"Oh, Kiki," she says softly. "There aren't any words."

"Ava, it can't be true. It just can't be."

"I know. It's too mind-boggling to comprehend."

Vic rushes back into the parlor. "Where the hell are the police?" he says to no one in particular. He glances over at Dan. "Did the operator give you any idea how long they would be?"

"She said a car was being dispatched, so I assume it won't be long."

"And until then we're just supposed to mill around in here?" Vic exclaims, lifting his hands in exasperation.

"Well, we can't go back out there," Dan says bluntly. "The police won't want us doing anything that would compromise the scene."

Compromise the scene. I hate how bossy he's trying to sound. Ava told me once that some of his clients write thrillers. Does he think that makes him some kind of crime scene expert?

Suddenly I'm on my feet.

"Vic, are you really sure it's too late?" I exclaim, fighting back tears. "Shouldn't we be trying CPR?"

"Kiki, I'm sorry," he says grimly. "But there's no way he could have survived his injury."

"What do you mean?"

"I hate being the one to have to share this, but it was a gunshot wound to the head."

I see Jamie then in my mind's eye—slumped in the front seat, blood gushing everywhere. The image makes me retch. I bolt from the parlor, race to the powder room, and after shoving the door closed behind me, kneel in front of the toilet. When it seems clear that I'm not going to be sick, I exit the room and make my way farther down the hall to the kitchen. I yank out one of the chairs by the table and collapse into it.

After a short while, I hear someone come up behind me, and when they touch my shoulder gently, I realize it's Ava.

"Let me make you some herbal tea," she says.

She fills the kettle with water, and as she's setting it back on the base, a new sound pierces the night— the wail of a siren. Ava freezes momentarily, holding the kettle in midair. She finally sets it back on the base, clicks it on, and settles next to me at the table. She lays a hand over one of mine.

"Do you think it was a robbery gone wrong?" I ask. "That someone was out there waiting for the guests to leave?"

"Oh, Kiki—I don't know," Ava says mournfully.

"It's all a terrible mystery. We're just going to have to let the police figure this out."

The kettle clicks off and she hands me a mug of tea, then says she's going to check to see what's happening. As soon as she leaves, I take a sip, but the taste makes me gag. I check my watch. Ten fifty-four. That means it's not even eight in Phoenix, where my mother's been living since my father died five years ago. But after her knee replacement surgery last month, she started going to bed super early, and despite how desperate I feel to speak to her, I don't want to take the chance of waking her.

When Ava returns a few minutes later, she explains that Vic has spoken to the patrol officer, who assured him that detectives will be here momentarily. After fixing a cup of tea for herself, she rejoins me at the table, keeping silent company with me as I wait in anguish. Though the kitchen door is partially closed, we can hear voices coming from the other end of the house.

About thirty minutes later, Vic reappears to say that he and Dan have been interviewed by a Detective Calistro, who would now like to speak to me alone in the kitchen. Ava will be interviewed in the dining room by a second detective, who's already spoken to Tori and Dan's wife. And then, within seconds, Calistro is here, and I rise to meet him. He appears to be in his midforties, about five nine or ten, with very short dark hair and a trim mustache. He's dressed in black slacks, a white collared shirt, and a dark gray blazer.

"Katherine Reed?" he asks.

"Yes, or Kiki, whichever you prefer." Unexpectedly, my heart has started to hammer.

Vic slips out of the room with Ava, who glances over her shoulder, offering a look of support. I trail her for a moment with my eyes, and while doing so, catch sight of Liam at the end of the hall, preparing to leave with Tori. His back is to me, so I can't see his face, but I can only imagine how devastated he must be. Has he informed his uncle Drew yet? This news will surely crush him.

"I'm very sorry for your loss," Calistro says, tugging my gaze back to the room. He motions me to be seated again, slides into a chair across the table from me, then flips open the pad he's carrying. His fingers are short, with shiny, buffed nails. "I know it's a difficult time, but I need to ask you a few questions while the events are still fresh in your mind."

Still fresh in my mind. Like tonight's a dish to be savored at the peak of perfection.

"Of course," I say, doing all I can to steel myself.

After taking down my contact information, he asks me to describe my connection to Jamie. I explain, haltingly at times, that we were romantically involved for two plus years and engaged for about half of that period. The relationship, I tell him, ended in March, and since I suspect he might get around to asking, I mention that I was the one who called off the wedding.

"Did you have any contact with Mr. Larsson tonight?" Calistro asks, glancing up from his notebook.

"Yes, we spoke twice, but only briefly each time."

"The final conversation was when?"

"Right before he left. I bumped into him in the solarium, and after we talked for a minute, he mentioned that he'd already wished Vic and Ava good night and was going to split. He went out the solarium door."

"Was he alone when he exited?"

"Yes." My eyes brim with tears as I'm flung back to that moment, realizing now that as I wished Jamie good night, he was only minutes away from his death. I picture him hesitating in the doorway, as if about to say something, then changing his mind and disappearing into the darkness.

"And how long after he left were you aware that something was wrong?"

"Within only a couple of minutes. I—I went to the front of the house to say goodbye to the Davenports, and as I was standing in the foyer, we heard what we thought was a firecracker. And then the car horn."

He nods, making more notes, and then returns his gaze to me.

"Did you notice anything out of the ordinary tonight, especially regarding Mr. Larsson?"

The question takes me aback. It sounds like he's considering something other than robbery, that one of the *guests* might have met up with Jamie in the field and killed him in his car.

"No, but I wasn't around him much. When we spoke in the solarium, he did mention that his date had left before he did, but he didn't seem all that bothered by it."

The girl will be a suspect, I realize suddenly. God, could she have killed him in some kind of rage? "I don't know her name, but Ava—Mrs. Davenport—will."

Calistro nods, looking down at his notes, and then glances back at me. His brown eyes are round and small like pennies, but they don't seem to miss anything.

"Was Mr. Larsson drinking this evening?"

"Um, he was having a glass of wine when I first saw him . . . but nothing later on. He's not—he was never a big drinker. . . . Why?"

"We're just trying to get a full picture of the evening."

"Okay."

"Can you describe the nature of your second conversation with Mr. Larsson?"

"As I said before, it was very brief," I reply, with my heart picking up speed again. "We acknowledged that the evening was a bit awkward for both of us, but he said he didn't mind that I'd come."

I'm certainly not going to volunteer anything about the conversation I overheard between Jamie and Sam.

"Was your ex-fiancé right- or left-handed?"

I hear the words, but I hesitate before answering, confused by the inquiry. And then, with a sickening jolt, I realize why he's asking.

"Right-handed," I say. "But *please*, I hope you're not thinking Jamie could have done this to himself. That's just not possible. Jamie was a very happy, very positive person. Talk to any of his friends or relatives and they'll tell you the same thing."

Calistro nods, as if in empathy, but his expression is still totally neutral. "When you were discussing the awkwardness of being here at the same time, did he seem morose to you?"

"No, nothing like that," I say, as my stomach twists. "He told me he was getting on with his life, and he didn't harbor any negative feelings. Jamie always looked on the bright side of things, and I promise you he wasn't the type of guy to let a breakup undo him. And—and tonight I even overheard him mention a bunch of fun plans he had for the rest of the summer."

I sound almost desperate, I realize, protesting far too much.

"Ms. Reed, we're simply considering every angle," he says, with kindness in his voice now. "A team from the state police will examine the scene here, and we'll investigate the situation as thoroughly as possible. And there'll be an officer on duty here tonight, keeping an eye on the premises."

"Okay," I say, relieved that the questions about a possible suicide were obviously routine. Jamie didn't even own a gun, for god's sake.

Calistro finally closes his notebook and offers me a business card, saying that I should call if I think of anything else. I'm so drained that my legs almost give out as I rise to say goodbye. Soon after he leaves the room, I hear a murmur of voices from the hall and then the click of the front door.

Moments later, Ava reappears in the doorway of the kitchen, dressed now in a cotton pullover and jeans. The house has turned eerily quiet.

"Where is everyone?" I ask.

"Liam took Tori home. Dan and his wife have gone to bed, and Vic's in his office."

"I should get back to the inn."

"Don't be silly, you're staying here tonight, Kiki. Unfortunately, we only have one true guest room, but there's a daybed in my office upstairs and I've already made it up for you. And you'll have a half bath to yourself."

I start to protest but quickly change my mind, realizing I'm in no shape to drive back to the inn on my own. Ava leads me upstairs to her office and hugs me good night. Though she'd whispered on the stairs that she'd left me a spare toothbrush and fresh washcloth in the bathroom, all I have the strength to do is peel off my dress and crawl beneath the sheets on the daybed.

For a few minutes I lie on my back, staring at the ceiling. Where is Jamie now? I wonder. In the morgue already, in a black body bag? And what about his killer: Is he—or she—back home, convinced they might have gotten away with it?

A sob catches in my throat, and I expect a flood of tears, but they seem trapped inside me.

I reach up with a hand and snap off the swinging wall lamp just to the right of the daybed. Within minutes, from sheer exhaustion and despair, I feel sleep overtake me.

When I wake the next morning, my mind is blank for a few seconds, the only thought in my head that the bed I'm lying in feels oddly unfamiliar.

And then my memory catches up, slamming into

me. I'm at Ava's . . . in her office . . . *because Jamie is dead.*

For a moment I lie very still, second-guessing myself. In this utterly quiet room, with the dull light of morning seeping in from behind the shades, it's almost possible to believe I've just woken up from the worst nightmare of my life. But the horrible knot in my gut tells me otherwise. I let out a moan and wrap my arms around my chest, squeezing hard.

My purse, I remember, is on the table behind me, and after twisting around, I drag it onto the bed and dig out my phone. The screen says it's only 7:12. I scroll quickly through my recent emails and texts. It's clear that news about Jamie has yet to reach anyone I'm close to. It's like I'm living in an alternate universe.

Summoning what little energy I have, I hoist myself up and stagger to the bathroom. There, I finally use the toothbrush Ava left and dab at my face with a wet tissue, removing the grungy traces of last night's makeup. Back in Ava's office, I slip on my dress and shoes and force my hair clumsily into a scrunchie from my purse.

For the first time since I've been in this room, I take it in—the soft yellow walls, the antique wooden desk, the built-in bookcase with all the volumes arranged so orderly. Exactly the kind of pretty but very functional office I would have imagined Ava having. I'm so grateful for all she did last night, but I need to get out of here and be by myself.

When I ease open the door, silence greets me. Everyone must still be sleeping, or they're huddled in their rooms, still shaken. I tiptoe down the stairs to the foyer, where, to my dismay, I spot the security system pad near the front door with a bright red light indicating that the alarm has been set. *Fuck*. I can't leave now without setting it off. Am I going to have to sit around in my party clothes until Ava or Vic surfaces?

My gaze drifts to one of the foyer windows and I spot a couple of police vehicles at the end of the long driveway. Now that it's daylight, the police must be making a closer inspection of the crime scene. A fresh wave of sadness crashes over me.

"Kiki."

I spin around at the sound of Ava's whisper. She's standing by the kitchen door, wearing a fluffy turquoise robe.

"Oh, Ava, did I wake you?" I say, keeping my own voice down.

"No, no. Vic and I have been up for a while, though Dan and his wife are still sleeping, I think. Why don't you come into the kitchen for a bit? Vic's up in his office but he'll be down in a while."

As eager as I am to be back at the inn, it will be good to have a couple of minutes alone with Ava. I nod and follow her into the dimly lit room.

"How about some toast?" she asks.

"Yes, god, I could use that," I say, realizing that my stomach is roiling.

Ava drops a piece of bread into the toaster, then pours us each a cup of coffee. Her hair is pushed back with a stretchy black headband, and her face is free of makeup at this hour, of course. Though Ava and I are close, our friendship started at work, and it's slightly disconcerting to see her in this context.

"Did you get any sleep last night?" I ask.

"Enough to get by on. And you, dear? This must be so brutal for you."

"I did manage to get some rest. . . . Do—do people know yet? I mean, like Jamie's uncle Drew?"

"Yes, Liam apparently broke the news to him last night, just as Drew and Heather were coming in the door from a charity event. Vic spoke to Drew soon afterward, though the man was too devastated to even say much. I think Vic might be talking to him again now because I overheard him say Drew's name."

I can't imagine how Jamie's uncle must feel.

"And what about Sam Morgan?" I ask. My heart lurches as I ask the question. "Has anyone reached out to him?"

"Liam was going to make that call last night, too."

The bread pops up, and Ava plucks it from the toaster.

"Ava, who could have done this?" I ask plaintively. "The police asked if I'd noticed anything out of the ordinary last night, as if they think the killer might have been someone at the party. Could that really be possible?"

"They asked us that, too, but it's so difficult to fathom," she says. "People adored Jamie." Since her back is to me, I can't read her face, but I've noted the slight hesitancy with her words. For the second time I wonder if there's something going on that I'm not aware of.

As she serves me the toast, footsteps approach and we turn in unison to find Vic in the doorway. His thick silver hair is standing on end in places, and his face is haggard, as if he lay awake most of the night.

"Any news?" Ava asks.

"Yes, that was Drew on the phone," he says, his voice uncharacteristically subdued. "The man's a wreck, needless to say, but he's doing his best to stay in the loop. He has a contact in the state police who's shared information that's not being released yet."

"And?" Ava says, worriedly.

Vic flicks his gaze a little to the left, so he's not making eye contact with either one of us.

"Nothing's final yet, they're waiting for the autopsy, of course, but—" His voice catches. "Jamie's death appears to have been a suicide. It seems he pulled the trigger himself."

5

Vic's words are like a hard kick to my gut.

"No," I protest, almost wailing. "It's not possible. Jamie would never do that—and besides, how would he have suddenly gotten his hands on a gun?"

"The gun was illegal, apparently, with no serial number," Vic says, "so he must have bought it on the black market, though we might never know when. I spotted it on the floor of the car when I checked Jamie's pulse, and the horrible thought crossed my mind at that point—that he'd done this himself."

"But the killer could have left it there," I insist. "Maybe he didn't want to risk being caught with it—or he dropped it in a panic. Don't you think this could have been a failed robbery?"

"Yes, Vic," Ava interjects, looking stricken. "Isn't that a possibility?"

Her husband shakes his head, looking reluctant. "Perhaps, but according to Drew, Jamie's phone and wallet were still on him. And robberies, let alone murders, are rare here. As shattering as it is, all the evidence is pointing in one dreadful direction."

Am I really supposed to believe that Jamie took his own life? That minutes after he told me he was through the worst of our breakup and had no hard feelings, he strolled out to the field, pulled out a gun he just happened to have in the car, and put a bullet through his brain?

If it *is* true, surely this all has to do with me. Because it occurred only minutes after our conversation. Something I said or did last night must have triggered his actions—either that, or my mere presence did. *Please*, I plead to the universe, *don't let that be the case.*

"Was—was there a note?" I ask weakly.

"Not in the car," Vic says. "Drew and Liam are going by Jamie's house today to see if there's anything there."

My body has started to boil over with panic, as if someone has come up behind me and thrown a hood over my head. Ava is speaking to me, I realize, but her words are a blur of sound.

"What?" I murmur.

"I said I hope you're not blaming yourself, Kiki," she says. "Because I won't allow that."

The mere fact that she's saying these words proves that the thought has crossed her mind, just as it will cross everyone else's.

"But . . ." I say, my voice quavering.

"Kiki," Ava says. "If there's one thing I know for certain, from both work and from life, it's that people are responsible for their own actions. We can't allow ourselves to think otherwise."

"Ava's right," Vic says, his voice subdued.

Isn't it possible, though, to push someone over the brink? By *your* actions?

"I should go," I announce, my voice shaky. "Thank you for all your help."

"Would you like me or Vic to drive you to the inn and then you can retrieve your car later?" Ava asks.

All I want right now is to be on my own, to be able to sob my eyes out and not worry about being seen or overheard. I need to call both my mom and my friend Megan to tell them what's happened.

I shake my head. "Thanks, but I'm okay."

"Let's check in with each other later," Ava says as I struggle up from the table.

After grabbing my purse, I hug my hosts goodbye. Ava's embrace is full and effused with her usual warmth, but Vic's hug is an awkward one, his body stiff with tension. Despite what he said, he might be blaming me.

With trembling hands, I back the rental car out of the driveway, past the empty police vehicles, and point it toward the Salisbury Inn.

The desk clerk greets me cheerily, paying no apparent mind to the fact that in my cocktail dress and stilettos, I appear to be doing a walk of shame. I'm the only guest in the lobby, but I can hear muted conversations emanating from the breakfast room down the hall, which also serves as a local café with a separate entrance.

I make my way upstairs and into my room, with its pretty gold-and-white-striped wallpaper and soft white duvet. Though I spent a couple of hours here before the party—reading, nursing a cup of tea, and prepping for several client meetings I have this coming week—I barely recognize the space. If it weren't for my roller bag on the luggage rack, I'd think I'd somehow gained entry into a stranger's room by accident.

After taking a swig of water from the complimentary bottle, I strip off my clothes and stagger into the bathroom to shower. For a few minutes I let the hot water soothe me, losing myself in the sensation. I'm sure that this is the moment when the tears will come gushing forth, but they still seem trapped deep inside me.

Back in the room, with just a towel around me, I sit on the edge of the bed and force my mind back to the party, realizing that some things aren't making sense to me. Don't people kill themselves when they're in the throes of depression? Jamie didn't *do* depression. I lived with him for more than a year, and I never saw even a sustained bad mood. Yes, the breakup upset him deeply, but that was nearly five months ago, and I believed him in the solarium when he told me he'd moved on. After all, his whole life has been about getting back on his horse again—like when he lost his mom early in his life, and then later his dad.

And I always thought the idea of suicide is something people agonize over for weeks or months, toy with, fantasize about, research online, and then plan out. Am I really supposed to believe that he was so upset by my presence at the party, which wasn't a surprise to him, that he walked out the door and on the spur of the moment took his own life?

Could the gut-wrenching information that Vic shared be wrong, the word of a police source who's not at the center of things?

It's now close to nine. I take a few more swigs of

water, dig my phone from my purse, and call Heather Larsson, the second wife of Jamie's uncle Drew, who's twenty years her husband's junior. It seems better to connect with her first since Drew must be incredibly distraught, and though I'm dreading this call with every fiber of my being, I can't let the day gain any more ground without making it. Not surprisingly, it goes to voicemail. The family has so much to cope with now.

"Heather, it's Kiki," I say. "I'm so horribly sorry for you and Drew. Please let me know if there's anything I can do. Anything at all."

My words sound lame to my ears, but I don't know what else to say. Next, I try Tori, who doesn't pick up, either. I leave her a message, too, explaining that I'm eager to see how she's doing.

It's too early yet to call my mom in Phoenix so I try Megan next. Not only has she been my closest friend since we met in college, but she's also a therapist, and I'm certain that speaking to her will help ease the pain. Because she's an early riser, even on Sundays, I'm surprised her phone goes to voicemail, too. There's no way I'm going to break the news in a voicemail, so I just ask her to call me as soon as she can.

Despair starts to overwhelm me again, in part because I feel so alone. *Get a grip*, I tell myself. The trip back to the city will take close to three hours, and I can't be a total basket case.

After dressing in jeans and a cotton V-neck sweater, I call downstairs to tell the desk clerk I'm checking out. Within minutes, I'm rolling my bag off the porch of the inn, headed toward the parking lot.

And then, with a jolt, I see someone I recognize; I can barely believe my eyes—it's Jamie's date from last night. She's striding across the parking lot from the café, dressed in tight jeans and a slim-fitting gray T-shirt, and carrying a take-out coffee. Though the expression she's wearing is as pinched as it was last night, it's hardly grief-stricken, suggesting she hasn't heard the news yet. She and Jamie obviously weren't a good fit, which means she might not be devastated when she learns what's happened, but still, it will be a terrible shock. I lower my head to make certain she doesn't get a glimpse of my face. I'm certainly not going to be the one to break the news to her.

As soon as I'm on the road, I try Megan again, thinking she might not have seen my message, but she doesn't answer. Next, I try the number for Detective Calistro, which I've programmed into my phone. Though that goes to voicemail, too, he returns my call minutes later.

"Is it true that you think Jamie Larsson's death is a suicide?" I say, after quickly identifying myself.

"Do you mind telling me where you got that piece of information?" he asks.

"From someone with a contact in the police force. Is it true?"

I hold my breath, hoping for a miracle.

"I'm not at liberty to share any specifics from the investigation at this time, but I will tell you there's been no ruling yet."

"Really?"

"The autopsy isn't scheduled until tomorrow. We're also awaiting results from a tox screen, which could take up to ten days. Please give us time to do our work, Ms. Reed, and we'll let the family know as soon as we've made a determination."

It's clear that Drew Larsson's contact in the police force spoke out of turn, and prematurely, and my shoulders immediately drop a little.

"I'm glad to hear there's been no ruling yet," I say, "because as I pointed out last night, I just can't believe Jamie would have taken his own life."

He thanks me for calling and signs off.

Though I'm almost ashamed for feeling a little better now, I can't help it. The idea of Jamie having been murdered is brutal, but if he'd taken his own life because of me, I won't be able to live with myself.

I'm about a quarter of the way into my journey when Megan finally calls me back.

"Hey, sorry to miss you earlier," she says. "I went out for a run and purposely didn't take my phone. What's going on?"

"Meg, it's horrible," I blurt out. "Jamie's dead."

"Oh my god, Kiki. What *happened*?"

"He was shot. And even more horrible, there's talk it was suicide."

"What? *No*. Was this in New York or Connecticut?"

I share a few details, but it's almost impossible to discuss the situation and navigate a two-lane country road at the same time.

"If you're not busy today, can we meet up after I drop off the rental car?" I ask. "I could really use your company."

"Of course. Text or call me when you're half an hour from your place, and I'll meet you there. But if you feel at all overwhelmed on the drive back, pull over and call me."

Megan is good to her word, waiting outside my building when I arrive. She's dressed casually and her chestnut-colored hair is tied in a high ponytail. We hug each other tightly, and as we separate I see that her bright green eyes are brimming with tears.

"Oh, Kiki," she murmurs. We board the elevator and take it silently to the ninth floor. As soon as we're in my apartment, Megan ushers me onto the living room couch. I'd been thinking that being in my own place would be comforting, but I haven't had much of a chance to fix it up yet, and it feels sparse and unwelcoming.

"Okay, first, what can I get you?" she asks. "Do you have any juice in your fridge? You look incredibly pale."

"What I'd love most of all is a coffee. I've had three sips of caffeine all morning and my head is pounding."

As she hurries into my galley kitchen, I remind her that there's a basket of coffee capsules next to the machine. She returns shortly with a mug full of coffee, milk added—we've been friends long enough for her to know how I take mine—and settles beside me on the couch.

Once I've had a few gulps of coffee, I pour out the whole story—the party, the conversation I overheard, my last contact with Jamie, and the awful hours since then, including my short conversation with the detective today. From time to time, Megan grabs my hand between her long, slim fingers, squeezing it for support, and her eyes well with tears again, the kind of tears I can't summon myself.

"This is mind-boggling," Megan says when I finish. "And it sounds like it'll be days before you know anything for certain."

"Right, but it can't be suicide, *can* it? You knew Jamie. Did he seem like the kind of person who would take his own life?"

Megan's lips part briefly, but then she closes her mouth again, hesitating. My heart sinks.

"*What?*" I demand.

"I agree with you, Kiki, I do. Jamie always seemed like such a well-adjusted person. And yet people suffering from depression sometimes manage to hide it really well, and that means friends and loved ones are not only clueless, but they're also denied any chance to help."

I shake my head. "But I dated Jamie for over two years and lived with him for a year of that. Surely I would have noticed at least a hint of depression."

"Not necessarily, if he was skilled at disguising it. And people who take their own lives don't necessarily have a *history* of depression. It can come on almost out of the blue if the person's suddenly struggling with a difficulty in their lives."

My breath hitches. "Like having your fiancée practically leave you at the altar?"

She hesitates briefly before speaking. "Being perfectly straight with you—because I know that's what you want—it's possible the breakup crushed him more than you realized and started him on a downward spiral. But any depression he experienced over the breakup could have been compounded by other factors that have nothing to do with you—like some kind of work setback or family conflict—which then led to suicidal ideation. And didn't his dog die recently?"

I appreciate Megan's support, but this is not what I want to hear. I need her to be as skeptical as I am.

"His dog did die, but when we spoke a few weeks ago, he told me he was thinking of getting another one. And from what I know, his work was still going great. He'd added a bunch of new clients earlier in the year."

I tug my hand gently away from hers, leap up from the couch, and begin to pace my living room.

"There's something else, something that began to crystallize for me earlier this morning," I say. "The suicide theory doesn't make sense on a whole other level."

"What do you mean?"

"Even if Jamie was more distraught about the breakup than anyone knew, and my presence at the party totally threw him, are we supposed to think he popped out of the house and on the spur of the moment shot himself? Don't people—especially careful, methodical people like Jamie—*plan* suicides?"

As I turn back toward Megan, I catch her letting out a gust of air. She glances over at me, her expression pained.

"*What?*" I demand for the second time.

"Okay, I'm going to continue to be straight with you. Yes, some suicides are planned, but believe it or not, the majority are impulsive. A person experiences something he views as catastrophic, finds it unbearable, and then takes his own life. Research shows that when people decide to attempt suicide, they might follow through within thirty minutes, in some cases as few as five."

As I'm digesting her words, it's beginning to feel as if a hand has gripped my heart and is squeezing it hard.

If there's nothing at all preposterous about what's happened, it means that seeing me at the party and exchanging a few words might have been enough to push Jamie over the edge. And he did all the planning he needed on the five-minute walk to his car.

6

Finally, the tears come, a sudden gush that gives no sign of stopping. I know that by laying it all out like that, Megan was only trying to help, but her comments have left me feeling even more unmoored.

"It's all my fault then," I manage between sobs.

Through my tears I see her quickly fish a few tissues from her purse—she carried them with her even before she trained to become a therapist—and jump up from her seat. She hands me the tissues, then wraps me in a hug.

"Oh, Kiki," she says. "You can't blame yourself for this."

"How can I *not*?"

"You didn't feel the marriage would work, so you did the right thing by breaking off the relationship.

Plus, as I said before, if Jamie really was depressed, there might have been other reasons for it. You said he had an illegal gun, which means he could have been having suicidal ideations for a while."

Or maybe just since March, I think. *When I pulled the rug out from under him.*

"Right."

"Please, tell me what I can do," she says. "Can I fix you something to eat?"

"Thanks, Meg, but I might just lie down and rest now. I'll eat something later."

"You want me to hang around? I could read here in the living room and then fix you a late lunch when you wake up. Or order something in for us."

"No, that's okay. I so appreciate you coming over and being straight with me, but I'll be okay on my own for a while."

Megan nods reluctantly and grabs her purse from the couch. We hug once more at the door and I promise to check in this evening. Though I do feel completely frayed and desperate for rest, I can tell within seconds of Megan's departure that I'm too wired to sleep. Plus, there are calls to make, and at some point I need to prep further for the two client Zoom sessions I have scheduled for tomorrow—though right now I'm dreading the very idea of them. I locate my phone and return to the couch.

I've yet to hear back from Drew's wife, Heather, and I try her a second time. When this call goes to voicemail as well, I leave another message, saying that I not only want to offer the family my condolences, but that I'd like to know when and where the funeral will be held.

Next, I call my mom and break the news, which triggers another wave of tears—on my part and also on hers. She always adored Jamie, and though she supported me during the breakup, she'd been shocked when I told her I was ending things.

"Oh, Kiki, I'm so terribly sorry," she tells me. "This must be devastating for you."

She asks a few questions about the party and aftermath, and though there's no judgment in her tone, I can't help but think she's wondering why I attended the party to begin with. My mom has a wonderful laid-back manner, but she's also practical and wise. If I'd thought to ask her advice beforehand, she surely would have advised me to stay home, give Jamie his space, and find another way to meet the literary agent.

"Honey, I'm coming to New York," she says once I've answered her queries. "I need to be with you."

"Mom, I'd love that more than anything, but there's no way your doctor would want you to be navigating airports so soon after your knee surgery."

"What if I could find someone to drive me?"

"From *Phoenix*? No way. Let's just say we'll stay in close touch by phone. Maybe I can come out there for a few days after the funeral."

"I'd love that, and I'm sure the change of location will be good for you. I'll check in later today."

"Thanks, Mom."

"And, Kiki, you have to promise me. You can't let yourself feel any guilt about this."

Here we go again. Someone else telling me that I'm not responsible. But if that's one of the first things that leaps out of people's mouths, it means that the possibility has crossed their minds. Does my mother just love me too much to betray what she's really thinking?

After we sign off, I take a few long, deep breaths and make myself an omelet along with a fresh cup of coffee. I manage to get down a little of each, then force myself to my workspace off the living room.

Following my breakup with Jamie, I'd been in a mad scramble to find an affordable apartment of my own, and thanks to a real estate agent friend, I managed to nab a decent one-bedroom in Manhattan's East Seventies. Though the building is on a blah-looking block, the apartment itself has a few nice features, including south-facing windows and a small anteroom outside the bedroom that I've been able to set up with a desk and a slim stand-alone bookcase on the other wall, giving the impression on Zoom calls that there's an actual office for Katherine Reed Coaching.

I open my laptop, spend a few minutes scanning the notes on each client I'll be speaking to tomorrow, but soon lose any interest. Almost without thinking, I find myself moving the cursor to the browser and typing in "recent homicides Litchfield County." Vic had mentioned that robberies and murders are rare in that area, but I want to see for myself.

After scrolling through a couple of online stories, it becomes clear that Vic was right. Though the county might not be Utopia, the crime rate seems low. And from what I can tell, there have been only two homicides in the past four years that weren't related to a domestic dispute.

Almost three years ago, a thirtysomething man was shot to death in a parking lot by a distinguished lawyer following some kind of disagreement, never fully explained. Obviously hoping to spare himself a long sentence, the lawyer took a plea and is currently incarcerated.

The other case is far more gruesome. Four years ago this month, a twenty-three-year-old woman named Jess Nolan was found in a wooded area near the grounds of a county fair with her head bashed in. Though she hadn't been raped, it appeared an attempt had been made to sexually assault her. One of the stories about this case features her photo, and I see that she was extremely pretty and sweet looking, with long light brown hair fanning out around her shoulders.

It's not surprising that I haven't heard of either case until now. Both of them occurred before I'd even met Jamie.

I also do a search for burglaries and robberies in the area, and though they turn out to be more common, I don't find any involving extreme violence. If Jamie *was* killed in an armed robbery, it would be an anomaly.

I spend the next hour or so tackling chores around the apartment—unpacking my roller bag, tidying my bedroom, Swiffering the floors—in the hope of distracting myself, but these mindless tasks end up giving my brain the freedom to kick-start a whole series of "What if . . . ?" questions. What if I'd never broken up with Jamie? What if I'd suggested therapy for both of us, to help us with any fallout from the split? What if I'd touched base with him a few times to see how he was doing? What if I'd never gone to the party? What if I hadn't stepped into the solarium just as Jamie was leaving? The answer to any of these questions could be that Jamie would still be alive.

I think back to what Megan said about depression. Could Jamie have been suffering during our time together without my even knowing it? Did he have demons I wasn't aware of? I didn't say this to Megan, but despite how easygoing Jamie appeared, there were occasional moments when I would catch him looking into the middle distance, his expression dark, troubled almost.

Everything okay? I had asked the first time I noticed it.

Yeah, yeah. Just trying to figure out how to handle a tricky client.

From time to time, I stop my busywork and sink onto the bed or the couch to weep. It would probably be good to finally let some of my other friends know what's happened, but I keep resisting the idea. They're not going to think I'm a monster, the way some of Jamie's own friends will, but I feel too much shame to talk to them just yet.

As the day draws to a close, I receive texts from Megan, my mom, and Ava, all checking on me. I write back, telling them I'm holding up okay. As much as I appreciate their support, it's draining to keep trying to sound less morose than I am.

Around ten, I wash my tearstained face and crawl between the sheets on my bed. As I'm shifting my body for the zillionth time, in search of a position that might summon sleep, my phone rings from the bedside table.

I fumble to reach it and the moment I see the screen, my heart freezes. It's Sam, Jamie's best friend. I have no doubt he's calling to dress me down for showing up at the party and wreaking havoc with Jamie's emotions. As tough as it's going to be to talk to him, I answer the phone anyway. Maybe what I really need today is the opinion of someone who isn't worried about my feelings and dares to speak the truth.

"Hello, Sam," I say. "I—I'm very sorry for your loss."

"Are you still in Connecticut?" he asks bluntly.

"No, I came back to the city. Of course, I'll drive back up for the service."

"I need to talk to you."

Here it comes. Will it be as short and blunt as a hammerhead? Or a long, red-hot tirade?

"All right."

"Are you going to be at your apartment tomorrow morning? I'm still in Connecticut but I plan to leave for the city at around six a.m."

God, he wants to do his takedown face-to-face. I don't think I can handle that. "Why don't you let me have it right now and get things over with?" I say.

I can almost see him flinch. "I don't have any intention of letting you have it, Kiki. But there's something you need to be aware of—concerning Jamie's death—and I want to tell you in person. Besides, I've been with his uncle all afternoon and I'm all talked out now."

"Okay," I say, wondering what it could possibly be. "I have a Zoom meeting between nine and ten but I'm free in the morning after that."

"I'll be there at ten."

I give him the address and apartment number, and he ends the call with not much more than a grunt. When I drop my phone on the table, I notice I'm holding my breath. If he's not reaching out so he can yell at me, it might mean Sam has doubts about the suicide theory, too.

Please, I pray, *let that be what he wants to discuss.*

Sam arrives at five past ten the next morning, and after buzzing him in from the lobby, I take a quick look in the mirror on the foyer wall. I managed to get about three hours of sleep last night, and though I applied a full face of makeup for my nine o'clock Zoom, it's done little to disguise my fatigue and grief.

Fortunately, my client, a twenty-seven-year-old manager in the packaged foods business, seemed thoroughly focused on the suggestions I offered for projecting confidence and speaking more succinctly in meetings, without long-winded introductions to her ideas, and she didn't appear to notice what a sad sack I am at the moment.

Opening the door to Sam's knock, I discover that he

looks as bad as I do. His dark brown eyes are blood-shot, his skin seems even paler than normal, and his longish brown hair is dull and lank, as if he's washed it with a bar of soap instead of shampoo.

"Do you want to come in?" I ask, a stupid question considering I've been expecting him, but his presence has already unnerved me. He steps into the foyer, dressed in black jeans and a wrinkled moss-green T-shirt, and then follows me into the living room, glancing around distractedly. At around six three, he's a couple of inches taller than Jamie was and seems to tower over my five-foot-six frame. "Can I get you something?" I ask.

At first there's no reply. I sense he's reluctant to be beholden to me in any way.

"Do you have any coffee?" he asks finally. "I barely slept last night."

"Yes, just give me a minute."

As I use my machine to fill two mugs, I steal glances at Sam through the kitchen doorway. He's now stand-ing by one of the living room windows, staring out at the rooftops and the overcast August sky. When my mother came east last year to help me shop for a wed-ding dress and ended up meeting Sam briefly, she noted how mismatched he and Jamie seemed as friends.

I knew what she meant, of course. Sam, an economics professor here in the city, is erudite, reserved, almost brooding at times, a real contrast to Jamie's affable, outgoing personality. Though Sam can turn on the charm when called for at dinner parties and events, he mostly listens and observes, his gaze unbearably intense at times. From what I can tell, he has never once suffered from the need to please.

Sam's parents have a house—more like an estate—in Litchfield County, and he and Jamie met as boys at a tennis and swim club there, to which they continued to belong as adults. According to Jamie, they connected instantly and bonded over a shared love of the outdoors and an appreciation of each other's wry sense of humor—and probably also due to that indefinable chemistry that helps forge enduring friendships. Like Jamie, Sam still spends his summer weekends in the area, at a cottage on his parents' property that they turned over to him.

By the time I reenter the living room, Sam is sitting in one of the two small armchairs, leaning forward with his hands clasped together. Though he's perfectly motionless, I can feel his nervous tension and I see it, too, in his eyes. What I'm not picking up on, oddly enough, is any blatant hostility.

I hand him a mug of coffee, and by the time I take

a seat on the couch across from him, he seems to have drained half of it.

I can't bear waiting any longer. "You said you had something to tell me," I say.

"Yes—about Jamie's suicide."

My heart sinks. So he's not dubious, then.

"Who told you that's how he died?"

"Drew. It's not official yet, but everything seems to be pointing that way."

"Did they end up finding a note?" I ask, the words catching in my throat.

"No. The police went by his rental house yesterday, and so did Drew, but didn't discover one. Drew and Liam are packing up the house today and they'll look more closely, but it doesn't appear Jamie left any kind of note."

"But how can people think—?"

"Look, Kiki, I didn't come to debate the matter. As much as the truth hurts, I'm trying not to kid myself."

"Then what did you want to tell me?" I say, puzzled. I'm looking in his general direction as I speak but not right at him, which feels too awkward.

Sam takes another swig of coffee and sets the mug back down. "I'm going to be blunt, because I don't know any other way to put it. I know you're probably beating yourself up, thinking that you might have caused his death. But I don't believe Jamie took his life because of you."

I pull back in surprise. Back in March I'd heard from people that Sam was livid with me on Jamie's behalf, and it's hard to believe he wants to let me off the hook now.

"What makes you so sure of that?"

"We talked a lot about the breakup. He was devastated at first—I mean, it really knocked the wind out of him—but he was definitely on the mend recently. And he knew that he'd dodged a bullet, that if you'd gone ahead with the marriage despite serious misgivings, you two would have ended up splitting up sooner or later."

"Then I don't get it—Why would he take his own life?"

Sam exhales loudly and presses his hands hard to his temples. "Something else was going on with Jamie lately," he says. "And it was eating away at him."

7

My stomach twists. What could have happened to Jamie? Had his life started to unravel, and if so, why?

"Do you think it had to do with his business?" I ask. That's one of the areas Megan had wondered about.

Sam shakes his head. "No, work was good for him. The matter seemed pretty personal, and I'm almost positive it related to something in Connecticut."

"Litchfield County specifically?"

"Yup. I first realized there was a problem during lunch at the club in, I guess, mid-July. Jamie looked agitated when he arrived and told me that an issue he'd been worrying about had just come to a head."

Since Jamie and I were no longer in any real contact

then, I can't even make a guess as to what it might have been.

"You didn't come right out and ask him?" I say.

"I did, point-blank. But he said it was premature to discuss it. And whatever was bothering him clearly needed sorting out. About a week later, almost out of the blue, he announced he was going to stay at his new rental for most of August. When I pushed him, he promised again to tell me what was going on, but not until he knew more."

I look off, thinking for a second. "Could it have had anything to do with the woman he brought to the party?"

"Her?" Sam shakes his head again, this time dismissively. "God no. He'd been out with her only a couple times and, long story short, she wasn't even supposed to be at the party that night."

"I wonder if it had something to do with his grandmother and the care she was getting. He mentioned at the party that her dementia was getting worse."

Sam shrugs. "Maybe, but I don't think so. He'd actually just come from seeing her that day at the club, and he made a point of mentioning how great the care facility was."

I rise from the couch and drift toward the same

window Sam was staring out of earlier. "How did he seem to you at the party?" I ask, switching gears a bit. If something was bothering Jamie enough for him to take his own life, it must have been boiling over Saturday night.

"He seemed okay to me."

"Okay good—or just okay?"

He shrugs again. "Overall, he seemed like himself that night, but to be honest, I didn't interact with him much. He was on the other side of the table from me at dinner, and then I had to bolt early. I ended up not even saying goodbye to him—and don't ask how *that* makes me feel."

Before I can raise anything more, Sam is on his feet, too, ending the discussion. This is clearly becoming too painful for him.

"That's all I had to tell you," he says bluntly. "I thought it was important for you to know, and I wanted to tell you in person."

He moves so fast toward the front door that I catch up with him only as he's reaching for the knob.

"Thank you," I say. "For coming . . . for what you told me."

It's just the two of us bunched in the small foyer now, and I feel my cheeks redden. Sam levels his gaze at me, and there's a sudden coldness in his expression.

"I thought you should know you're not responsible, but that doesn't mean I can forgive what you did to Jamie. He didn't deserve to be kicked to the curb that way."

And then he's gone, leaving me with only the bite from his parting salvo. I probably should have expected something like that, but during the past few minutes I'd let myself believe that some of the ice between us had melted.

As I carry the mugs to the kitchen, my mind is churning. Does Sam have it right? Was something seriously troubling Jamie this summer, something beyond the fact that, in his words, I was nothing but a fraud? Jamie knew plenty of people in Litchfield County, but for the most part they were casual acquaintances, and his only close friends in the area were Sam and, to a lesser degree, Vic, so even if a problem had arisen with someone—from the club, for instance—it's hard to imagine it getting to him in a profound way.

So that leaves his family to think about.

If I had to, I could certainly envision an issue bubbling up with one of his relatives. Drew, a successful portrait artist, can be pompous at times, and—at least from what I saw—not inclined to compromise when it comes to his own needs. Then there's his cousin Liam. I always got along with him myself, but he struck me as fairly rigid and set in his ways and focused on only three things in life: Tori; his son, Taylor; and his company. Though he and Tori belong to the same tennis and swim club Jamie did, I rarely saw Liam hanging out there.

Yet Jamie had seemed to navigate situations with his family really well, and our times with them—birthday celebrations, summer holiday barbecues, occasional dinners—were always devoid of drama. Plus, when I force my brain to return to Saturday night, I recall Jamie saying that Tori had been picking his brain about a birthday gift for Drew. Hardly a sign of any trouble brewing among family members.

For the rest of the morning, I do my best to respond to emails and then brace myself for my second client Zoom of the day. This one is with a woman in her early thirties who often makes me wonder why she hired me because she always seems to know better than I do. True to form, within minutes she's challenging some of my suggestions about how to deal with a difficult co-worker. It's a relief when the hour is up, and I conclude by saying I'll send her a recap of the session, hoping I can make my suggestions less muddled in writing.

"Yeah, okay," she says, then adds, "Are you all right, by the way?"

"What do you mean?" It comes out with a curtness I didn't intend.

"I just thought you might not be feeling well."

"Uh, no, I'm fine, just a little tired. Thanks for asking."

"You should drink extra fluids today. You look really dehydrated."

Great, now she's coaching *me*.

As soon as I've signed off, my day goes from bad to worse. There's a text waiting from Drew's wife, Heather, and my heart sinks as I read it.

Katherine, I got your messages and I know you mean well, but please, let us deal with our horrific grief on our own. Drew does not feel comfortable with my speaking to you. We are planning a memorial service, of course, but we intend to keep it private, just family and very close friends.

Meaning I'm not going to be invited. Surely Jamie's uncle and aunt are eschewing contact with me because they blame me for his death, like I'm some kind of pariah.

I try to concentrate on work again and do my best with the recap for the difficult client—so she won't decide to drop me—but my mind keeps fighting its way back to Jamie and Sam and the dismissive text from Heather.

Something plops onto my keyboard and I realize I'm crying again. I grab a tissue from the rattan box on the desk and wipe my eyes, but as soon as I've soaked up the tears, more come, and before long I'm fighting to catch my breath. Sam said that I shouldn't feel guilty, that I wasn't the cause of Jamie's distress, but I have no proof of that. How am I going to be able to function over the next days and weeks? How am I going to do my job or go on with my life?

I briefly consider calling Megan or my mom, but I know hearing their voices will only go so far. I need comfort, but I need answers even more.

Dropping the tissue, I tug out the single drawer in my desk. Nestled among the paper clips, pens, and neon Post-it notes are two sets of keys—a spare one to my apartment and my old set to Jamie's place, which I never got around to returning.

I'm going there, I decide. Even though Drew probably intends to have someone pack up the apartment as soon as possible, I doubt that plan is in place yet. Whatever was tormenting Jamie, perhaps he left a clue in the apartment. And I need to get my hands on it.

8

Shortly after two, I hail a cab to Jamie's apartment on West Twenty-Fourth Street. It's going to cost plenty, but I don't have the mental stamina right now for a forty-minute trip by subway, which would involve switching trains at one point. Plus, this way I can get in and out by four o'clock and be less likely to run into any of Jamie's neighbors coming home from work.

The trip south is straightforward enough, but we hit crosstown traffic after turning west, and by the time we pull up to his building, I'm nearly jumping out of my skin. Beyond my fear of possibly bumping into someone Drew has dispatched, I dread being back in the apartment, especially knowing that Jamie won't ever be returning there.

After exiting the cab, I loiter a minute on the sidewalk,

making sure that no one I recognize is about to enter or leave the building. Fortunately, there's no doorman to contend with, and if a former neighbor spots me, they might not give my appearance a second thought. Anyone who asks themselves why this is the first time they're seeing me in ages could conclude I've been traveling a lot over the past months or that my schedule just hasn't aligned with theirs. Even if they somehow knew that Jamie and I had broken up, it's possible they'll assume we've gotten back together again. But over the next few days, some residents will probably get wind of the tragic news, and if one spots me today, they might mention my presence to the super, who might in turn tell Jamie's family.

Once I'm sure the coast is clear, I dart into the small lobby, unlock the door, and board the elevator. It stops on the seventh floor with a loud groan, as if empathizing with me. Before exiting, I poke my head out to check that the corridor is deserted, then make my way to 7G and nervously rap on the door. When no one answers, I turn the key in the lock and quickly enter the apartment.

I can't believe I'm here, standing in a place I thought I'd set foot in for the last time months ago. I survey the foyer—the mint-colored walls, the small wrought-iron table, the jade-green bowl sitting on top of it where we always dropped our keys when we returned home. I'm suddenly overwhelmed by the most ferocious sadness. The bowl will never hold Jamie's keys again.

For the first time I wonder if he might have left a suicide note right here in the apartment, then realize I may be about to find out.

I take two steps into the living room and then freeze, listening carefully. My heart is beating so loudly, I can hear it between my ears, but after a minute I'm certain I have the apartment to myself. It's almost oppressively warm in here, probably because the AC hasn't been run lately. I tiptoe farther into the space and finally exhale.

At a glance, it doesn't seem like anyone has been here yet. The place is tidy, just as Jamie must have left it when he set out for his weeks-long stay in Litchfield County. He is—no, he *was*, I remind myself with a horrible pang—a bit of a neatnik, though he never complained about the splayed books, scraps of paper, and coffee cups I left in my wake.

A sob catches in my throat. Part of me wants to flee, to forget this crazy idea, but I can't. This is my chance to figure out if Sam is right and that I wasn't the source of Jamie's recent distress. Because otherwise I'll never let go of the guilt, no matter how much Megan and Ava and my mother assure me I should.

I drag my gaze around the room, absorbing the

details. Though the building is fairly modern, the apartment itself has several touches that prevent it from seeming austere—lead-paned windows, oak floors, and a small arch above the doorway that leads to the bedroom corridor. Jamie bought the apartment about four years ago after breaking up with a long-term girlfriend who'd moved to Hong Kong for a dream job. The colors he chose for the decor, mostly creams and pale greens, give it a relaxed, comfy vibe. I liked the apartment from the start and was always at ease in these rooms, at least during those early months before doubts began to slither into my head.

As I stand here, though, it strikes me that being at ease is not the same as being at home, and that in certain ways I always felt a bit like a houseguest. Since I'd moved into the apartment as a stopgap measure until we found a place of our own, I'd put almost all my belongings in storage and never added any personal touches—not even so much as a favorite tea towel.

Maybe that should have been a red flag for me.

My eyes inch across the room, and I realize it looks mostly the same, but with a few changes I can't help but notice. Jamie's replaced the slightly battered coffee table from his previous apartment with a sleek model of burled wood. There's also a new piece of art—composed of metal and what looks like gold chimes—on a wall that used to be bare.

With a start, I spot one more thing. The silver-framed photos that once sat on a wooden Parsons table against the far wall have been removed and replaced with a couple of houseplants. It's no surprise that he got rid of the pictures featuring the two of us, but I can't imagine why he took away the others—shots of him with friends and of course his late parents.

Is that telling? I wonder, anguished. Had he moved those photos because he was redecorating a little or was he beginning internally to sever ties with the world and was afraid gazing at loved ones would cause him to second-guess his terrible plan?

What I don't see is any kind of farewell note.

I quickly turn and duck into the small, white-tiled kitchen. Somehow, it's even more painful for me here, since Jamie always loved being in this room, whether he was firing up the Nespresso machine with the towel from his morning shower still tied around his waist, or making us dinner, something he did frequently.

You up for turkey chili? he might ask and then lift his eyebrows. *Or are you pining for something truly gourmet?*

The kitchen, like the living room, is neat as a pin. On impulse, I open the dishwasher and peek inside.

The only item in it is an espresso cup on the top rack, obviously placed there on his last morning in the city.

And then as crazy as I feel doing it, I tug out the expresso cup and press the rim to my lips. Another sob catches in my throat. *Oh, Jamie,* I wonder, *what were you thinking as you brought this to your own lips? How terrible of a problem could you have been facing?*

So far, nothing I've seen here is giving me any indication.

As I turn to leave the room, I spot Cody's leash on the hook by the door and my heart squeezes at the sight. Obviously, Jamie couldn't bring himself to part with it.

I head next to the second bedroom, a space Jamie had set up initially as a home office for himself and then, when I moved in, for the two of us. My desk is missing, of course. That's the one thing I'd brought with me and then hauled away when I left. In its former location is a new, waist-high bookcase. I stoop down to peruse the thirty or so books that have been arranged in an orderly fashion on the shelves. I recognize most of them as biographies and popular histories, including the six Vic wrote before his latest. While I lived here, these books all had homes on different shelves or tabletops around the apartment, so it seems Jamie was suddenly eager to fill the space. Maybe he didn't want to be reminded of my absence.

I turn back around and walk toward his sleek wooden desk. My eyes focus immediately on the mango-colored Post-it note stuck to the desktop. Stepping closer, I recognize Jamie's handwriting and see that he'd scrawled the words *chargers, contact lenses, weights*, obviously a reminder to pack those items for his monthlong stay in Connecticut.

The rest of the items on top of the desk are simply the usual suspects: a black mesh container for pens and pencils, a stapler, a tape dispenser. Nothing that tells me anything. There's no laptop, of course. He would have taken it with him.

I reach down and tug open the single built-in file drawer. Though the idea of looking through Jamie's files makes me queasy—I would never have even considered doing it when we were together—I realize that if I'm going to find any hints to the source of his troubles, they're probably not likely to be in plain view. Jamie stored almost everything digitally, but he did keep a few paper files.

At first glance, nothing seems revelatory. The tabs on the files are all totally mundane: "Medical," "Vet bills," "Mortgage," and so on. When I thumb through one or two, I see that the paperwork is from the aughts, meaning much of what's in here is from a period before statements and notices were sent electronically.

One file tab does grab my attention: "Active." I tug it from the drawer and flip it open.

To my disappointment, it's almost empty. Is that revealing in itself? Was there no need for an "active" file because he wasn't planning on a future? I lower myself into the desk chair and pick up the first item.

It's a ragged piece of white butcher paper, torn off, I would guess, from one of those table coverings in bistro-style restaurants. "Duolingo," it says, in feminine-looking handwriting. "Online Spanish lesson app. Fun!"

Improving his Spanish had been one of Jamie's New Year's resolutions, and it appears that someone he'd had a recent meal with had recommended a resource for it. Was she a client? Or maybe a date, a woman he'd begun seeing here in the city?

The second item is a renewal form for the New York Historical Society Museum and Library and the last is a sheet of lined yellow legal paper with a list of addresses—nine altogether—scribbled down in Jamie's handwriting. There's a variety of towns represented, and all but two of the town names are ones I recognize as being in Connecticut, within thirty or so miles of the house Jamie was renting when I met him.

My first thought is that they must be houses Jamie looked at before he settled on his latest rental. Or perhaps he was even in the market to buy. Since I was out of the picture and we were no longer purchasing an apartment in Manhattan, he might have decided to try to invest in a weekend home after years of renting.

But the last two addresses, I suddenly notice, are in Florida. Maybe as an alternative, he saw himself snagging a winter getaway.

Regardless, if he *was* toying with buying a second home—either in Connecticut or Florida—it certainly doesn't jibe with him wanting to exit the world.

I take a photo of the page and then stick the file back in the drawer. As I rise from the chair, a brief noise tears me from my thoughts. It seems to have come from the living room—was it the sound of a door clicking shut? My heart skips. Is someone else inside the apartment?

I sneak a nervous peek into the corridor and after hearing nothing else, I tiptoe back toward the front. There's no one in the living room or the foyer. I stand stock-still, with my ears perked. After a couple of seconds, I hear the sound again, and realize it's the ice maker in the fridge, dropping cubes into the compartment below. I lived here for a year, so I should have known.

It's a reminder, though, that if I intend to be gone by

four, I need to get my ass in gear. But there's still one more space I haven't entered: the bedroom. I return to the hallway beyond the arch and force myself in that direction. Oddly, the door is closed, and I hold my breath as I push it open.

There's a change in here, too, which presents itself at first glance. Jamie has removed the sage-green duvet I helped him pick out and replaced it with a cream-colored one. Had he never liked that duvet as much as he said he did—or was it simply too much of a reminder of our time together?

I take a quick look around the tidy space and en suite bathroom but find nothing significant. I could look further—into bedroom drawers and bathroom cabinets—but that feels way too intrusive.

Without really thinking, I lower myself onto the bed. How many times did Jamie and I make love in this room? Surely hundreds, in the two and a half years we were together.

I'd been physically attracted to him the instant I laid eyes on him. We'd "met cute," arriving simultaneously at a Citi Bike rack where only one bike remained.

"You take it," he'd said gallantly, smiling his full-wattage Jamie smile.

"Wow, so chivalry isn't dead," I'd replied. "Thank you."

"There's just one hitch."

"You want to ride on the handlebars?"

"No, you have to let me take you out for coffee within the next forty-eight hours."

"Sure," I said, smiling back. The moment felt straight out of a rom-com.

Our initial sexual encounters turned out to be nice enough and mostly physically satisfying for me. They weren't, however, truly electric, and I was left with the nagging sense that something was missing. I told myself that sex would get better as we grew even closer, and when that didn't happen, I decided it was unrealistic to expect the type of sex women had in movies, especially when they were having it with Brad Pitt.

It worked for a while—until I found myself constantly fantasizing about another man, one who'd unexpectedly walked into my life one day. I never so much as kissed this person, let alone slept with him, but the mere thought of him left me breathless.

And that eventually led to the awakening that changed everything: I cared about Jamie deeply, and I'd regained even more of my confidence in the many months we'd been together, but our relationship lacked any true spark for me, in or out of the bedroom. Most of the time, in fact, he seemed more like a friend than a lover.

By then, though, he'd already popped the question,

and we'd set a date for a small wedding. With a sinking heart, I knew I had no choice but to pull the plug. I broke the news on a cold March morning.

My hand drops to the duvet and I stroke the fabric a couple of times, letting myself imagine Jamie peeling it back and sliding into bed, and then sleeping with his right arm lifted above his head on the pillow, as he always did.

Why didn't you want to come back here? You bought a new coffee table and bookshelf and a fresh-start duvet. Was something troubling you enough to make you want to take your life?

I'd come here today looking for insight, but all I have are more questions. Certain small details—the missing photographs, the almost empty "active" file—hint at sadness, maybe even depression, and yet the list of houses I found suggests Jamie had hope for the future. I don't know what to think.

I reflect back on what Sam said—that whatever was tormenting Jamie was in Litchfield County, in the area he'd known since he was a boy.

And I realize that the only chance I have of figuring out what was going on is to return there as soon as I can.

9

I leave for Connecticut midday on Thursday, a bit later than I would have liked, but it took me a few days to get all my ducks in a row. I'm just praying I haven't lost valuable time.

So far, no official cause of death has been announced, I've heard from Ava. Though the autopsy was conducted earlier in the week, the police must still be waiting for the toxicology report, which Detective Calistro had mentioned would take at least ten days.

Ava also told me the memorial service was held yesterday, a private event at Jamie's uncle's house to which only family and a couple of very old friends of Jamie's were invited. Jamie's body was cremated, which means there's not even a gravesite to visit. Some of his New York friends are arranging a memorial in the city this fall, so at least I'll have that to attend—if I'm invited.

One reason for my late start was trouble locating a place to stay. I decided against a room at an inn or a B&B, because of both the price and the fact that I'd have to eat all my meals out. That left Airbnb, and there were slim pickings this late in the season. But something finally popped up on Wednesday—a small, simple house in New Burford, one of the many small towns that dot the county—and I grabbed it. Fortunately, I won't be far from Jamie's old rental, so I'll mostly know my way around, and Ava and Vic are only a twenty-minute drive.

Though it's cheaper than a hotel, the house, along with the car rental, is going to cost a bundle, and I've had to tap into savings I created five years ago with a portion of my dad's life insurance payout, which my mom was kind enough to share with me. But I don't care what it's costing. As the days have gone by, I've felt even more desperate for knowledge. I'm having trouble sleeping and eating, and work has felt impossible. During one session yesterday, I found myself staring at the obnoxious young male client and thinking, *Why don't you grow the fuck up?*

When I'm halfway to my destination, Ava calls to check in. I'd let her know midweek that I'd decided to come back for a short while, but I decided not to mention what Sam had divulged or that I'm on a quest for answers. Instead, I told her that I needed a break, and that being in the area Jamie loved would be a comfort to me.

"Are you sure you wouldn't like to stay with us?" she asks now after we've exchanged greetings. "The guest room is free for the next couple of days."

"Thanks so much, Ava, but the house I found looks just fine. And it's probably good for me to spend some time alone right now, with everything I need to process."

All true, but beyond that, I wouldn't feel comfortable interrupting her summer with Vic or possibly distracting him while he's busy promoting his new book.

"Can we at least have lunch tomorrow here at the house?" she asks.

I tell her I'd love that, and we agree on one o'clock.

As I've spoken to Ava over the past several days, appreciative of her attempts to console me, I've been trying to be mindful of the fact that she and Vic are suffering, too. Not only had Vic been tennis friends with Jamie, but I know he and Ava must be devastated that the death occurred at their home. How long will it be before Vic can catch sight of the barn without picturing the gruesome scene he discovered behind it? Maybe never.

And what will it be like for *me* to be on that property again? *I'm just going to have to steel myself*, I think—because I need time with Ava.

Nearing New Burford, I make a short detour to a local gourmet market, where I pick up fresh vegetables, milk, yogurt, and butter, as well as sliced turkey, shrimp salad, and a couple of chicken breasts. It's a place I sometimes shopped with Jamie, and a wave of sadness rolls over me as I settle up with the familiar cashier.

From the parking lot, I text Clarissa, the manager of the house I've rented, to let her know I'm close by. The couple of times I've used Airbnb with friends, we've always retrieved the key from a lockbox on-site, but this rental requires a person-to-person handoff.

As soon as I reach the address on Ash Street, I spot Clarissa on the stoop, but I take in the property first. The house is a white clapboard with hunter-green trim, and though it's small, it appears to be in as good shape as the online photos indicated. There's a decent-size front yard, and though there are neighbors on each side, they aren't so close that I'm going to hear the *Jeopardy!* theme song through an open window every night.

Clarissa seems to have left her car on the street, so

I pull into the driveway to the right of the front door. After exiting the car, I cross the yard and greet her. She appears to be about fifty, with lightly curled brown-and-gray hair, and a wide, soft face. Though it's over eighty degrees today, she's paired her jersey pants with a matching jacket.

"You must be Katherine," she says with a pleasant smile, stepping down from the stoop to greet me. "Did you have any trouble finding the place?"

"Please call me Kiki. And no, none at all, thank you."

"What did we ever do without GPS, right? Do you want to grab your bags before we go in?"

"Why don't I just stick my groceries in the fridge, and come back for the rest later?" I suggest. I want to get the formalities over with so I can have the place to myself.

Inside, the house is even more charming than promised. The downstairs features a small living room that runs across the front of the house, a pint-size dining room, and a kitchen with white wooden cupboards, butcher block counters, and plenty of sunshine. The walls appear freshly painted, and the place is decorated in a slightly old-fashioned but inviting country style—rag rugs on the wide-plank wooden floors, faded chintz fabrics, table lamps with beige or black paper shades, and a rattan umbrella stand by the back door filled with walking sticks. I take a minute to place my perishables in the fridge before Clarissa resumes the tour.

The second floor is reached by an enclosed staircase from the living room, and as advertised, there are two bedrooms. The primary one, which I'm planning to use, faces the backyard and offers a lovely view from one window of several leafy maple trees. It feels a little like I've stepped into the pages of a fairy tale.

While we're in the main bedroom, Clarissa takes a minute to discuss the contents of the linen closet and show me how to operate the white portable AC unit, whose accordion-like hose fits into a panel on the window.

"The owners opted for this instead of a window unit because it blocks less of the view and can be moved out into the room a bit if you want." She smiles, resting a hand on the air conditioner. "Plus, it works just great, you'll find."

The machine bears a striking resemblance to R2-D2 from *Star Wars*, which might make me laugh if I wasn't feeling so heartsick.

Back downstairs, she goes over a few more details, including the Wi-Fi password, TV remote instructions, recycling rules, and where the ant traps are stored.

"Any questions?" Clarissa asks once she's gone through her spiel.

"I think I'm all set. I just feel lucky this place turned up this week."

"The owners mainly rent to friends or friends of friends, and only use Airbnb when they have an unexpected vacancy. I'm so glad you happened to see it."

As soon as she's departed, I unload the car, needing two trips for my roller bag and the totes I've used to transport dry food, wine, and work supplies. I unpack it all, and just as I'm wrenching open the living room windows, my phone rings. I'm pleased to see Megan's name on the screen, but I also feel a twinge of guilt. When she called me yesterday, I was so crazed preparing for the trip that I didn't have a chance to get back to her.

"Hey, hi," I say. "Sorry we didn't connect yesterday."

"No problem, though I admit I've been worried about you. I was hoping you might be up for dinner tonight. Colin wants to see an old college friend who's in town so it would just be the two of us."

"Um, that's so sweet of you, Meg, but I'm in Connecticut at the moment. At an Airbnb."

"Wow, have the Larssons agreed to see you after all?"

"Nope, from what I know I'm still persona non grata. But I started thinking that if I spent some time in the area, I might be able to get a better sense of things, and even talk to some people who knew Jamie."

"Talk to a few people?" she says. "You mean for closure?"

"Uh, yeah. I guess that's part of it. But also, I still have so many questions."

"I can understand that, Keek," she says. "But be aware that you might never find answers to some of the biggest ones. That's one of the hardest parts of grieving a suicide. We never fully understand the person's motivation. And even if we did, it wouldn't necessarily make things any better."

"I know. But for my own peace of mind, I just need to be here. Anyway, can I take a rain check on dinner? Maybe in a week or so?"

"You're staying that long?"

"I have the Airbnb for nine nights but I have an option to extend. I'll keep you posted."

"Okay. Let's talk soon, okay?"

"You bet. Thanks for everything, Meg."

As I set down the phone, I experience a flutter of unease. Megan clearly wonders what the hell I'm doing, and if I'm being honest with myself, the reason I didn't tell her about my plans is that I worried she might try to talk me out of coming.

It's a little early for dinner, but there seems no point

in waiting. I retrieve the shrimp salad from the fridge, slice one of the tomatoes I bought, and then make up a plate.

As I'm pulling out a chair at the small kitchen table, my phone rings from its spot on the counter. To my surprise, I see Tori's name on the screen. I never heard back after my message on Sunday and had assumed that she had no interest in talking to me, like Jamie's other relatives. Of course, it's possible this isn't going to be a friendly conversation. I take a deep breath before accepting the call.

"I'm sorry not to have called sooner, Kiki," she says after we've said hello to each other. "But you can imagine how it's been."

I exhale, grateful there's no animosity in her tone. "I understand completely. It's just good to hear from you."

"By any chance, did I see you outside Phillips' Farm Market today?"

"Oh—yeah, that was me. I didn't see you, though."

"I tried to wave, but you were concentrating on backing out your car. Are you still up here, then?"

"I actually went home and then came back today."

I hear her breath catch. "Don't tell me the police have more questions for you."

"Not as far as I know. To be honest, I thought being here might help ease my grief a little." I decide to be direct. "Does this mean you and Liam don't think the worst of me?"

"Right now, Liam is too stunned to discuss what he's feeling, but I don't hold anything against you, Kiki, and I'm sure he doesn't either. You did what you felt you had to do."

It's not exactly a reassurance, but I tell her thank you.

"How long are you planning to stay?" she asks.

"A few days or so. I can work from here easily enough."

"I take it you'll be spending time with Ava."

"Some, though I know she and Vic are busy. Mainly I just feel that if I'm here, answers will come to me faster than they would in New York."

"Answers?"

I've let down my guard too quickly and said more than I should have. If Sam is right and Jamie's worries centered on this area, they might very well have been related to his family. The last thing I want to do is open a can of worms with Tori.

"Oh . . . just answers to questions I have in my heart—about me and Jamie."

"Right," she says. "Well, I should let you go. But maybe we could have coffee while you're here?"

"I'd love that, Tori. Just let me know when might be good for you."

I eat my dinner in the silent kitchen. It's only seven o'clock when I finish, and the evening seems to stretch forever in front of me. I could watch something on Netflix, but the TV in the living room offers no streaming options, and I don't feel like looking at the small screen of my laptop.

On the spur of the moment, I decide to walk into town. The main strip is only about fifteen minutes away by foot, and though New Burford's center isn't as over-the-top picturesque as some of the others in the area, it's pleasant enough, with a few nice shops and cafés. After grabbing a cotton sweater and locking up the house, I step out onto the porch. It's still warm outside, and something about the fading light and the balmy, fragrant air floods me with memories of August evenings as a girl, playing Hide-and-Seek and Sardines with neighbor kids in the small town in eastern Pennsylvania where I grew up, and praying my parents would never call me indoors.

I'm on Main Street in even less time than I'd thought, and after securing an outdoor table at the local bistro, I order a glass of wine. Though there are more than a few people ambling along the sidewalk, chatting and laughing, it's not too crowded tonight.

Reaching behind me to where my purse is hanging from the chair, I dig out the pen and small pad I always carry. I need to make a game plan for the next few days and set goals for myself.

Tomorrow is my lunch with Ava, and though I don't want to be forthcoming yet about my purpose here, I'm eager to hear anything she has to share. By now, she might know some more about Jamie's death than she's felt comfortable sharing over the phone.

And then there's Tori and her invitation to coffee, which I can use as an opportunity to see what *she* might have learned. After all, she spoke with Jamie only minutes before he left the party, and perhaps he said something to her that seemed unimportant at the time but has great significance now.

At some point soon, too, I'm going to have to summon the nerve to touch base with Sam. He might be up to the same thing I am—trying to figure out what was weighing on Jamie—and I want to hear about whatever he stumbles on.

I set down my pen. It's almost dark now, and the strings of fairy lights above the outdoor tables have blinked on. At any other time, it would be a pleasure to sit here and watch the evening unfold, but I'm too restless tonight. I pay the bill and set out for home.

On my way into town, there had been people on some of the porches I passed, but everyone seems to have retreated indoors now. Lights are glowing in many of the homes, sometimes along with a blue cast from a TV screen, but others are totally dark. For the first time, I experience a twinge of nerves about sleeping in the rental alone. This will be my first time, I realize, on my own up here. Whenever Jamie traveled for business, I always stayed in New York.

I reach the house, and much to my aggravation, the front door lock resists the key. Instinctively I check behind me, then reassure myself that this is a nice neighborhood and I have nothing to be worried about. Still, the street is dark and empty, and I don't like standing out here by myself. After thirty more seconds of wiggling, the key finally turns, and I push the door open.

I'd remembered to leave one of the living room lamps burning, so at least I don't walk into a pitch-black house. With a start, I notice that the overhead light in the kitchen is also on, though I could have sworn I turned it off before leaving. I take a few cautious steps in that direction. Nothing is amiss. Obviously, I'm just remembering wrong. It's clear that if I'm going to feel comfortable staying alone, I'll have to chill out and be as focused as possible.

After double-checking that the front and back doors are both locked, I head upstairs, flicking the stairwell light on as I do. The heat in the house has risen and my bedroom is stiflingly warm. Using the remote control,

I activate the AC unit, but it sounds like a blender on "ice crush," so I turn it off, knowing I'll never be able to fall asleep with that racket. Instead, I wrest open the two windows and pray the breeze will find its way in.

The double bed, at least, turns out to be inviting. It's got a firm mattress with soft cotton sheets, and there's a faint lavender scent coming from the pillowcases.

Before turning off the light, I sit propped against the headboard, sipping from a glass of water and glancing at the notes I scribbled an hour ago. There's so little there, I realize, and nothing I've listed promises many answers. What was I thinking—that once I crossed the Litchfield County line, revelations about Jamie's life were going to emerge from the woodwork and fall right into my lap? No, I'm going to have to be more proactive about finding them.

As I drop the notepad next to my phone on the bedside table, my mind flashes back to the addresses I found in Jamie's drawer. I'm still confused by that list. If life had become too much for Jamie, why was he looking at properties here and in Florida? Maybe checking them out will tell me something, at the very least, about his recent state of mind.

That's a next step, at least. And I can get started tomorrow morning.

10

I wake to soft summer light pouring in from the windows. I've somehow managed to sleep through the night, even though the room isn't much cooler. I take a quick shower, eat breakfast, answer a few emails, and then set out just after nine, with a printout I made of the photo of the address list.

The first house I plan to see is the farthest away, but I've decided to work my way more or less backward from there so I'll eventually end up at Ava's for lunch. Based on my calculations, I'll be able to see four of the properties this morning.

My journey takes me along a series of two-lane country roads, lined in many areas with weathered split-rail fences or old stone ones that probably date back at least a hundred years. The landscape is both lush and serene, a mix of farm fields, orchards, woods, and rocky outcroppings, with blue-green hills rising gently in the distance. I pass through a few small towns not unlike New Burford, but mostly I'm in rural areas punctuated with farmhouses, weathered barns, and silver silos, as well as the occasional historic clapboard house. For a few miles, there's a stream on my left, sparkling in the morning sun, and then I pass a field populated with at least thirty black wild turkeys that seem almost prehistoric.

I'm in for a surprise when I pull up to the first property. It's a fairly small, nondescript blue house, set close to the road, and not at all what I could imagine Jamie considering as a weekend home, either to rent or to purchase. Maybe some artful online photos had tricked him into thinking it had possibilities.

I keep moving, and the next two places turn out to be just as confusing, though in a totally different way. They're both ranch houses, not a style I can picture Jamie ever warming up to, and each needs some work. Maybe he was thinking of living in one for a year or so and sprucing it up, then flipping it to buy a house that was more his style. After all, if Jamie wanted something badly enough, he was more than willing to roll up his sleeves, do the necessary grunt work, and bide his time if necessary. But I feel sure he had enough money saved for a down payment on something a bit closer to his dream home.

The last house on my way back toward Ava's completely throws me for a loop. It's a two-family dwelling, which wouldn't have been right for Jamie at all. The idea of him house hunting seems more and more remote. Unless . . . unless he decided to kick off his search by canvassing absolutely everything in his price range. He was a methodical guy, after all. But it still seems like a stretch.

As I drive away, something else occurs to me: none of the houses had a For Sale sign in the yard. Of course, not everyone chooses to put one out, but what are the chances that all four of the sellers would have decided to skip that, or that the houses have all been sold?

Twenty minutes later, slightly on the early side, I arrive at Ava's. I'm prepared for the sight of the house to be tough, but it's even worse than I expected. My heart immediately begins to race, and my breath becomes trapped in my chest. The barn, thankfully, is hidden behind the house and several large trees, but I still see it in my mind's eye. I'm just going to have to do my best to maintain equilibrium and take what comfort I can from being in Ava's presence.

There are two cars in the driveway, Ava's white

Audi and a black sedan. It must be a new car of Vic's because Ava had mentioned that they wouldn't have any houseguests this week. I park my car farther down the long driveway in case Vic will need to go out before I leave.

I'm ten feet away from the front door when it swings open, and to my shock, Tori and Liam emerge. I freeze on the flagstone path, not sure how to respond. Even if Tori's holding nothing against me, Liam might be a different story. And I'm standing between them and what must be their car.

"Kiki," Tori murmurs, as the two continue toward me and we cluster together in the driveway. There's a lack of surprise in her voice, suggesting that Ava told her I was coming.

"So good to see you," I say, and give her arm an awkward squeeze. She looks drained, with her eyes slightly bloodshot, and she hasn't even bothered with her usual swipe of lipstick today.

I quickly shift my attention to her husband. "I'm terribly sorry for your loss, Liam," I say.

Based on his rigid body language, I decide to forgo an arm squeeze in his case.

"Thank you," he says evenly. It's almost impossible for me to read his expression, because his sunglasses have mirrored lenses, providing a glimpse of my sad eyes instead of his. His jaw looks tightly clenched, though, and I sense he's not too thrilled to see me.

"How hard this must be for Taylor, too," I say to him. "I remember you mentioning once that he really looked up to Jamie."

"Yeah, it's been brutal for him. What about you? This can't be easy—even if you weren't a couple anymore."

"No, it's been very hard," I say.

"And you're up here to . . . ?"

"Spend time with Ava," I say, "and to try to find some peace."

"Right. Well, good luck then."

Difficult to tell whether he's just being his no-nonsense self or there's a snideness beneath his words.

He turns to his wife. "Meet you at the car, Tor?"

She nods, follows him with her eyes as he heads toward the black sedan, and then returns her attention to me.

"Ava mentioned she was expecting you," she says. "We should have called her first, but we were nearby and decided to stop in and see how she and Vic were doing."

"No problem. And I hope you and I can have that coffee."

"Yes, I'll give you a call."

I wait for their car to pull out of the driveway before ringing the bell. Ava opens the door dressed in flowy beige pants and a short-sleeved peach top. She looks dressed for a perfect summer afternoon, though of course this won't be one of those.

"Oh dear," she says, staring briefly at the car backing out of the driveway. "I was afraid you might bump into them. I had no idea they were coming, and thought it would be too obvious if I grabbed my phone to text you a warning."

"That's okay," I tell her and attempt a smile. "It went better than I thought."

She pulls me into a hug and then leads me down the hall to the dining room, where three places have been set at the end of the antique wooden table. I suspect she's picked this room for lunch rather than the solarium, which has a clear view of the barn.

"I want to hear everything. But first let me get you a drink. How about an iced tea?"

"Perfect." As she pours us each a glass from the pitcher on the table, I settle into a chair and survey the food she's laid out: a bowl of chicken salad, a platter of sliced bright red tomatoes dressed with pesto sauce, a small dish of black Greek olives, and a sliced baguette.

Though my appetite has been mostly in hiding this week, the sight of this lovely spread makes me suddenly ravenous.

"By the way, Vic wants us to start without him," Ava says, taking a seat across from mine. "He's on a call with his publicist about an event early next week."

"Totally understood. I'm just so glad to be here, Ava. It feels good to be taken care of."

"You deserve that, Kiki. I can see in your eyes how much this is troubling you."

I nod. "It just seems horribly wrong that a person as good as Jamie isn't in the world anymore."

She squeezes lemon into her iced tea, her hand cupped over the wedge so it doesn't splash on me. In the years we worked together, she taught me how to interview and evaluate job candidates, but I also learned a lot about poise and manners by observing her.

"Yes, that's what Vic and I are struggling with too," she says, looking as though she's had her share of sleepless nights. "Jamie was such an interesting and engaging person, and we're going to miss him terribly. Especially Vic."

"They were playing a lot of tennis this summer?"

"Yes, and the two of them had gotten into the habit of grabbing lunch at the club afterward. As you know,

Jamie was a history buff and to Vic, he was his ideal reader. He loved picking Jamie's brain."

So, thanks to Vic, Ava might have more insight than I realized into Jamie's recent state of mind. I don't feel ready to raise Sam's concerns with her, or admit to searching his apartment, but I decide to feel her out a little.

"I can't help thinking about Jamie's last days up here. From what you know, was he house hunting in the area, looking for a place of his own?"

She furrows her brow. "Hmm. . . . I know Jamie was extremely committed to the region, in part because of his uncle and grandmother, but I hadn't heard anything about him wanting to buy something yet. We can ask Vic when he joins us."

She passes me the bowl of chicken salad and then the tomatoes, and we take a minute to load up our plates.

"These tomatoes are exquisite," I say. "Are they from your garden?"

"Yes, straight off the vine. I had Vic pick them this morning. I—I just couldn't bear to do it myself."

I realize with a sickening sensation that the tomato vines must be out near the barn.

"Are the police done with the property?" I ask gently.

"Yes, they seem to be, thank god."

That's good for Ava, but I just pray it doesn't mean the detectives are finished with their investigation.

We've just begun to eat when Vic comes into the room, dressed in jeans and a white collared dress shirt that he's left untucked. His thick silvery hair is pushed back from his face by a pair of red reading glasses. Though he looks as exhausted as his wife, his body seems propelled by a nervous energy today.

"Kiki," he says. "Good to see you."

I rise from the table to hug him and notice that like last time, his body feels stiff.

"Let me make you a plate, darling," Ava tells him and begins preparing one.

"Yes, thank you, love, but I'm afraid I'll have to take it back to my office with me. I need to jump on the phone again."

"No worries," she says, handing the loaded plate to him. "But come down for coffee if you can."

"I'll try," he says and turns to me again. "I'm sorry I can't join you, Kiki, but Ava will fill me in later."

"Before you go," Ava says, "Kiki had a question you might be able to answer. Do you know if Jamie had been house hunting up here?"

Vic cocks his head to the side, his eyes pensive. "If he was, he didn't discuss it with me. He did mention that he'd downsized his rental, and though the new place was smaller, it apparently suited him."

"Do you know where it was?" I ask, a hint of desperation in my tone. I feel a longing to drive by the house, to see where he was living in his last days.

"I don't, no. But Liam told me he and Tori helped Jamie's uncle pack up his belongings early this week. They're planning to address the Manhattan place next week."

Ava passes him a glass of iced tea, and with his hands full he turns to leave.

"Vic," I say, "just one more thing, if you don't mind. Was . . ." I hesitate for a moment, finally convincing myself that if there's anyone I should feel comfortable asking about Jamie's mood, it's Vic and Ava. "Do you know if there was some kind of issue that Jamie was dealing with up here—besides, of course, our breakup?"

An odd expression crosses Vic's face—concern, or annoyance—and then it's gone in a flash.

"Did someone say that?"

"Uh, not in so many words, but I was wondering if—"

"I know it would be good to have answers right now, Kiki," he says, cutting me off. "For god's sake, we all want them. But unfortunately, we're not about to get any. And we're only going to prolong the nightmare and drive ourselves nuts if we keep telling ourselves they're out there."

"I know, it's just—"

"For god's sake, Kiki," he snaps. "Let it *go*."

His words, along with his cold, blunt tone, send blood rushing to my cheeks. As he turns and hurries from the room, I slide my eyes over to Ava, sensing she's taken aback, too, and see that her lips are parted in surprise.

"Kiki, please don't take that personally," she says quietly. "As I mentioned, Vic has been badly shaken by this."

"Don't worry," I say. "I can only imagine what this might be like for both of you."

Ava tries to shift gears, mentioning a trip she hopes to take to Manhattan in September. She also asks if I've written to Daphne, her literary agent friend, and I explain that the most I've done is send her an email saying that due to a personal situation, I have to delay submitting the proposal.

But I'm still shaken by my exchange with Vic, and I find it tough to maintain any semblance of normalcy throughout lunch.

For dessert Ava brings out a bowl of clementines and a plate of chocolate chip cookies, but I only eat half a clementine and then take my leave, thanking her pro-fusely for being there for me.

I had told myself that some time with Ava would ease my grief a little, but somehow I feel worse than when I arrived.

11

I'd planned to check out the rest of the properties on Jamie's list today, but as I pull out of Ava and Vic's driveway, I'm overwhelmed with a desire to return to the quiet and peace of the rental house on Ash Street.

Once I'm back, I fill the teakettle with water and open the kitchen windows. From somewhere in the trees comes the shrill, insistent whine of a dog-day cicada, a sound I found mesmerizing as a girl but that feels unsettling today. Maybe I *do* need to let it all go. If I strip away the hurtfulness of Vic's comments, I realize they echo what Megan said on the phone earlier: looking for answers is often fruitless. But often doesn't mean *always*, I tell myself. Maybe there are answers somewhere, and if I can uncover them, I'll come to some sort of understanding and acceptance.

I just have to figure out where they're hiding.

I make a mug of herbal tea and sit with it at the table, trying to decompress. My mom had texted while I was at Ava's, so I write back with a promise to call her soon. I also scroll through the latest batch of emails from friends and acquaintances, offering their condolences. Most seem genuinely sorry on my behalf and appear to recognize how weirdly complicated the situation is for me, though I'm sure a few are gossiping among themselves, wondering if I'm the catalyst for Jamie's awful death.

Without warning, I'm ambushed by fatigue. Leaving the mug behind, I wander into the living room, kick off my sandals, and stretch out on the couch. I tell myself I'm only going to rest my eyes for a couple of minutes, but almost immediately I find myself drifting off.

I wake to the sound of a ringtone. With one eye open, I pat the coffee table, searching for my phone, but with a start I realize that the sound is actually the doorbell. Since no one except Clarissa knows my exact address, I assume it must be her dropping by to check on me or it's a door-to-door salesperson.

I struggle up to a sitting position, having no idea how long I've been asleep but noticing that the back of my top is damp with perspiration. The doorbell chimes again. I push off the couch and make my way to one of the two narrow windows that frame the front door. It's not Clarissa on the stoop outside, but rather a pleasant-looking woman in her late thirties or early forties. She must have come to the wrong address, because she doesn't look like someone about to pitch me on solar panels or better lawn care options.

"Yes?" I say, after opening the door.

The instant our eyes connect, the woman offers me a friendly smile. Her wavy brown hair, ribboned finely with gray in places, is loose around her shoulders, and she's wearing a midcalf-length floral dress, which she's paired with blue sandals.

"Hi," she says. "I'm Gillian Parr. I—hope I've come to the right address."

"Are you interested in renting here at some point?" I say, keeping my tone cordial. Maybe she learned it's sometimes listed with Airbnb.

I glance over her shoulder and notice she's pulled her white four-door sedan into the driveway, and there's a dog sitting in the back seat. As soon as he notices that I've spotted him, he sticks his head out the window and rests his chin on the door, a sweet, yearning look in his eyes.

"No, no, I live around here," she says. "I'm looking for Jamie Larsson."

I let out a small gasp, shocked by her words. Is she a

friend of Jamie's who hasn't heard the news? Someone he was dating? But why has she turned up at my rental house to ask me about him?

"Oh god, you haven't heard," I say. "Jamie passed away last Saturday night."

As her eyes widen with distress, one hand flies to her mouth.

"Oh, dear, how awful," she exclaims. "I guess I should have known something was wrong when he didn't get back to me."

"He was a friend of yours?"

"More of an acquaintance. I'm so terribly sorry."

"Thank you. But I don't understand. Why did you come here? Did someone tell you that you could find me here?"

Her brow wrinkles. "No, I didn't know anyone else would be here. I was looking for Jamie himself. This is the address he gave me."

There are a few seconds when nothing computes, when it feels like she's presented a riddle that's impossible for me to solve. And then, seconds later, the truth goes off in my brain with all the force of a firecracker.

Jamie was staying here, in this very house. *This* is the property he started renting not long after we split up, and his death is the reason the house showed up online midweek, seemingly out of the blue. According to Ava, Jamie's belongings were packed up early in the week, and the owners must have put the house on Airbnb immediately afterward.

I touch a hand to my temple, feeling woozy. I've been living in the same house Jamie had stayed in, breathing practically the same air he had before he died.

"Are you okay?" Gillian asks.

"Um, yes, thanks. My name is Kiki Reed, by the way. It's just a shock. We were a couple once, and I rented this place this week not knowing it was where he'd been staying."

"Oh dear, that *must* be a shock," she says and shakes her head. "I should get out of your hair. Again, I'm so sorry."

She turns to leave, but I raise my hand, indicating I'd like her to wait.

"What was it you needed?" I ask. "I mean, maybe I could be of help."

"It's actually fairly sad," she says. She glances over her shoulder and then returns her gaze to me. "He was going to take Maverick, the little guy in the car."

"What?"

"I work at a local animal shelter, and Jamie adopted Maverick from us."

She's caught me totally by surprise. When Jamie had told me about Cody dying, he mentioned he'd probably get a new dog, but I had no idea he'd actually gone ahead and done it. But then, I wasn't part of his life anymore.

"I'm the outreach coordinator," she continues. "I don't usually deal directly with adoptions, but since we hadn't been able to reach Jamie, and I live not far from here, I decided to swing by with Maverick."

I glance at the car again and see that the dog's ears have perked up, probably from hearing his name.

"Can—can I see the dog?" I ask.

"Of course." She touches my arm lightly in a show of support, and then leads me to the car, where Maverick jumps up enthusiastically in anticipation of our arrival.

She opens the door cautiously, quickly grabs the leash, and leads Maverick from the car.

My heart nearly breaks at the sight of him. He's a mutt, for sure, but one with some Boston terrier mixed in, just like Cody. Maverick darts toward me and presses his snout between my legs.

"God, he's a sweetheart," I say, reaching down to pet him.

"He really is. Jamie was totally besotted with him, and the feeling seemed mutual."

"And you're saying he actually adopted him? He wasn't just thinking about it?"

She nods. "The adoption was finalized a week ago.

He'd completed all the paperwork, provided references, and paid the fee."

"But why didn't he take Maverick with him?"

"Maverick developed a skin infection, and we didn't want to release him right away. When he improved earlier this week, we left several messages for Jamie, obviously not knowing what had happened. I feel sick about this."

And at that moment everything sinks in for me, making my heart hammer. Jamie had fallen in love with a dog and gone through the adoption process. He was waiting to bring Maverick home. Which means there's no way in the world he would have killed himself.

12

I drop to my knees so I can get closer to Maverick, but I'm really buying a moment to slow the colliding thoughts in my head.

"What if I take Maverick—at least for now?" I say, glancing up at Gillian. She looks like the kind of woman I'd enjoy grabbing a cup of coffee with if circumstances were different. *Jamie didn't take his own life*, I tell myself again. *He didn't take his life because of me—or for any other reason.*

Which means someone *else* took his life. It's what I thought at the very beginning. He was murdered.

"I wish I could say yes," Gillian says sympathetically. "But everyone is required to go through a formal application process before we turn over a pet. What I can do is give you one of our cards, and if you're interested, you can fill out an application."

Rising to stand, I accept the card. "Thank you," I say.

"Again, I'm so sorry about Jamie. He seemed like such a lovely man. He'd even done some volunteer work for us several years ago, helping us come up with a strong financial plan."

I try to smile. "That sounds like Jamie."

"We'll return the adoption fee, needless to say. I'll have it credited to the card he used."

She turns, giving Maverick a gentle tug and ushering him into the car again. Once seated, he gazes at me with mournful brown eyes, as if on some level he knows that he's going back to his cage at the shelter, where he'll have to begin the process all over again. I have to fight off the urge to weep in front of him.

As soon as Gillian drives off, I hurry back into the house, grab my phone, and scroll through my address book for the number I saved for Detective Calistro. It goes straight to voicemail, but five minutes later, as I'm pacing the kitchen, he returns the call.

"Good afternoon, Ms. Reed," he says. "How can I be of help?"

Wasting no time, I present what I've just learned, doing my best to sound calm and rational because I know my theory might strike him as flimsy. Hopefully Calistro is a dog lover who will understand the significance.

There's a pause after I speak, and I pray it means the detective is carefully weighing my words.

"Thank you for the information," he says finally, with perfunctory politeness. "I'll make sure it's passed along to the state police, who, as you know, are working in conjunction with us."

"Today?"

"Pardon me?"

"Will you be able to share it with them today?" I say. "Because . . . doesn't each day matter tremendously in this type of investigation?"

Does he think I sound ridiculous, spouting off some nugget I've picked up watching Investigation Discovery shows?

"I assure you, Ms. Reed, that we're taking the incident very seriously and doing as thorough a job as possible."

The *incident*?

"It's just . . . you have to understand," I say, unable to hide the pleading in my tone, "there's no way Jamie would have adopted a dog if he wasn't going to be there for him. Which means someone shot Jamie in cold blood that night—and is still out there. The killer could hurt someone else."

"I hear your concerns," he says, clearly trying to sound empathetic now. "And I realize how hard this must be. Would you like to speak with someone in victim services, Ms. Reed? They can be very helpful at a time like this."

Oh my god, he thinks I'm having serious trouble coping. Part of me wants to press him, but my gut tells me that it could backfire, making him see me as someone whose grief is clouding her judgment.

"I'm okay, thank you," I say. "I just wanted to make sure you had this information. Why don't I follow up in a few days?"

"Sure. We appreciate you keeping us informed."

The call over, I toss the phone on the table, feeling defeated. Maybe I should have gone in person, wearing the "I mean business" pencil skirt I tossed into my roller bag at the last moment. Stupidly, I'd ignored the advice I offer clients: the phone and Zoom might be easy and fast, but if you want to be convincing, it's often better to show up in person and dressed for the part.

My gaze drifts around the kitchen. Jamie stood in this room only days ago, drinking his espresso and cooking his breakfasts. This is where he was going to make the pomodoro sauce he talked about at the party. And maybe he would have sat at the table while it simmered, planning that trip to Scandinavia in search of his family's Nordic roots.

Everything I believed about him turns out to be true—that he was a guy who knew how to get back on his horse again, that he would never let a breakup derail him, and that this summer was a fresh start for him. Until someone took his life. The cops might not buy the idea, but I'm finally sure of it.

So now what? I certainly can't track down the killer myself, which means I'm going to have to find a better way to make the police take this more seriously.

Megan, I think. Maybe she'll have insight into how to convince Calistro. She's brilliant with people—I swear, she can read my thoughts across a room, sometimes even before I've had them—and part of her work as a therapist is motivating people to take essential steps in life. Besides, I'd promised I'd be in touch. I snatch my phone back and call her.

"I was hoping that was you," she says in lieu of hello. "How are you feeling today?"

"Slightly discombobulated, actually. I need your advice on how to handle something."

I tell her about Gillian and Maverick and what it all means, and how my call to the police seemed to fall completely flat. I also confess that though I thought instantly of adopting Maverick, there's no way I could take on a dog right now, and that breaks my heart.

"You must be reeling," she says when I finish.

"Reeling, yes, but I need to *do* something, Meg. Tell me how to push the cops in the right direction."

She takes a beat before responding, and I use those moments to catch my breath.

"It sounds like you've done all you possibly can for the time being, and you just have to be patient," she says.

"*Patient?* Meg, if the detective didn't take my information seriously, it's hard to imagine patience will help."

"He might have been more invested than you realized. Aren't cops supposed to come across as noncommittal, so they don't give anything away?"

I'm clearly not conveying how uninterested Calistro sounded. "Maybe, but he sure didn't seem it. Do you think I expected too much from him—that it might be hard for a stranger to understand how Jamie felt about dogs?"

"Possibly. I know Jamie adored Cody. But I'm also worried you're putting more stock in this than you should."

"Are you saying that this doesn't prove Jamie was murdered?" I ask, finding it hard to keep the frustration out of my voice.

"You could very well be right, Keek. But people who take their own lives don't necessarily want to die. They're suffering from deep emotional pain or hopelessness that interferes with their thinking and decision-making. Jamie might have been in such distress that the dog receded from his mind, or he could have convinced himself the dog would be better off without him."

"Meg," I say, "if you'd seen Maverick and heard the woman from the shelter talk about how besotted Jamie was, you'd be able to see I'm right. He would never have abandoned that dog, no matter how unhappy he felt."

"I just don't want you to get sidelined with this theory about murder and let it interrupt the grieving process."

Wow, my best friend thinks I could benefit from victim services, too. The last thing I need is any contentiousness between us right now, though, so I decide to wrap up the call before I say something I'll regret.

"Thanks so much for your input, Meg. Look, I do want to catch up some more, but I'll have to call you back later, okay?"

"Has something happened?"

"A client just texted with an emergency," I lie.

"All right. But let's plan to talk again soon."

"You bet."

I let out a groan of frustration as soon as the call

ends. On the one hand, I know that Megan is simply looking out for me. She was there when I got fired—when it practically took the Jaws of Life to uncurl me from the fetal position on my couch—and she's clearly worried I'm sinking into another state of despair. But when I needed her to see this from my perspective, she couldn't.

Should I call Jamie's uncle, I wonder, and tell him what I learned? Though it would be traumatic for Drew to think Jamie was murdered, it would also be a hell of a lot better than what he's wrestling with now. But as far as I know, he and Heather don't want to hear from me, and they might not even take my call.

There *is* one person I may be able to count on: Sam. As much as I dread speaking to him, he was Jamie's best friend and will surely see it the same way I do.

He doesn't answer, so I leave a voicemail saying that I need to speak to him urgently. It's not until two hours later, when I'm wondering what to do about dinner, that he calls back.

"What's up?" he says bluntly, like I'm someone he's eager to chase off the phone.

"Are you somewhere you can talk privately?"

"Yeah." He doesn't volunteer his location, but a second later I hear birds chirping in the background and realize he must be at his cottage outside Salisbury.

"There's something I need to share. I'm almost positive now that Jamie didn't kill himself."

The silence on the other end seems to last forever.

"Are you still—"

"Yeah, I'm here. What makes you say that?"

I fill him in briefly about the dog—without giving away that I found out because I'm at the house Jamie rented.

"And the adoption—it was a done deal?" Sam asks after I've finished.

"Completely."

Another silence. I picture his forehead creased, his dark eyes narrowed.

"So, what you're saying is that Jamie was murdered."

"Yes. Because that's the only alternative."

"But *why*? Who would have any reason to kill him?"

I can't believe Sam is sounding dubious. I have to make him understand.

"Could it have been an accidental shooting during a robbery?" I ask. "Right from the start I wondered if someone had been waiting in the field, planning to mug a guest who was getting into their car, and then—"

"I don't think Litchfield County is a hot spot for muggings," he says. "And Drew said Jamie's wallet and phone were still on him."

I keep thinking. "Maybe once the robbery went wrong, the killer bolted before stealing anything."

"But there was gunshot residue on Jamie's hand. Are we supposed to believe the killer took the time to stage a suicide?"

God, he's right, I think, biting my lip. This theory doesn't add up.

"Then he was murdered for some other reason," I say. "And the person did his best to send the police in the wrong direction. Sam, please, I need your help."

He lets out a ragged sigh. "I hear you about the dog, I do. Even if things had become too much for Jamie, it's hard to believe he wouldn't have at least let the shelter know he was backing out. But I need time to think this through. Where are you—in New York?"

"Um, no. I'm in Litchfield County too."

"Litchfield?" He sounds surprised. "All right, I'll get back to you later. I'm here as well—for most of the rest of the summer."

There's still a gruffness in his tone, but at least he's not rebuffing my entreaty.

"Thank you, Sam."

"Right" is all he says in response.

I exhale, relieved that Sam seems willing to pursue the topic further. He's not likely to have any more luck with the police than I did—but once he's thought this through, he can relay the information about Maverick to Jamie's uncle. Drew has plenty of clout in the area—and as Vic revealed, he has a contact in the state police—and I'm hoping he can make the authorities see the light of day.

I make a quick meal for myself, and after pouring a glass of white wine to go with it, settle at the table. There is a terrible truth now staring me in the face.

As Sam said, no thief would have taken the time to stage a suicide, which means the killer had to have been someone Jamie knew. That person had either learned Jamie would be at the Davenports' and lay in wait outside or had been at the party themselves. And, for a reason I can't fathom, they wanted Jamie gone from this world.

I close my eyes and summon my memories of the party. As painful as it is to be back there, I can still see the amber glow, the candles alight on nearly every surface, the guests circulating through the inviting warren of rooms. Jamie wasn't always in my sight, but I certainly don't recall anyone glowering at him behind his back, and when I did see him interacting with others, they appeared to be enjoying his company.

In my apartment the other day, Sam suggested that a family issue might have been weighing on Jamie during the second half of the summer, and with a chill I think of Liam. Liam, who left the party early and could have driven part of the way home and snuck back on foot. If he'd suddenly slipped into the front seat of Jamie's car, Jamie might have been surprised to see him, but not concerned enough to jump out.

But as I've already worked through, I never once witnessed tension between the two cousins, and when their lives overlapped, it was mostly at their uncle's house.

Someone else suddenly muscles her way into my memory. Jamie's date. I picture her long, stick-straight hair and small hazel eyes, but also the disgruntled expression she wore. Jamie seemed to pay zero attention to her that night, and when he'd spoken about her to me in the solarium, his tone had been dismissive. And, of course, she'd left the party early too.

But according to Sam, they'd only gone out briefly and it's hard to believe that getting the brush-off from Jamie would have triggered a murderous rage in her. Women who get jilted after a few dates might trash the guy to any mutual friends or, if they've got anger issues, even key his car. But murder just seems so extreme as to be unlikely.

In general, Jamie wasn't someone who went around asking for trouble. So maybe it wasn't hatred per se that motivated the killer. Could one of the guests at the party have thought Jamie posed a threat? Maybe Jamie had stumbled onto troubling information about that person and he—or she—found out what Jamie knew and decided to do something about it.

I think suddenly of the list of addresses. Perhaps they're significant in a way I can't imagine right now. Seeing the first four houses in person offered no insight, but I decide to return to that task—as soon as I'm up tomorrow.

Because maybe if I see the final three, a pattern will emerge, and it will offer a hint about why Jamie was killed.

13

By the time I head upstairs with my iPad, planning to read in bed, I still haven't heard from Sam, and I feel more than a pinch of annoyance. How much thinking could the man have to do?

The phone rings, though, just after I've changed into a nightshirt.

"I hope it's not too late to be calling," Tori says.

"No, not at all," I reply, surprised but at the same time grateful. When she'd suggested we might get together, I wasn't sure she'd follow up.

"I was thinking we could set up that coffee date—if you're still planning on being here."

"Yes, I'd like that. And I'll be around for at least a few more days."

"How about tomorrow then—nine o'clock at the Salisbury Inn?"

I ask if we can make it ten thirty, adding that I have some things to take care of beforehand. She agrees, which I'm happy about. I'm eager to talk to her and learn if she saw something at the party that could be illuminating, though I have to be careful how I ask the questions. The last thing I want to do is give her any idea about what I've discussed with Sam.

The call over, I set the phone on the bedside table and before I've even taken my hand away, it pings with a text from Sam.

Let's meet in person to discuss. 7:30 tomorrow night.

My annoyance flares again. No "Does that time work for you?" Just a command. And why the delay? Is he in the same camp as Megan, thinking that murder is something I've concocted in my grief-addled mind? Still irritated, I reply agreeing to the time, figuring we'll pick a place to meet tomorrow.

I read for an hour, then pray for sleep to come quickly—but it rebuffs me. Tossing and turning, I think of Jamie sleeping between these same soft white cotton sheets, with no sense of the horrible fate that awaited him.

Despite how ragged I feel in the morning, I'm out the door by eight. Two of the addresses I plan to check out are east of me and the other is farther south, in a town I've never been to. I decide to start with that one, figuring that the whole trip will consume about two hours.

The first house turns out to be another ranch, not unlike the two I saw yesterday. Though it's freshly painted, it's far too suburban-looking for the rural road it's located on, and not the kind of place Jamie would have coveted for a weekend retreat.

The next place I check out is a medium-size, two-story clapboard house, and so is the final one. They're both in decent condition and freshly painted, it seems, but without any of the rustic charm Jamie found so appealing. I'm left with the same impression I had yesterday: I can't imagine him seeing photos of these properties on real estate sites and deciding they were worth a look, even for a sense of what area homes were selling for these days. Like yesterday's batch, none of these have For Sale signs in their yards, either. I'm now even more convinced that he wasn't house hunting—and that leaves the list a mystery. A very odd one.

What I should do next, I decide, is google all nine of the properties and see if the search offers any kind of explanation or connection between them. At the very least, I'll discover if the houses are on the market.

As I start my journey home, I realize I'll be driving through Sharon, the town where Jamie's uncle lives in a stunning white clapboard house just a couple of blocks off the main street. Drew's a very successful portrait painter, but he was able to afford such a grand home in part because his first wife, who died almost twenty years ago, inherited a substantial sum from her parents.

Jamie loved being in that house and in his uncle's company. Though he never had children himself, Drew was paternal toward Jamie and a huge support after he lost his mother so young, and then again five years ago when his father died. And Drew's an appealing guy—tall and slim like Jamie, with longish dark blond hair that's turned pale with age, and quite attractive and energetic for a guy in his early seventies. Yes, he can be pompous at times, but it's hard to resist his zest for life. We were invited to parties, barbecues, and charity events at Drew's home, as well as laid-back dinners around the honey-colored wooden table in the kitchen.

The only drawback: Drew's fiftysomething wife,

Heather, a former yoga instructor, whom Jamie was never a fan of. Dressed in flowy clothes, Heather would act laid-back and easygoing one minute, and the next come across as totally entitled, talking with clipped tones to a handyman or someone helping in the kitchen for a party. Jamie was happy, though, that his uncle had found someone he adored after the devastating loss of his first wife, and he was also grateful Heather hadn't tried to box him out. She never seemed to warm to me, and I'm a hundred percent sure that after I broke off the engagement, she burned a sage leaf in the kitchen, trying to dispel any trace of my presence from the house.

The minute I enter Sharon, the sight of its graceful clapboard houses, church steeples, and lovely village green overwhelms me with sadness, and on the spur of the moment, I make the turn that will take me down Drew's street. Perhaps seeing Jamie's uncle's place one more time might do my heart good, helping me envision the memorial service that was held there. I understand why I wasn't included, but over the past few days I've realized that being denied the chance to honor Jamie with the people closest to him has added to my sadness and sense of disorientation.

As soon as I'm on the street, my pulse begins to race, and as I approach the house, it spikes. That's because

Drew is standing under the portico at the front of the house, along with Heather and another man, perhaps someone who dropped by to offer condolences. I slink down in my seat a tiny bit, while still being able to see the road. Though I feel the urge to pick up speed, I resist, knowing it might call attention to the car.

I exhale loudly once I'm past the house, pretty sure they didn't notice me. So much for that doing my heart good.

At the first stop sign, I check the time and see it's just after ten. Feeling a little frayed, I'd like nothing more than to head home, but I have my coffee date with Tori and there's no way I'd blow that off.

I end up arriving ten minutes early, but Tori is pulling into the parking lot of the Salisbury Inn at the same time.

"Thanks for suggesting this, Tori," I say after we greet each other on the blacktop. She looks even more fatigued than she did yesterday, with purplish, bruise-like half-moons under her eyes. "And also for accommodating my schedule."

"Glad we could do it." A few beats later she smiles in that hesitant way of hers. "Did you have errands to run first thing?"

"Yes, kind of."

After ordering cappuccinos in the café section of the

inn, we take our drinks to the wide porch that runs along the front. There's a man working on a laptop at the far end, but otherwise we have the space to ourselves.

"Is this one of your regular free days?" I ask once we've selected our own table. She's casually dressed in a sleeveless, pale yellow top, shorts, and sandals, an outfit I doubt she'd wear for her job at the library.

"No, I took some time off," she says somberly. "I felt Liam needed me—and I didn't want to have to answer any questions at work about Jamie."

As she pops off the lid of her drink, I notice her ragged cuticles. In the period I've known her, I've never seen Tori with a manicure, but based on a photo I saw of her and Liam at Drew's house, I think she used to primp a lot more. That wasn't the only difference I noticed between her during her real estate days and now. She looked really stylish in the picture, dressed in a bright white pantsuit with her hair in waves. I wonder, not for the first time, if the air of disappointment that's overtaken her since is related to her marriage. I can't imagine spending my life with someone as tightly wound as Liam, but then who am I to question anyone's romantic choices.

"Is Liam okay with us getting together?" I ask. Even if I never set eyes on her husband again, I hate to think of him harboring any animosity.

"He headed into work just for the morning and I didn't have a chance to tell him, but I doubt he'd mind. He's shattered, we all are. But like I told you before, Kiki, he doesn't blame you."

"That's so good to know," I say, then pause. "Would—would you mind telling me about the memorial service at Drew's? I completely get why I wasn't included, but I'd love to hear a little bit about it, if you're open to sharing."

She nods, staring into her cappuccino. "Drew kept it very simple. There were about thirty people in all, I'd say—a few very old friends of Jamie's, including Sam, but mostly family. A cousin on Jamie's mother's side flew in from Buffalo and so did Liam's sister from Chicago. Unfortunately, Taylor has been dealing with a bad case of strep throat, so we discouraged him from coming up for it."

"What about Liz?" I ask, referring to Jamie and Liam's grandmother.

"No." She shakes her head. "Drew decided not to tell her about Jamie. He doesn't think she'd be able to grasp it, and if she did, it would be too upsetting."

"That makes sense. She loved Jamie so much."

I take a sip of my drink and set the cup back on the metal table. It's now or never, but I need to proceed delicately. "I-I'm sure you've given some thought to the party the other night."

"Of course," she says as her expression darkens.

"Did you see Jamie interacting with anyone?"

"Now and then, but I was busy keeping Liam company, and then after he left, I talked with someone I know from the library."

"When Jamie *was* in your line of sight, how did he seem to you?" I ask. "Did you notice anything odd?"

What I want to ask is whether she saw anyone acting contentious with him, but it would give too much away.

Tori furrows her brow. "Is something not sitting right with you about the investigation?"

"No, no, just curious. I've been trying to make sense of things in my mind. For my sanity's sake."

"That's understandable." She takes a sip of her own drink, then hesitates before speaking again. "Though does it really help to relive it?"

"Maybe not, but my brain hasn't let me stop. Before Jamie left, he mentioned to me that he'd been talking to you—about a birthday gift for his uncle."

"Yes, more or less."

"What's the more part?" I ask.

"We chatted about a gift, but I think he mostly just wanted to connect."

"Was something worrying him?" I ask, trying to establish eye contact, but she thins her lips and looks away.

"*Please*, Tori. It would help for me to know."

She finally locks eyes with me. "Are you sure you want to hear this?"

My heart has started to pound. "Yes, whatever it is, please tell me."

"Jamie was far more upset than he'd expected to be by your presence at the party. I could tell it was extremely painful for him, and I think he needed some moral support, especially after Sam left."

"Gee, that's not the impression I got," I say, trying not to show how flustered I am.

She shrugs. "Well, you know Jamie. The master of keeping up a good front. He was like that when his father was killed, even though he was falling apart inside."

I take another sip of cappuccino, trying not to betray my distress.

"Oh dear, that's why I hesitated before saying anything," Tori says, clearly reading my face. "But you said you were trying to make sense of things."

I run my hands through my hair, undoing my ponytail and then securing it back into the scrunchie.

"Thank you, Tori, I'm glad you told me," I say, not sure if I'm lying. "But you know, I should get going soon. I have some work I need to get to."

"Understood. When are you planning to go back to the city?"

"Um, I'm not sure yet."

The next moments are incredibly uncomfortable. After we rise and offer each other awkward hugs, Tori's paper cup tips over, emptying the remains of her cappuccino onto the table.

"Don't worry, I'll get it," she says, as I dab clumsily at the spill with my napkin.

I give her a quick wave and take off, hurrying to the parking lot, and in my haste to leave, I nearly ram the rear of my car into a dumpster.

By the time I reach Ash Street, I'm still rattled by Tori's revelation. Chances are she shared her impressions with the cops when they interviewed her, and it could easily be part of the reason they seem invested in the suicide theory. But I tell myself not to let it throw me off course. Jamie might not have liked me being at the party, but that's not why he's dead. Someone killed him, and I need to focus on making the police take action.

I enter a house that's hot and airless. I quickly hoist open a few windows and then hurry to the kitchen, where I pour myself a glass of sparkling water and drink it leaning against the counter. Though I was desperate to leave the inn, I wasn't lying when I told Tori

I had work to do—and I also need to google the addresses on Jamie's list. But first, I decide to change out of my top. It's damp and sweaty from the long car ride, as well as the tense conversation I've just had.

I push off from the counter and trudge upstairs. The door to my bedroom is completely closed, something I must have done without thinking, because it will mean it's especially stifling in there. I twist the handle, step inside, and jerk to a stop.

The room isn't hot, it's ice cold, as if I've stepped into a walk-in freezer.

14

I glance behind me, not sure what I'm expecting to see, and then look back at the bedroom. It seems as if the AC had been running all morning, except that can't be the case. I've run the floor machine only once, and briefly, on my first day here.

I step inside and look beneath the back window, where the AC unit is sitting in its usual spot, totally silent. Good, so I haven't lost my mind. But why does the room feel like a freezer?

It takes a few seconds for my confusion to morph into unease, for me to realize that something's wrong. Since there's no way a blast of arctic air mysteriously traveled south and blew into the bedroom while I was gone, someone must have been in here, turned on the AC for more than a few minutes, and shut it off before

I returned. This seems batshit insane, but what other explanation could there be?

I back out of the room and scramble downstairs. I check the back door to see if it might have been jimmied when I was out this morning, but both the lock and door are intact. I stand in the middle of the room, arms crossed tightly, trying to decide what to do.

Calling the police won't help. I mean, what would I say—that my bedroom is now twenty degrees cooler than the rest of the house and I need the cops to deduce why? And is that what I want at this moment in time, when it's essential for them to think of me as a rational person?

No, I need to get hold of Clarissa. She might even have an explanation, though I can't imagine what it could be.

To my chagrin, my call goes straight to voicemail. I leave her a message saying there's a problem at the house and I'm hoping to speak to her as soon as possible.

Thankfully, she calls back a few minutes later. "So sorry you're having trouble," she says, her voice perfectly calm. "How can I help?"

"Something weird happened in the bedroom today," I say and describe what I discovered when I arrived home.

"Hmm, it sounds like the room just managed to stay cool from last night."

"But I didn't run the AC while I was sleeping," I tell her, "and even if I had, the room wouldn't still be this cold. Is it possible for you to drop by so I can show you what I mean?"

I think I hear a small sigh, though perhaps I'm projecting.

"All right," she says. "But I'm twenty minutes away."

"Not a problem. And thank you, Clarissa, I really appreciate it."

I've no sooner tapped the off button when the phone rings in my hand. Sam. Oddly, just seeing his name quells some of my agitation.

"We need to pick a place to meet tonight," he says after a brusque greeting.

"Um, there's a café on the main street in town. And a small restaurant a few doors down," I add, thinking of the bistro where I had a glass of wine the night I arrived.

"That sounds too public. This area is rife with blabbermouths."

Is he afraid of people gossiping that they've seen him with Jamie's ex? Or does he have some new information that he fears will be overheard?

"Do you want to come here, to my Airbnb?"

"Yeah, that's probably better."

"I need to warn you, though—I'm actually in the New Burford house that Jamie was renting," I say, realizing this fact has to come out sooner or later. "I had no idea when I booked it that he'd been staying here."

"On Ash Street?"

"Yes." There's a long pause, as he seems to process this piece of information. "All right," he says finally. "I'll be there. Seven thirty as planned."

The call ends without a goodbye, which I'm starting to get used to. Clearly he's not wild about having to spend time with me.

While waiting for Clarissa, I make half a turkey sandwich and eat it absentmindedly as I inspect all the windows on the lower level. There's no sign that any of them were tampered with. So if someone did get into the house, how did they manage it?

Clarissa arrives exactly when promised. Her hair has been shaped into a large bouffant and appears to be defying the humidity thanks to several layers of extra-hold hair spray.

"Why don't we go right up," I say and lead the way to the bedroom, in a reverse of our roles from the other day.

"It *is* a little cool in here," she says once she's stepped into the room. "But I wouldn't call it frigid."

"The room's warmed up since I called you," I say, realizing that in order to make my point, I should have closed the door before scurrying downstairs. "But still, it's over eighty outside and the room should be about the same temperature, or even higher since it's on the second floor."

Her gaze shoots over toward the window and little R2-D2.

"I actually haven't been using that since I've been here," I say. "It's too noisy for me. Is there another reason the room could get so chilly?"

Clarissa crosses to the unit and lays a hand on the vent at the top. "It's cool to the touch," she says. "Like it was definitely running earlier."

I close the distance to where she's standing and lay my own hand there, something I should have thought to do earlier.

It *is* cool.

"I promise you I haven't touched it," I say. "The machine might simply feel cool because of how chilly the room's been."

Clarissa nods lightly, her gray eyes pensive. I have to hand it to her as a property manager: though she might be starting to think I'm a little nuts, she's giving nothing away. Stepping away from the unit, she gazes around the room, and I see her eyes land on the bedside table. Along with my iPad and an empty water glass, the remote control for the AC is lying there, in the exact spot I left it the other night. Clarissa approaches the table, picks up the remote, and presses a button.

As the machine fires up, she gives a quick nod, as if everything's starting to make sense. "You know what I think happened," she says over the whir. "You must have accidentally hit the on button right before you went downstairs today."

Really?

"But even if I did accidentally turn it on, how did the unit turn *off*?" I ask. "Because it definitely wasn't running when I came home."

"I've heard from a few renters that this remote can be fickle at times," she says, bobbing the device in her hand. She points it at the machine again and presses the off button. "Like it's got a mind of its own. And of course, it's programmed to shut itself off in certain circumstances."

Next she's going to tell me it can summon Obi-Wan Kenobi if I need him. "What circumstances?" I ask.

"If the room reaches the programmed temperature, just like a window unit would."

"But wouldn't that same internal system have triggered it to kick back on once the room started to warm again in the last half hour?"

She looks up to the left, clearly thinking. "Why don't we go back downstairs and see what the manual says?"

Clarissa leads the way this time, and after entering the kitchen, she tugs open an overstuffed drawer she pointed out to me on Thursday. After rummaging through it for a minute, she shakes her head.

"Well, we seem to be missing it," she says, and I notice her sneak a quick peek at her watch. "But maybe the machine's only programmed to run for so long. Or, like I said, it was being fickle."

The machine with a mind of its own. As we stand side by side in the kitchen, my eyes drift around the room, and I think of the overhead light I found on on Thursday night, the one I could have sworn I'd turned off before leaving.

"Clarissa, does anyone besides you have keys to the house?" I ask. "Like the cleaning person, maybe?"

"Only the owners," she insists. "And they're out of the country right now. When we're between clients, I open it up for the cleaners and then come back later to see them out."

She pinches her lips together, and for the first time, I sense I might be trying her patience.

"I really don't think you have anything to be alarmed about," she adds. "This is a very safe area, and no one's ever had any issues with the house."

There's no point in trying to make any more of a case with her—because she clearly doesn't buy there's a problem. And even *I* can admit it's hard to believe someone would sneak into the house just to run the AC.

"Well, I appreciate you dropping by," I say. "I guess I just have to consider the cold air to be a fluke thing." *Or a ghost*, I think but don't say. Aren't cold spots one sign of their presence in a house?

"Yes, just a fluke. I'll let you get back to what you were doing. But don't hesitate to call if anything else crops up."

I trail behind her to the front door. "Can I ask you one more question before you go?" I say, then give her a second to turn around and face me again. "Is it true that Jamie Larsson was staying here before he died?"

The question clearly catches her off guard. "Um, yes, he was. That's why the house became available so suddenly."

"So I guess you had a chance to meet him."

"Just briefly. What a nice young man, and of course I was very sad to learn what happened. Were you two friends?"

"We were once," I say, realizing I have no right to say it. I swing open the door for her, and we wish each other goodbye.

As soon as she's gone, I return upstairs and unplug

the AC unit from the socket near the floor, so there's no chance in hell of me mysteriously activating it again. Just to be sure, I also move the remote to the top of the old wooden dresser.

Back downstairs, I settle at the dining room table with my laptop and look up the manual for the AC unit online, but it doesn't clear up my confusion. It confirms that that machine turns off when it reaches the desired coolness but should turn back on again once the room temperature is too high again.

Then, before I even realize what I'm doing, I drag the cursor to the search bar and type in "unexplained cold areas/ghosts?" I don't believe in ghosts, not for a second, but I need to see what turns up.

Those four words summon endless hits, links to stories about ghosts and signs of their presence. Some of these articles are even on reputable media sites like *U.S News & World Report* or those that cover the real estate market, obviously because most people want to avoid purchasing a haunted house.

According to the first few pieces I skim, cold spots are one of the most common signs of paranormal activity—because, according to one so-called expert, spirits draw energy and heat from a room in which they're present. Other indicators include: a sense of being watched or of not being alone; strange noises;

phantom smells; objects moved around; unexplained stains; or interference with the electromagnetic field, like a flickering light.

Or, I wonder, a burning light that you swore you turned off earlier?

I tell myself to close the browser window, that even though I don't believe in ghosts, I'm going to upset myself if I continue down this rabbit hole. And though Clarissa's explanation isn't sitting any better with me, this experience is clearly some kind of strange outlier.

For the next couple of hours, I do my best to concentrate on work that's piled up, responding to several prospective clients who've inquired about my rates and finally starting an article I was assigned days ago for a career website. The topic—how to conduct a job search without tipping off your current employer—is straightforward enough, but when I reread what I've written, it's as dreary as one of the owner's manuals in the kitchen drawer.

Shortly before seven, I make my way around the house, turning on lamps and opening a few more windows to let in the cooling evening air. I brush my hair and swipe on mascara, blush, and lip gloss, hoping to look less fatigued.

Sam arrives on time, and the mere sound of his car pulling up behind mine in the driveway makes my body tense. As I open the front door to his knock, my hand slips a little on the knob, and I realize it's damp from perspiration.

He's dressed in a weathered gray T-shirt and rumpled khakis, his hair is tucked messily behind his ears, and his dark scruff looks like it's been ignored for days. He seems even more like an absent-minded professor than usual, but I'm sure it has to do with Jamie's death.

"Can I get you something to drink?" I ask. "Water, a glass of wine?"

"Wine," he says, ambling past me into the room. His request surprises me. Maybe he's really willing to sit and talk through what we need to do.

When I return a minute later with two glasses of wine, he's scanning the room.

"I assume you've been here before," I say.

"A couple of times," he says bluntly, accepting his drink. "To watch Wimbledon one afternoon. Another time for a few beers. Mostly when Jamie and I hung out this summer, it was at the club—or a few times at my place."

"I keep telling myself that he probably felt really comfortable in this little house. I've liked being here, too."

"So, this was all a coincidence?" Sam says, with an edge to his voice. "You had no idea he'd been renting it?"

"None."

"Why is that so hard to believe?" he says.

"I don't know, Sam, but I assure you that no one, including Jamie, told me where he was staying. I wasn't having any luck finding a rental on Airbnb, and then suddenly, on Wednesday, this place popped up."

He squints, studying me skeptically.

"And even if I'd known this had been Jamie's," I continue, "would it have been wrong of me to rent it? Are you worried I'm sullying his memory by being here?"

"Maybe."

I shake my head as anger overrides how flustered I feel by Sam's presence. "Why are you acting so hostile?"

"Why? Other than the fact that you dumped Jamie during breakfast one morning with some vague explanation about you not being right for him?"

I gulp a sip of wine, gathering my nerve. "Do you think it would have been better for me to marry him even though I didn't feel what I should have felt?"

"Maybe it was only prewedding jitters," he says with a disdainful shrug. "Something that would have sorted itself out over time."

Oh, that's funny—the never-married professor's got some wisdom for the brides-to-be of the world. I feel my pulse start to race. "Not if you find yourself drawn to someone else."

He frowns. "You had an affair?"

"No, quite the opposite. I felt something for someone else, but never acted on it."

He takes a long drink of wine himself, sets the glass down on a small side table, and crosses his arms. "Who was it, then? This mystery man?"

I take another breath, closing my eyes for a second and then leveling my gaze at him.

"Please don't pretend you had no idea. It was you, Sam."

15

S am pulls back, biting his lip. I don't know him well enough to read his response—whether he had an inkling and is just playing dumb, or he's truly shocked and appalled.

I didn't meet Sam until over a year into my relationship with Jamie. He'd been on a sabbatical in California until then, meaning my only exposure to him was seeing his photograph in the apartment and hearing his voice on speakerphone in the car a couple of times. He looked and sounded too erudite to be much fun, but since Jamie was such a fan, I'd figured I'd at least be able to tolerate him.

Our first meeting was at Jamie's apartment, not all that long after I moved in and Sam had returned to the East Coast. He was fresh from tennis in Central Park with Jamie, still a little sweaty and with his hair swept back off his face. Inexplicably, and without an ounce of warning, my heart hurled itself against my rib cage.

I certainly did my best to hide my attraction to him, especially when—despite what steps I took to fight it—that attraction swelled from twinge to vague, troubling crush, and eventually to a shameful infatuation. But Sam is an observer, and highly intuitive, and I was sure he must have decoded things like my regular failure to hold his gaze and the frequency with which I begged off from dinners that would include only the three of us or double dates with him and the concert violinist he was seeing for a while.

"I'm sorry," Sam says finally. His tone sounds heartfelt, with no edge at all this time. "I wasn't aware, Kiki." He shakes his head and drifts over to a window, looking out, even though there's little to see. "I take that back. I did wonder a couple times, but I suspected it was all in my head. I swear that's the truth."

"No, it wasn't in your head."

"But *that's* the reason you called off the wedding?"

"Not entirely. But what I was feeling helped crystallize something I'd begun to suspect—that as much as I cared for Jamie, I wasn't in love with him. Back in my twenties, something happened at work that really knocked me for a loop, and in hindsight I realize that

I gravitated to him partly because I was still craving a safe harbor."

He turns toward me and cocks one of his thick, dark eyebrows. "You want to say what that something was?"

"Maybe another time. But—I'm glad to have cleared the air. We have to get to the truth about Jamie, and that means we need to be in sync."

"All right," he says quietly. "Let's be in sync then."

I nod, and as I take a seat on the couch, he crosses the room and lowers himself into an armchair across from me.

"You really think the dog adoption means Jamie couldn't have killed himself?" he asks.

It's hard not to be frustrated by how dubious he sounds. "Don't *you*?"

He lifts a shoulder, not quite a shrug. "As horrible as it is to think someone murdered him, I can believe that theory over him taking his own life. But is the adoption enough to prove it was a homicide?"

"No, but it's something to start with, and I feel we have to act on it."

"How?"

"You could talk to Drew."

"Why not the cops?"

"I tried," I tell him. "I called the detective yesterday, and though he promised to pass along what I'd learned, he didn't sound very invested, and my guess is that they've made up their minds about Saturday night. And to some degree I can't blame them. They've apparently had, like, two murders in this area during the past four years."

Sam leans back in the chair and then glances off into the middle distance. I try not to stare because looking too closely at him risks stirring things up in me, bringing back feelings I hated myself for.

"Jess Nolan," he says finally.

"What?"

"Jess Nolan. That must be one of the two people you mean. She was killed in the woods behind the Foxton County Fair."

Yes, that was the girl I read about. And I know that fair, I realize. I wanted to go with Jamie last summer.

"Did you know Jess at all, Sam?"

"Only vaguely. She worked at the tennis club, and I'd seen her around a bit. People were really shaken up by what happened."

"She worked at the *club*? Jamie never mentioned her to me. Though of course it was before we met."

"Right. And I remember him saying that her photo didn't ring a bell for him. She worked as an attendant in the women's locker room, so not everyone at the club crossed paths with her, but I ended up chatting with her once when we were both walking up from the lake to the clubhouse."

"What was she like?"

"A really nice kid. She was doing classes at the community college and working to pay her way through school."

"How tragic. And they never caught the man who killed her?"

"Uh-uh. She'd been seen at the fair earlier, and some people thought she must have been attacked by one of the workers who came with the rides and then left town right after." He shakes his head. "I'm digressing, though. I'm happy to speak with Drew, but I'm not sure what you would want him to do with the information."

"Go to the police himself. I know he'll have more sway with them than I did."

"I'll give it my best shot. Drew clearly doesn't want to think Jamie took his own life—maybe because it means he might have failed Jamie somehow—but on the other hand, he feels the evidence all points in that direction. He said he even consulted with a shrink, who told him that happy-seeming people can have demons without anyone being the wiser."

"That jells with what my friend Megan told me right after Jamie's death, but we've now got evidence saying something else."

Sam takes a final swallow of wine but continues to hold the glass, running his thumb absentmindedly around the rim.

"Do you want a little more?" I ask.

"No, I need to go soon, but I wanted to clarify something with you. Since we've dismissed the idea of a robbery gone wrong, are you assuming the killer was at the party that night?"

"I'm not assuming *anything* at this point, Sam. The person who did it might have heard Jamie would be at the party that night and was waiting outside for him, though it seems more likely the killer *was* at the party—and able to track his movements. It's totally possible it's someone we both know."

He looks off again, appearing to digest my words.

"Yeah, agree," he says finally. "It's just tough to wrap my head around."

"As far as you're aware, did any of the guests harbor animosity toward him?"

He shakes his head hard. "Not anyone *I* know. Jamie, as you're well aware, got along with everyone and he didn't go around provoking people."

"The other day you said something was weighing on him, though. What if he'd come across disturbing information about someone and the person was aware he had it?"

Sam cocks his head and flips his hands over, palms up. "Yeah, I guess that's a theory worth considering."

"We shouldn't forget about the girl who was with him, either. What was her name?"

"Percy. And West is her last name, I think. But like I told you before, she meant nothing to him. She ended up leaving in a huff that night."

"Why was he ignoring her? It seemed fairly rude of him to just box her out."

"She *deserved* to be boxed out," he says, slapping his thighs lightly with his hands. "He originally asked her to come as his date, but when he changed his mind and told her he didn't have a plus-one invite after all, she just showed up anyway."

"Why did he change his mind?"

"He was beginning to think there was something not quite right about her."

Goose bumps sail up my arms. "Define 'not quite right.'"

"She told him a bunch of things about herself that he discovered weren't true, including that she was a high-end landscape designer when she really was a clerk at the garden center in Salisbury. He was annoyed at himself for being taken in by her."

A memory bobs lightly in my mind, like an empty glass bottle on the surface of a stream, and I'm suddenly replaying Jamie's words to Sam in Ava's mud-room: *She's a complete and total fraud, not at all who she pretended to be—but I've got no one to blame but myself.*

And I now realize that those words were never about me. It was this woman Percy he considered a fraud.

"What?" Sam asks, clearly having noticed my shoulders sagging without knowing it's a gesture of relief.

"Uh, I'm just thinking about that night. . . . You said Percy meant nothing to Jamie, but what if he meant something to *her*?"

"They'd had, like, three dates, and one of them was her showing up unannounced at his house with a pizza, so it's hard to picture her deciding to murder him because he'd given her the cold shoulder."

"Still, the police should be told about her. Can you mention that, too, when you speak to Drew?"

"Sure. . . . Look, sorry, but I need to go." He pushes himself up from the armchair. "We can talk more about this later."

I rise from my seat too. "Do you think I'm totally off base, Sam?"

"No, I don't. But as I said, it's a lot to take in."

I see him to the door, and when we end up reaching for the doorknob simultaneously, our hands accidentally touch. My breath catches in response.

"I'll call you tomorrow, okay?" Sam says. "After I speak to Drew."

And then he's gone.

As I listen to the sound of his car driving off, my mind's a jumble of emotions, some scuffling with each other. It's a relief, cathartic really, to have finally unburdened myself of a secret that tortured me for well over a year and left me ashamed and remorseful. And with it finally out in the open, it means that I can talk more easily to Sam. But at the same time, there's a whole new awkwardness to contend with. Was he embarrassed by what I said? Does he pity me?

Based on his reaction tonight, it seems pretty clear that my attraction to him wasn't reciprocated in even the smallest measure, that he never experienced what I felt. *Feel.* Yes, feel, because there's no way to deny what's going on with me now. Despite five months of working hard to banish the man from my brain, two short encounters with him this week have rekindled my infatuation, as if it's been lying stealthily beneath the surface for all these months. I'm going to have to do my best to squash those feelings—because I need Sam's help right now, and we have to interact with as little clumsiness as possible.

I pour another half glass of wine and wander from one room to the next in a circle, reflecting on what Sam said about the party. Even if he didn't notice anything out of the ordinary, someone clearly arrived at the house either furious with or threatened by Jamie.

And I can't dismiss Percy as easily as Sam did. Maybe there was even more to the relationship than he knew, and she was enraged to find she was being jilted. Plenty of men have died at the hands of a woman they dumped. I need to find out more about her.

Reaching the dining room for the third time, I take a seat at the table and use my laptop to do a google search for Percy West, Litchfield County. The only relevant link I find is to an Instagram account. When I click through, I see that it's public, with her appearing to post a couple of times a week. It's definitely the woman who was at the party. She labels herself a "garden guru," and her posts—both photos and reels—mainly feature her posing with plants or flowers, looking playful, even flirty. She doesn't mention her actual job title and she doesn't tag her workplace.

But there's nothing about the posts that makes her appear, in Sam's words, not quite right.

Why had she lied to Jamie? To make herself more appealing in his eyes? I search next for the Salisbury Garden Center, a place I'm familiar with—and from my time in this neck of the woods, I'm pretty certain it's the only place like it in the town. According to the website, the doors open at eight thirty tomorrow morning.

As I lean back in my chair, my gaze drifts aimlessly over the table, surveying the files and notepads I've scattered there. Lying in the midst is the list of properties I found at Jamie's apartment. I've been so preoccupied this afternoon and evening that I lost track of my plan to google them.

That will be a top priority tomorrow, when my brain isn't as fried. But so is learning more about Percy. I'm going to head to the garden center as soon as it opens.

And then, just out of curiosity, I look up Jess Nolan, reading a few more stories about her murder. It doesn't seem as if the police ever had a suspect, at least as far as the local press was aware. According to the accounts I read, one person who knew her casually recalled seeing her at the fair, and several people reported noticing a woman fitting her description, but she'd been alone on each occasion. So what Sam said could very well be true. That she struck up a conversation with a guy who worked at the fair, perhaps on the fringe of the fairgrounds so they hadn't been noticed, and then snuck off into the woods with him—where he assaulted and killed her.

Before going upstairs, I make one last loop around the first floor, double-checking that the doors and windows are securely locked. Thanks to Sam's presence, I'd managed to put the frigid room episode out of my mind, but as I head to bed it's all I can think about. *Don't be silly*, I think. As I assured myself earlier, there's no such thing as ghosts. And no one breaks into someone's home to run their AC.

I sigh gratefully when I enter the bedroom a few minutes later and find that it's hot as hell.

Four Years Ago

He grabbed the rock and carried it with him as he tore through the woods. It was a risk, he knew. It was covered with hair and blood, and some other gunk, too, and since it was big, he could only wedge half of it into his pocket. He had to cover the rest with his hand.

But he'd heard enough about forensics to know that his fingerprints might be on the rock or his DNA, something to fuck him up. It would have been stupid to leave it behind.

His car was at the far end of the parking lot, which he was relieved to see was pretty empty, and he'd noticed earlier there weren't any cameras. He walked casually, like he had all the time in the world, but he could feel the sweat pooling on his back and on his hands, too.

He reached his car and slipped into the front seat, and within a minute he was pulling out onto the road. As soon as he was back at the house, he stashed the rock and his clothes behind the furnace in the basement and then took a shower so hot it almost burned his nuts off, scrubbing his skin until it was nearly raw.

In the morning he was on the road soon after six, though not in his own car this time. It took him only fifteen minutes to reach the Massachusetts state line, and then he kept going, another thirty minutes past Great Barrington. He ended up hurling the rock into a field that looked like it hadn't been farmed in decades, and then heaving the clothes he'd worn last night into a dumpster at the edge of a town.

He'd never planned for things to turn into a fucking shitstorm, though maybe he should have. Because after weeks of smiling and flirting and finally dropping the hint about the fair, she'd started this coy, clingy routine: *Why can't we drive there together? Don't you want anyone to see us? There's no actual rule at the club that says we're not supposed to hang out with each other.*

It had started to work his last nerve. And then it got worse as the night wore on—her getting all coy again and being weird about being in the woods, and then making it clear she wanted to get out of there. The worst was when she'd bolted like a deer, as if he was some kind of monster. And he knew she would just run and tell everyone how he was a loser and she'd ditched him right then and there.

16

I wake to the sound of rain, light but resolute, like it's determined to last the whole day. Throwing off the top sheet, I realize I'd been having a dream about Jamie's rescue dog. I sink back down on the mattress and squeeze my eyes shut, trying to summon it once more. The dog didn't really look like Maverick, but I was sure in the dream that it was him standing in my kitchen in New York, watching me intently with mournful eyes and his head cocked to the side. It seemed as if there was something he wanted to communicate, but I didn't have a clue what it was.

By the time I finish breakfast, it's only eight o'clock, and I still have a little time to kill before heading to the garden center. I decide to call Ava. She's an early riser and probably won't mind, and I want to ask her about

Percy. We've been texting over the last day or so, but this will be the first time we've spoken since the lunch at her house that ended so awkwardly.

"Kiki, hi," she says warmly after picking up. "I was planning to call *you* this morning, just to check in. How are you?"

"Getting by," I say. "There are times when I'm busy working and I'll forget what's happened and then it hits me like a sledgehammer."

"Oh, Kiki, I'm so sorry."

"How about you?"

"I've experienced the same weird disconnect you've had at moments, but I'm trying to engage with life again, working on the library fundraiser, assisting Vic with his book launch. . . . Speaking of Vic, I keep coming back to what he said at lunch the other day. I hope you can forgive him for speaking to you that way."

"Of course," I say. Though that doesn't change how much his comment stung.

"He's just been thrown so badly by Jamie's death and that it happened here—and keeps asking himself if he could have said or done something to prevent it."

So she and Vic have obviously accepted the suicide theory.

"Has he been able to keep up the promotion for his new book?"

"He's been giving it his best shot—recording podcasts and preparing for a talk tomorrow night at the Harvard Book Store. Dan, his agent—who you remember from the party—is coming for moral support. He'll spend the night here, and then the three of us will drive to Boston right after breakfast."

"I'm glad you have someone going with you."

"Me too, and the change of scenery should do us both good."

I take a moment to choose my words.

"Ava, I know Vic doesn't want to dwell on what happened to Jamie, but I hope you won't mind if I ask you one more question for my peace of mind. What do you know about Percy West, the woman who was at the party? I hear Jamie disinvited her, but she showed up anyway."

"Yes, that's all true. Jamie was embarrassed and worried that it might be awkward for me, but other than pouting the whole night, she didn't cause any problems."

Other than possibly killing Jamie.

"Do you know anything about her?"

"Only that he hadn't known her very long. Kiki, I hope you're not letting this woman get under your skin. She obviously meant nothing to Jamie."

She clearly hasn't suspected why I'm probing, and this isn't the moment to explain.

"Don't worry, I'm not. I've just found it helpful to piece together Jamie's last few days," I tell her, then change the subject. "Will you have any time for us to get together once you're back from Boston?"

"You'll be here still?"

"Yes, for at least a few more days."

"Oh," she says, sounding surprised.

"Being out of the city has been good for me, and though it might seem odd, staying in an area Jamie loved so much has been helpful, too."

"You need to do what's best for you. But . . . there's something I should tell you."

My heart skitters. "Okay."

I hear the faint squeak of a chair, and she asks me to hold while she closes her office door. Obviously so there's no chance of being overheard.

"It's about Drew and Heather," she says after a few seconds. "According to Vic, they found out that you were in the area, and they expressed some confusion—or maybe the right word is *discomfort*."

"*What?*" I say, totally dismayed. "How does my presence here affect them at all?"

For a split second I wonder if Drew spotted me yesterday and thinks I've been staking out his house, but I'm nearly positive he didn't.

"You have every right to be here," Ava reassures

me, "but they're probably so crazy with grief that they aren't thinking straight. I'm sorry to burden you with this, but I felt you should know, in case you bump into them."

"Yes, thank you, Ava. I should let you go."

We wrap up the call, with Ava saying that she'd love to get together at some point Tuesday, and she'll let me know possible times when she's got a better sense of her schedule. I set the phone down feeling disheartened.

It's distressing to think that Drew and Heather are bothered by my being here, so bothered, in fact, that they've complained to Vic. But almost worse is the fact that someone's felt the need to tattle on me. Was it Tori, or Liam? Vic himself? Of course, it might have come up in passing, not shared with the intention of stirring up trouble. That, however, doesn't alter the family's sentiments.

But I can't worry about that right now. It's 8:15, and time to head to the garden center. I grab my bag and lock up the house, then take off for Salisbury. I know exactly where the garden center is because I stopped by there a couple of times when I was living with Jamie to buy flowerpots for the front steps of his old rental house as well as herbs for the kitchen counter.

Despite how insistent the rain seemed this morning, it's come to a complete stop now, and there's even a filmy smear of sunlight in the sky. Reaching Salisbury, I discover that the town has yet to fully awaken, though there are a few people having coffee on the porch of the inn. I bear left at the fork where the inn is situated, make a turn farther up the road, and pull into the parking lot of the garden center a few minutes later.

As I'm sliding out of the car, I end up grabbing my baseball cap from the passenger seat. It seems silly to resort to a disguise, but I don't want Percy to recognize me from the party. That is, if she's even working today.

I decide to start with the large barn-red wooden building at the front of the center, where, from what I recall, the registers are located, along with shelves of garden tchotchkes. There are several salesclerks inside, dressed in khaki pants and hunter-green polo shirts, but Percy isn't one of them.

I make my way quickly across the space until I'm at the back exit. As I reach for the door, my gaze falls on a large bulletin board to the right, tacked with flyers and posters for local summer events. With an uncomfortable flutter in my stomach, I realize one poster is for the Foxton County Fair, the same fair Jess Nolan attended before her body was found in the adjacent woods. It's taking place right now.

I push open the door and venture outside. In front of me are endless rows of plants, and the air is ripe with the scent of flowers, mulch, and potting soil. I search the area with my eyes. Percy isn't here, either. *Damn. Please don't let this be her day off.*

The last place to check is the large greenhouse off to the left, and I've barely stepped inside when I spot her. She's dressed in the same green shirt and khaki pants as the other salespeople, a far cry from the low-cut cocktail dress she was sporting the night of the party.

I lower my head as I continue to study her. She's chatting with a gray-haired male customer who's dressed in a polo shirt himself, though his is light pink and probably has a little polo player on the front. The guy nods every few seconds in response to what she's saying, his attention glued to her face.

I proceed a bit farther into the greenhouse, and then turn down an aisle of floor plants that backs up to where Percy and the customer are standing. Within seconds, I'm right behind them, mostly hidden by foliage, but just to be safe I turn my back to them and pretend to read something on my phone.

"I agree," I hear Percy say. "Fiddle-leaf trees look great, but they tend to be pretty finicky."

Her voice is deep and her tone playful, like she's enjoying the exchange.

"In other words, it'll be dead in no time," the customer replies.

"Yup, I think there are better options for you."

I sneak a peek through the cluster of bright green leaves. Despite the uniform, she's clearly taken pains with her appearance today: her hair is in a polished ponytail and she's wearing lots of blush and lip gloss, plus superlong lashes that must be fake. Though she's not unattractive, the sharp angles of her face—especially her overly arched brows—suggest a hardness in her, or at the very least a tendency toward prickliness. Or do I see it that way because I've already decided I don't like her?

"Okay, time for a little quiz," she says, wagging a finger. "On a scale of one to five, how important is each of the following to you? Number one: filling an empty space in your living room."

"Five," the man says.

"Next, making a bold statement with the decor." She sounds like she's auditioning to be an HGTV host.

"Um, three. No wait, maybe four."

"Okay, now here's the last one," she says, chuckling a little. "Getting in touch with nature inside your own home."

The man chuckles, too. "Can I say zero?"

Percy offers a full laugh this time. "Of course. I've got the perfect solution: a Chinese money tree. Unfortunately, it doesn't actually *grow* money, but it has a braided trunk that makes a great statement, and you only need to water it every few weeks."

From the corner of my eye, I watch as she leads the customer away and across the floor, her ponytail swishing as she moves.

Though I only heard a couple of minutes of conversation, it was enough to give me a read on Percy. She not only seemed upbeat, but downright flirty. Her demeanor hardly suggests someone who's either choked up over a date's death or concerned that a murder might be tied to her.

It seems, at first glance at least, Sam called this right. There was probably no relationship to speak of between Percy and Jamie, and though she left the party after getting the cold shoulder, it was most likely in a huff, not a murderous rage.

I exit the greenhouse to the outdoor area and wander for a bit down the rows of plants: mostly brightly colored mums, as well as marigolds and zinnias, the flowers I always associate with fall. I realize that the summer has rushed by with me barely experiencing it, coming to an end on the most tragic note.

"Hello, Kiki." The words come from behind me.

I spin around and find Percy standing only a few inches away. I'm so shocked I can't summon a reply.

"Did you think I wouldn't recognize you?" she asks,

as I struggle for the right response. I don't want her to guess I've been suspicious of her, or even *curious* about her, which means I need to play dumb right now.

I cock my head to the side. "Oh, you were at the party at the Davenports'?" I say finally. "I'm sorry not to have recognized you."

She offers a tiny cat smile, as if she knows I'm being disingenuous and is amused by the fact, even eager to play along. For a second her hazel eyes hold mine and won't let go.

"Well, you were very busy, if I'm remembering correctly," she says, with an odd edge to her voice.

"You—you heard the news, I assume."

"You bet I heard. I was Jamie's date that night."

But she wasn't. Does she actually believe it, or is she intentionally lying to see how I'll respond?

"It must be hard for you, then, dealing with what happened."

"Of course, and on top of everything, I need to put on a big fake smile at work every day. I just wish there was more I could have done for Jamie that night."

"*Done* for him?" I say, taken aback by her comment.

"Yeah." She shrugs a hunter-green shoulder. "But it was hopeless. That's why I left the party early. I finally saw that I couldn't give him what he needed."

"And what exactly did he need so much?" I ask, now even more confused.

"Support. Understanding. . . . Forgiveness."

"*Forgiveness?* Forgiveness for what?"

She purses her lips into a tiny pout. "It's really too private to discuss, but you should know that he and I shared an awful lot with each other." Her arched eyebrows lift even higher. "Which means I know all about you, Kiki. And what happened between you and Jamie."

Her words leave me feeling unbalanced, like I'm crossing one of those swaying jungle bridges you see in movies, made with wood slats and rope for handrails. But turning around is just as scary as going ahead.

"And what—"

Her gaze has shifted over my shoulder, as if a customer or a manager has caught her attention.

"I really need to get back to work." And without another word, she strides away.

My heart is racing as I pull out of the parking lot a few minutes later. Had Percy noticed me spying on her through the foliage, like I was playing at being Veronica Mars or Nancy Drew? The thought makes me cringe.

But the embarrassment isn't what's left me shaken. It's her implication that she and Jamie had a relationship and that she had knowledge of his private thoughts—about me and more. I know from Sam that she's a liar. So maybe everything she said to me just now was a lie, an attempt at malice, or a game played to get a rise out of me.

But what if Sam has it wrong, and her connection to Jamie was deeper than he realized?

I need to know what was really going on between her and Jamie. And beyond that: What on earth did he want to be forgiven for?

17

As soon as I'm back at the house, I make a fresh pot of coffee and return to my usual spot at the dining table. I do another internet search on Percy, wondering if I missed something, but I don't turn up anything else. When I talk to Sam next, I'm going to see if he knows any other details about her, anything he forgot to tell me or didn't want to share at first.

What I should do next is prep for my Monday client calls and finish my blog post, but I decide to postpone both of those tasks. Instead, I finally google search the properties I went to see, the top question in my mind whether they're even for sale. I type the first address into my search bar. Though it pops up on several local Realtor sites, it was last on the market a year ago in August, with an estimated closing price of $245,000.

Staring at the listing photos, I'm struck again by how the house, one of the ranches, isn't the kind of place Jamie would have been interested in, even if it had been for sale.

I go through the rest of the list, including the two apartments in Florida, both of them in medium-size condo buildings. Though these eight properties all show up on at least one Realtor site or on Zillow—all in roughly the same price range—none of them has been on the market within the past year. In fact, one of them was last sold seven years ago.

Okay, so now I'm totally confused. What's the common denominator on Jamie's list, and why did he put it together?

If I knew who owned each house, it might tell me something, but unfortunately there's no personal information available on the listings. I spend a few minutes googling how to find out who owns a particular piece of property, and though there are companies that purport to help you, they all charge a small fee for each search. Since I can't tell if they're legit, I don't want to offer up my credit card details.

Giving myself a chance to think, I head to the kitchen, splash a bit more coffee into my mug, and then place a call to a guy named Kevin whom I met in my stint in human resources. Our department used to hire him to do sensitive background checks on certain job candidates.

"Hey, Kiki, what a surprise," he says, sounding pleased to hear my voice.

I tell him how nice it is to connect after all this time and explain what I need his help with, though I refrain from explaining why. Experience has taught me that Kevin knows how to find out almost anything about anyone, so I'm not surprised when he assures me he can show me how to determine who owns a given piece of property.

"The one hitch," he says, "is that California and Connecticut make it tough to find owners' names, so in general, you gotta go through a back door. You start by logging on to the town's website, then locate the link that takes you to property assessments, and then type in the address of the property you're curious about. For tax reasons, the law requires that the value of a property be public, so the town needs to provide that information—along with the owner's name."

"Whoa, that seems complicated," I say, though I've taken notes as he's spoken.

"It's not as hard as it sounds. I'll show you—just give me one of the addresses."

I recite the first one and hear Kevin's computer keys clicking away.

"Here we go," he says in next to no time. "You got your pen ready?"

"Yeah."

"The owner's name is Liam Larsson."

I sit up straighter in my chair. I'm not sure what I was expecting to hear, but it wasn't that. And though it's not far-fetched that Liam would own a piece of property besides the house he and Tori live in, I can't see why Jamie would have that house on a list.

"You still there?" Kevin asks.

"Yeah, just a little surprised."

"Want me to try another?"

"If you don't mind, that would be great."

The next address I rattle off takes him longer, and while typing he explains that the websites for some towns are more advanced than others. Finally, the clicking stops.

"Okay, got it," he says. "And, huh, guess what? It's the same guy."

"Liam Larsson?" A silly response because he just told me as much, but I'm startled.

"Yup."

Kevin asks if he should continue, but since I don't want to hijack any more of his time, I explain I'll take it from here and thank him profusely. After we sign off, promising to meet for coffee this fall, I make my way through the list. I have no luck with the first house I try on my own, but the website I pull up for the fourth town on the list is simple enough to navigate, and I quickly locate the homeowner's name. Liam Larsson.

I jump ahead to the two Florida apartments—one in Fort Myers, the other in Hallandale Beach—and the information I want pops up quickly. Liam owns these, too, each of them worth around $330,000. It's possible, I realize, that he bought the one in Fort Myers for his son, Taylor, who moved there several years ago, though Tori had said he'd recently relocated to the Miami area. I check the distance between Miami and Hallandale Beach: nineteen miles.

I've still got a few properties to check, but there doesn't seem to be any point in doing it right now. My guess is that Liam is the owner of those as well.

It's hard to absorb the fact that Liam has so many properties. I've been in his home on a couple of occasions, and though he must make a decent living running his own business, nothing explains how he could have ended up possessing nine extra properties with a combined value of—I quickly calculate—approximately two and a half million dollars. Even if he's receiving rental income from each place, where would he have found the money for the down payments? And why did his side career as a landlord never come up in the time I've known the family?

Jamie, I realize, must have asked himself these same questions after somehow pulling this list together. Had he then broached the subject with Liam? A faint siren of alarm goes off for me.

Before I do anything else, I need to let Sam know. I tap his name on my phone and when he answers with a rushed hello, I'm pretty sure from the background noise that he's in his car.

"I know we said we'd talk at some point today," I say, "but I've come across some information that couldn't wait. It—it might be the reason why Jamie seemed troubled recently."

"What is it?" Sam demands.

"It'll take a minute—do you have the time now?"

"I'm driving, so it's not ideal. It'll be better if I come by—though I can't make it there for an hour."

He doesn't seem thrilled at the prospect of showing up here—I'm sure he's even more uncomfortable being around me now that I've bared my soul to him—but at least he's coming.

"Okay, see you then."

I force myself to focus on work for a while, making

another stab at the article I've got due. I also agree to an emergency Zoom session late this afternoon with a client named Michelle, whose boss arranged a surprise meeting with her at eight thirty tomorrow morning, giving no reason why. She's terrified she's about to be fired.

Forty-five minutes later, I open the storage closet off the kitchen and drag out two of the folding aluminum chairs that Clarissa pointed out to me on the tour, and lug them to the backyard, along with a small folding table. There's a flat, grassy area under the big maple tree, and I set everything up there. I return for my laptop and then text Sam to tell him to come around to the back, thinking that maybe he'll feel less awkward if he doesn't have to be in the house alone with me.

It isn't long before I hear a car pull up behind mine in the driveway, and moments later Sam rounds the corner of the house. I hate how much my stomach churns at the sight of him.

"Hey," he says, offering a faint smile as I rise from my chair. Though it's nothing to write home about, it's the first smile he's given me since I ended things with Jamie.

"Hi. Is this okay—I mean sitting out here?"

"Yeah, fine." He drops into the empty chair across

from me, with its slightly tattered green and white plastic strips, and stretches his long legs out in front of him on the grass. He looks a little less unkempt today, dressed in khaki shorts and an unwrinkled heather-blue T-shirt.

"So, what's going on?" he says, not wasting any time.

I start by coming clean, confessing that I had snuck into Jamie's apartment last week, hoping to learn what had been troubling him this summer, and found the list. Sam lifts an eyebrow as I'm speaking but doesn't comment. Then I grab my laptop, click the pages I've saved, and show him one by one, demonstrating that the properties all belong to Liam.

"It just doesn't smell right to me," I say.

"Huh," he says, his brow furrowed. "I've never thought of Liam as someone with a lot of dough to splash around. Could he have inherited money?"

I shake my head. "His father was a veterinarian in the area, and though I believe they had a comfortable life, they weren't wealthy. And from what I heard, Tori grew up modestly."

"So then where'd he get the money?"

I nod. "Exactly. What I've been wondering over the last hour is whether he got it from his grandmother—without anyone being the wiser."

"*Liz?* You think he took advantage of her cognitive decline to talk her out of money?"

I let out a long sigh. "The truth is, he wouldn't have had to do any talking. Jamie told me once that Liam is the one who handles their grandmother's finances, which means he keeps an eye on her accounts and pays her expenses at the assisted-living facility. She apparently has a pretty nice nest egg."

"How did Liam end up with that responsibility?" Sam asks.

I stretch my own legs out across the grass. As tense as I am, it's calming to be sitting in the backyard after so many hours cooped up inside the house.

"From what I know, Drew asked him to take over the task because Liam lives around here, and so it seemed to make more sense for him to be in charge instead of Jamie. And for what it's worth, Drew lets Liam draw a monthly fee for his efforts."

"Was there any oversight of the arrangement?"

"Well, not by Jamie, or he would have mentioned it when he was telling me all this."

"It makes sense that Drew would farm out the job—I've heard him say more than once that he doesn't have a head for numbers—but there should have been oversight. Regardless, this list suggests that

Jamie stumbled on something that made him suspicious of Liam."

"Right. And don't you think this could be what was troubling him so much the weeks before he died, that he suspected his cousin was defrauding his grandmother and wasn't sure how to handle it without causing a massive rift in his family?"

Sam scrunches his mouth to one side. "Maybe. And here's something else. Remember how I said that the first time I noticed Jamie seemed troubled was during lunch at the club, and that he'd just come from seeing Liz?"

Something clicks into place for me. "Apparently, she still has lucid moments, so what if she said something that tipped Jamie off?" I sigh. "God, is it really possible Liam stole from her, and Jamie found out?"

"There could be a perfectly legit explanation for Liam owning the properties," he says. "But let's say there isn't. Would your next thought be that Liam murdered Jamie to prevent him from exposing what he learned?"

"Yes, I guess it would be," I say, though the idea nearly leaves me breathless. "And he left the party early, which means he had opportunity."

"This is pretty fucking awful—that Jamie might

have been shot by his own cousin. And what are we supposed to do about it?"

I shake my head, bewildered. "If Drew can get the police to start viewing this as a homicide, they'll have to take a closer look at all the party guests, and who in that group might have had a motive. Because he left early, Liam is going to grab their attention, and at that point I'd feel obligated to turn over this list to them. . . . Have you spoken to Drew, by the way?"

Sam looks confused.

"About the *dog*," I say. "And the fact that Jamie couldn't have killed himself."

"Not yet," he says. "But I will. I think it's important to do it in person, and I have to find the right moment."

His response triggers a prick of impatience in me. What's he waiting for? As if sensing my feeling, Sam suddenly grabs hold of the chair arms and pushes himself into a standing position, obviously ready to split.

"Maybe I should stop by Drew's now and see if he's home," he says.

I'm glad he's following through, but his departure seems abrupt. I rise as well and trail behind him toward the driveway.

"Sam, wait," I call out. "I need to ask you something else—about Percy West."

He spins around, looking surprised. "What is it?"

"I was at the Salisbury Garden Center today and she came up to me and started talking about Jamie."

His eyes bore into mine for a few moments. "I'd stay away from her, Kiki," he says finally.

"Is there something about her you're not telling me?"

"No, nothing, other than the fact that I never got why Jamie asked her out in the first place."

I've been asking myself the same question. Maybe he met her one night when he was hanging at a bar in the area and, newly single, fell for one of her flirty quizzes.

"Do you think he was seeing Percy longer than you realized—before he figured out she was a phony? She seemed to know stuff about me."

"There are only so many ways I can say it." Sam exhales loudly. "He barely knew the woman."

"Had he slept with her?" I know it's awkward for me to ask this, but it feels relevant.

"He told me he hadn't, and he wouldn't have had any reason to lie."

"Then why did she say she couldn't give Jamie the forgiveness he needed?"

Okay, now he's starting to look annoyed. "*What?* Jamie didn't need forgiveness—from her or anyone else."

Then he's gone, and a second later I hear his car back out of the driveway and emit a small screech as it makes the turn. Does he not like me pressing him about Jamie? Or did he take off so quickly for a second time because he knows I want something from him that he'd never be able to give?

Leaving the chairs and table behind, I trudge inside with my laptop. Maybe it makes no sense to question Percy's role in Jamie's death. She's simply, as Sam suggests, an odd, unpleasant woman who lied to Jamie when he first met her, only to reveal her true nature a short time later. And she decided to get a rise out of me by pretending that the two of them were closer than they were.

Clearly the person I should be focusing on is Liam. But all I can do right now, it seems, is wait for Sam to contact Drew and hope the police will be galvanized into action, action that will eventually cast a light on Liam.

I despise holding patterns, in part because they remind me of the assault by R and how my failure to act made it even worse for me in the end. I convinced myself that I was doing the right thing by not reporting the situation, that it was smart to let sleeping dogs—so to speak—lie. R seemed to avoid me after that night, and when our paths occasionally crossed, he never made eye contact. *See*, I told myself. *Good call.*

Before long, however, I felt my certainty morph into dread. Was this simply the lull before the storm? Was R, emboldened by my silence, orchestrating a scheme to get me alone so he could try again, even more aggressively this time, or was he concocting his revenge? His lack of eye contact became ominous rather than reassuring, and soon I spent each workday welded to my desk, waiting for the other shoe to drop. I was no longer simply passive, I was practically unable to move, to perform. When I was fired soon after, I was positive R was behind it, but because of the dip in my performance, I didn't see how I could push back against the decision.

I can't do that kind of waiting now, I decide. Yes, on the one hand it seems ludicrous that Liam killed his own cousin. Perhaps he's more successful financially than I ever imagined, and Jamie had the list because he was considering buying an investment property himself and wanted advice. On the other hand, maybe Liam's a thief, one who would do anything to prevent being found out.

If only there was a way to learn more about the properties—but I have only a handful of days left here in the house, and I'm not sure what I'd be able to find out from my apartment in New York.

Wait, maybe there is a way. It will involve retracing some of my steps and summoning some chutzpah. But I'm game for both.

18

As eager as I am to execute my plan, I've got my client Zoom call coming up and after that it will be too late in the day. I'm going to have to cool my heels until first thing tomorrow morning.

I return to the pile of work in front of me, then at five minutes to five, I change into a blouse for my appointment and head to the dining room, laptop in hand. I like Michelle. She's talented and hardworking, but she lacks confidence, and that's prevented her from not only coming across as effectively as possible but also advocating for herself.

After we greet each other, I tell her not to be alarmed, that the meeting request might be simply an impromptu one. I suggest we run through various reasons her boss might want to get together and then play out a response to each, including an appropriate one if she is indeed let go. We seem to make a lot of progress over the next thirty minutes, but as we wrap up the role-playing, Michelle lets out a long, anxious sigh.

"Do you want to talk it through a bit more?" I ask.

"No, that's not necessary." She grimaces. "It's just—well, I know you've encouraged me to speak up more and to ask for opportunities, but I'm wondering if it's backfired somehow, that I've come across too aggressively. And now they think I'm a bad fit for the organization."

Her comment totally throws me. "I doubt that's it," I say, trying not to appear as offended as I feel. "From what you've told me, it sounds like everything you've done lately has gone over well. Try to put the meeting out of your mind for now, unwind over a nice dinner, and text me tomorrow once you know what's up."

"Um, okay. Thanks, Katherine."

As soon as the call ends, I drop my elbows on the table and sink my head into my hands. Could Michelle be right? Have I misread what she's told me about her company's ecosystem and pushed her to be more assertive than is warranted? I was sure I was guiding her correctly and felt proud of the sessions I'd done with her, but what if I actually fucked things up for her?

I urge myself not to worry yet, since I won't know anything until Michelle reports back to me tomorrow.

It's nearly six now, and after a short but comforting call with my mom, I wander into the kitchen. Mindful of the advice I gave Michelle about unwinding over a nice dinner, I thaw a chicken breast in the microwave, coat it with a beaten egg and a ton of breadcrumbs, and sauté it in olive oil. I also make a tomato salad. On the spur of the moment, I load the finished meal onto a tray and carry it to the backyard, along with a citronella candle.

It's turned out to be a beautiful evening, in total contrast to the morning. There's a light breeze now, and the air is ripe with the smell of citronella as well as the intoxicating, jasmine-like scent of honeysuckle.

Almost imperceptibly, dusk dissolves into twilight. Fireflies begin to blink in the grass, and before long they're glowing everywhere in a dance that almost looks choreographed. For a few brief seconds, I could be twelve years old again and back in Pennsylvania, hanging outside after dark for another game of Capture the Flag to begin. It seems like any minute now, I'll hear one of my parents' voices calling me inside.

I try to relax and savor the moment, but it's next to impossible. For one thing I can't look at the chair across from me without thinking of Sam sitting there earlier and being reminded that my feelings for him are completely ridiculous. I'm also still agitated from the day's events—my unsettling encounter with Percy, as well as the discovery I made about the properties on Jamie's list and what they might mean.

It's more than that, though. This small backyard might be lovely, but it's not where I belong. I should be back in the city—seeing friends, getting to know my new neighborhood, having coffee in the afternoons at the small café near my apartment building, and working out of my own little home office, where I can be clearer headed about my work.

But I can't leave. Not until I've done everything I can to ensure Jamie's killer is apprehended.

I'm up early again on Monday, and after a quick breakfast, I'm on the road by seven thirty, dressed in one of the nice tops I brought and a cotton skirt.

My plan today is to revisit some of the houses on Jamie's list and see if I can talk to anyone who's living in them. I've set out early so I can catch residents before they leave for work. I'm not sure what kind of success I'll have, but I'm hoping that speaking to someone living in at least one of the properties will shed light on the matter. Are the houses owned solely by Liam, for instance, or has he partnered with anyone, which would have made them more affordable? Are they definitely being rented out? I assume that's the case, but I want to be sure. And maybe I can even stumble onto revelations beyond that.

I stop first at the closest house on the list, but I'm out of luck. Though the place appears occupied, the driveway is empty, and no one answers the door when I knock. My second try, at a house about fifteen minutes farther west, is also a bust. Then, thanks to getting stuck behind a tractor on a two-lane road, it takes me nearly half an hour to reach the third spot, one of the ranch houses I saw on Friday. To my relief, there's an SUV in the driveway, so I park along the road. After climbing out of my car, I walk up the sidewalk and, taking a breath, rap on the door. After a short wait, my knock is answered by a bearded guy is his late thirties or early forties, about five ten and stocky. His dark brown hair is styled in a mullet, and something tells me it's not a tongue-in-cheek homage to the '80s.

"What can I do for you?" he asks without a smile, as if he's hoping my answer will be "Nothing." He's holding a metal travel mug, which suggests he's planning to hit the road soon.

"Good morning. I'm trying to find a house to rent and—"

"Let me stop you right there," he says, kicking up his chin. There's a jagged white scar on it, shaped like the blade of a saw. "You must have been looking at an old listing—this place is rented now."

"Yeah, I thought it might be," I say and beam a smile. "But I heard the guy who owns it has other places for rent, and I was hoping you could give me the name of his company or tell me how I can get in touch with him."

He stares at me, scrunching his mouth to the side. "You new to the area?"

"No, I'm renting a place around here, but the owner is thinking of selling." On the drive from Ash Street, I'd decided not to say I was from New York. I figured that if anyone I talk to ends up mentioning to Liam that a woman dropped by asking questions, it will have been best not to draw attention to being from the city. "I'm sorry to show up out of the blue, but I'm feeling kind of desperate. There's so little inventory these days."

"The guy who rents it is on his own, not with a company," he says after a brief hesitation, "but yeah, I guess I can give you his number." He seems to have lowered his guard, and I sense he's buying my story.

He tells me to wait and disappears into the house. Without him acting as a barrier, I get a better look at the entryway area. It's freshly painted, but dusty, and the floor is cluttered with work boots and sneakers. After a few seconds, the house smells finally reach out to greet me, a combination, I think, of weed, bacon, and dog fur.

"Okay, here ya go," the guy says, returning shortly with a crumpled envelope. He shifts his gaze to read from the back of it. "The owner's name is Liam Larsson."

"Great, thanks," I say, taking my phone out for show and typing in the number as he rattles it off.

"I think he does have other places," the guy adds, "but I have no clue if they're available."

"Well, it can't hurt to ask." I pause, wondering if there's anything else I can extract with the right question. "Uh, what's he like, anyway? Is he easy to deal with?"

"Yeah, a straight shooter. Responds pretty quickly when something leaks or falls apart."

"Good to know."

"Listen, I wish I had all day to chat, but I really don't, okay?"

"Of course, thanks again for your help."

I make my way to the car, sensing eyes on my back. I don't have a lot to show for my efforts, but at least it seems that Liam is the sole owner and is using this particular house to generate income, suggesting that's probably the case with all of them. There's still the chance, of course, that his son lives in the Hallandale Beach condo and that he and Tori use the other condo part of the winter for themselves.

Regardless, this would all add up to a big chunk of rental income annually, which would help defray interest charges on the mortgages. But it doesn't explain where Liam got the money for the down payments.

"Hey, hold on a sec."

I spin around to find the renter still standing on the threshold. *Please,* I think, *don't let him have decided that something fishy is going on.*

"Yes?"

"How'd you find out about this property anyway?"

"Uh, gosh," I say, scrambling for a plausible answer. "I think someone I know must have mentioned the address, and it ended up on this big list I compiled."

"Do you know where this person heard about it?"

"I don't. I've been jotting down any leads that come my way."

He shakes his head, looking irritated. "I'm starting to wonder if the owner might be pulling a fast one and trying to rent this place out from under me."

"I doubt it," I say. "I just made a mistake."

"No, something's going on. Because you're not the only person who's wanted to know. Some dude showed up a few weeks ago and asked pretty much the same question."

My breath catches. "Was the guy who came by in his late thirties?" I ask, taking a few steps closer to the door again. "Tall, with blondish hair?"

He nods, his expression wary.

"Oh, that was a friend of mine who was helping me look," I say, hoping it doesn't sound as lame to his ears as it does to mine. "I'd given him my list, and he must have forgotten to tell me he stopped by. I'm so sorry for any confusion. Like I said, it's all a mistake."

I sense him still watching me as I continue to the car, but I don't look back and try to seem casual as I slide into the driver's seat. When I've gotten a few blocks away, I pull over to the curb, put the car in park, and sink back into the seat with my eyes closed.

The *dude* who came by was obviously Jamie. He must have set out one day like I did, hoping to find someone to speak to who could illuminate the list of properties for him.

By knocking on this door and possibly others, or by searching online—or both—he must have figured out that Liam owned at least some of the properties and asked himself where the money could have come from. And then surely, just like me, he wondered if Liam had used their grandmother's nest egg to turn himself into a minimogul—without anyone in the family being the wiser.

19

I shudder, realizing that the hunch I shared with Sam—that Liam murdered Jamie—could very well be right. If Liam was stealing, he would have utterly panicked when he figured out that Jamie was onto him, not knowing whether his offense would be dealt with discreetly by the family or he'd be reported to the police. In the case of the latter, it could mean serious jail time for him.

According to the guy with the mullet, Jamie stopped by the house several weeks ago, and that fits with what Sam said about Jamie making the decision in late July to spend most of August in Litchfield County. He was obviously planning to investigate the matter further, then act on what he learned. Had Jamie confronted Liam at the party? If so, my guess is that Liam left early, drove home, and returned with a gun. He might even have had the gun in his car. However, from what I saw at least, there didn't appear to be any tension between Jamie and Liam, or Tori, that night.

Or: What if Jamie decided to stay quiet until he had the full picture, but Liam learned from one of the renters that he was snooping around? That would have put Liam against the wall. If that's the case, he might have gone to the party with a plan in place to take off early and lie in wait, then ambush his cousin. When he left the house, he'd probably driven a short distance away, parked his car where it wouldn't be noticed, and then made his way back on foot, gun in hand.

Of course, the plan would have been derailed if Jamie had departed earlier, heading to the field at the same time as other guests. But . . . but what if that was why Tori grabbed Jamie to ask about a birthday gift for Drew—to stall him and delay his departure? That means she might have been in on it too.

I shudder again. Tori seemed curious about why I decided to come back here. Though I've been careful in speaking to her, she might have picked up on my suspicions and shared that with Liam. If so, I could be in danger—and so could Sam, if they know I've been speaking to him. I have to protect both of us.

With my stomach churning, I grab my phone and text Sam.

I have an important update. Can you call me?

I give it a couple of minutes, hoping for a response, but nothing arrives.

As I start to drop the phone into my purse, I notice that my client Michelle has texted with an update: her boss wanted to meet, it turns out, to give her a special assignment, a plum one that will be great for her career. She's eager to set up a call to discuss. I shoot her a thumbs-up emoji, but tell her that I'm in the middle of something and will email her later to arrange a time to speak.

My main objective right now is figuring out how to get enough information to prove that Liam had a clear motive for murder. I could drive to the other houses on the list, hoping to speak to additional tenants, but I'm not sure what more there is to discover that way. Besides, making contact with additional renters will only increase the likelihood of my snooping getting back to Liam.

Without warning, an idea blooms in my mind, one I can't believe I'm thinking. At first, I push it aside. It seems like a big risk, and perhaps even a violation, and yet I can't ignore the thought as I drive, barely noticing the lush farmlands on either side of me. Before I know it, I'm taking a left turn onto another road, a turn that clarifies that I've made a decision. I'm going to the assisted-living facility where Jamie's grandmother lives.

I spent time with Liz on at least a dozen occasions while Jamie and I were together, first at Drew's house, when she still felt comfortable going out, and then more recently at the residence, when I sometimes accompanied Jamie on his visits. According to Jamie, Drew encouraged his mother to move in with him after his father died and her house became too big for her to handle alone, but she valued her independence and opted for a retirement community. Initially she had a roomy two-bedroom apartment, allowing for plenty of autonomy, but as her dementia revealed itself, she was moved into the facility's memory care center.

From what I recall, that section has very generous visiting hours, but not anyone can just show up. You need to be on a list. Fortunately, Jamie placed my name on that list, and I can't imagine him having bothered to ask for it to be removed.

The drive takes about twenty minutes, and I pull into the parking lot just before eleven. I take a moment to touch up my makeup in the rearview mirror, and once I've exited the car, I smooth out my skirt. From what Jamie told me at the party, Liz's condition has worsened since I last saw her, but I'm praying that a chat might reveal a detail or two about her visit with Jamie, the one that led Sam to believe something was really troubling him. Had he come right out and asked her about Liam?

As I cross the parking lot, with the odor of hot asphalt filling my nostrils, I have second thoughts. What if my visit upsets her? What if it makes her wonder about Jamie and why he hasn't been to visit her over these past days? But Liz—at least Liz-before-her-decline—would support what I'm doing. She and Jamie were extremely close when he was growing up and became even more so after his mom passed away.

Since the temperature is already in the mideighties, it's a relief to step into the attractive lobby of the building, where the AC is going full blast. I glance quickly around. The reception desk is on the right, and farther ahead of me, the lobby widens considerably, with passageways shooting off in different directions to the independent living section, as well as the library, beauty salon, and gym.

It looks busy ahead, with people coming and going and others stopping to chat with each other. My heart instantly picks up speed. *Please*, I think, *don't let me run into one of the Larssons today.* I have no idea how often Liam visits, but I know Drew stops by a couple of times a week. I just have to hope Monday morning isn't one of them.

I head to the reception desk, where a pretty brown-haired young woman on duty raises her head and smiles in greeting.

"Good morning," she says pleasantly.

"Morning. My name is Kiki Reed, and I'm here to see Liz Larsson. Is this a good time?"

"Let me check." She types for a moment on the key-board of her desktop computer, pauses to read what comes back on the screen—hopefully a verification of my presence on the list—then types a little more before offering another smile. "Mrs. Larsson is in the day-room at the moment, so your timing is perfect. Do you know how to get to the memory care area?"

"Yes, thanks, I do."

"Great, if you just sign in, you'll be all set."

I reach for the clipboard with the sign-in sheet and surreptitiously scan the names of everyone who's checked in before me this morning. Fortunately, no members of the Larsson family are here at the moment. And since the sheet is a daily one, it means that as long as none of them visits later on, the Larssons aren't likely to find out I've been on the premises. I sign my name illegibly and then proceed into the larger section of the lobby, my guilt intensifying with each step. I can't believe I'm doing this, but at the same time I know it's the right thing.

I keep going until I reach a more remote area that leads into a separate small lobby. A locked door there is marked with a sign saying MEMORY CARE, PLEASE CALL FOR ENTRY and a phone number.

A friendly voice answers when I call, and after I give both my name and Liz's, I'm asked to please wait. About five minutes later, a female staff member opens the door and politely ushers me inside. Unlike the receptionist, this woman looks vaguely familiar, and I spot what seems to be a flicker of recognition in her eyes.

She leads me immediately to the sunny dayroom, where about ten residents and several staff members are seated, and I spot Liz immediately. She's in a comfy-looking chair by the window, wearing a floral top and loose cream-colored pants, with an unopened book in her lap. Her short, wavy white hair is nicely styled. From a distance, she seems pretty much the same as she did when I first met her—curious and serene at the same time. But as I approach the chair, I notice that there's a vacant look in her pale blue eyes.

"Liz, Katherine is here to see you," my escort says. "Isn't it great to have a visitor this morning?"

Liz glances up, her expression blank, but after apparently registering my presence, she offers a vague smile.

"Liz, hello, it's so wonderful to see you," I say. And it is. But with a terrible ache, I suddenly recall that the last time I was here was in early March, when I'd finally acknowledged to myself that my relationship with Jamie was doomed. Racked with self-reproach over what I'd soon be doing, I listened to him regale his grandmother with plans for a wedding that would never be.

After suggesting I take a nearby chair, the attendant wishes us a nice chat and tells me she'll be on the other side of the room if I need her.

"You're welcome to stay as long as you'd like," she adds quietly to me. "But we've been finding that she tires after about ten minutes. She can also become a little agitated—if that happens, just signal for me."

"Thank you," I say and drop into the nearby chair.

As soon as the attendant walks off, I return my attention to Liz. My decision to come was so spur of the moment that I haven't given any thought to what to say. But I realize my first step should be making Liz feel as comfortable as possible in my presence.

"Liz, how is your day going so far?" I say, smiling.

She stares at me, her expression blank.

"Your outfit is lovely. Is it a favorite of yours?"

Again, no reaction. Her condition must have worsened more than I'd imagined since I was here last.

Desperate for a way to engage, I glance down at the book she's grasping with pale, gnarled fingers. The title is *The Picture Book of Birds*.

"What a charming cover. And I know you've always been an avid birder."

In a flash, the blankness leaves her eyes and there's an inquisitiveness there now, as if I've somehow triggered a moment of lucidity.

"I saw a bullfinch today," she announces. "A male with a red-orange breast."

"Oh wow," I say, surprised by the specificity. "Did you see a picture of it in the book or was the bird outside?"

"Outside."

"That's wonderful. What other birds did you spot this morning?"

She doesn't respond.

"Well, I'm glad you got to see the bullfinch at least."

Her gaze slides off my face, and I realize I'm losing whatever ground I gained.

"Liz, I need to ask you a question. Has anything been bothering Jamie lately? Has he mentioned any concerns to you?"

I hate myself for even breathing Jamie's name. What

if she's missed him and is wondering why he hasn't been to visit her? And yet, I remind myself, the Liz I know would be urging me to find the truth.

She suddenly shifts her attention back to me. "What is your name?"

"Kiki. I'm Kiki Reed. I used to come visit you."

"Are you a friend of Tori's?"

"I know Tori, for sure. Was Jamie worried about Tori? About Liam and Tori?"

"I don't know you," Liz says. Her voice is cold now, and her eyes flicker a little, as if in fear.

"We don't know each other well, but we've met on numerous occasions. I came to vi—"

Without warning, she lets out a high-pitched keening sound, one that seems to get louder each second, like a siren piercing the night.

"Liz," I say, reaching over to touch her hand. "Please, you *do* know me, I'm Kiki."

But the keening doesn't stop. By now everyone in the room is glancing over, and the staffer who escorted me here is on her feet, moving fast in our direction.

"I'm so sorry," I tell her. "She doesn't seem to know me and it's scaring her."

The woman speaks softly to Liz, offering words of comfort that immediately calm her, then turns back to me.

"It's not your fault. But it's probably best that you end your visit now."

"Yes, understood." I look into the woman's eyes, trying to keep the shakiness I feel out of my voice. "You won't say anything to her family, will you? I'd be so embarrassed to have them know."

"Don't worry," she says, "and please don't take this personally. Sometimes small things can stress her out."

I murmur goodbye to the attendant, but I don't dare address Liz again. Though I feel frantic, I force myself to walk toward the door at a leisurely pace, so as not to draw even more attention to the situation. By the time I reach the parking lot, my heart's racing and shame has blistered inside me. It was wrong of me to come. Wrong and callous.

The drive home is a blur, and once I reach the house, I slink inside like a dog with its tail between its legs. Though I showered already today, I take a second one, this time with lukewarm water. It cools me down but does nothing to wash away my distress. I pray that Liz is feeling okay now, and that the attendant was sincere when she said she won't report my visit to Drew. Because that could make matters even worse.

Over a late lunch, I google "bullfinch," wondering if there was any significance to Liz bringing it up. The male of the species turns out to be absolutely gorgeous, with a pinkish-red breast, gray back, and black cap, but it's found only in Asia, parts of Europe, and the UK. So Liz must not have seen one today but had tapped into a memory from years ago, perhaps when she was visiting Europe with her husband.

The moment hadn't been truly lucid after all. Which means that even if Liz hadn't become upset today, she probably wouldn't have been able to share coherent or credible information about Liam. And she might not have told Jamie anything of value, either.

There doesn't seem to be any way for me to get proof of Liam's guilt on my own. I have to count on Sam's ability to convince Drew to go to the police and urge them to delve deeper. Once the cops start taking a closer look at the party guests and wondering who had a motive, I can, as planned, turn over the list of addresses to them, and they'll surely zero in on Liam.

The rest of the day drags on, with me doing my best to concentrate on work but failing miserably. I can't stop thinking about what I've learned or worrying whether Liam and Tori suspect that I've been out there digging into their lives. Each time I get up to make a fresh cup of tea or grab a piece of fruit from the kitchen, I take my phone with me in case Sam calls or texts, but there's no word from him. At the very least, I thought he'd fill me in about his visit to Drew.

By nine, I can barely keep my eyes open. Before heading to bed, I double-check the locks on both doors, reassuring myself that even if Liam and Tori have their suspicions, they don't know where I'm staying. There's still no word from Sam, and as I mount the stairs with my phone in hand, I can practically feel my anger pulsing in my fingertips. He doesn't share my sense of urgency about finding the truth, and I don't know how to fix that.

As I'm pulling back the bedspread, my phone pings with a text. I'm sure this finally must be Sam, but it's Ava.

Hello dear one. Bookstore talk over and done with. Headed back tomorrow, how about an early dinner at the club? 7:00? Dan's staying on for a couple of days, and he and Vic will do a working dinner so it can be girls only!

I'd love that, I write back. But the club only lets members pay and I don't want you to have to treat me.
You can treat me in the city.
Deal.

I smile to myself, glad that I'll be seeing her again soon. Despite how warm the bedroom is, the sheets are cool, and I let my body sag in relief as soon as I'm between them. I'm so exhausted that sleep soon overtakes my swirling thoughts.

When I next open my eyes, it's pitch-black and, I sense, not even close to morning. Flipping onto my side, I squint at the bedside clock: 3:45. Since I don't need to pee, I'm not sure why I've woken up. Was it because of a dream? Or an odd noise?

With bated breath, I strain my ears to hear. The only sound I notice is a light wind rustling the tree leaves. But as I lie in the tangle of sheets, I suddenly realize what's roused me: a smell drifting from the open doorway to the hall.

The smell of smoke.

20

I bolt up, flinging the top sheet off me, my heart galloping like it might burst free from my body at any second.

Hold on, I tell myself. *Maybe it's all in my head, because what could possibly be burning? I ate leftovers tonight and didn't use the stove.*

I flick on the bedside lamp, swing my legs off the mattress, and stumble out into the hallway. The smell's more noticeable out here, but not super strong—and thankfully there's no smoke wafting up the stairs.

I step back into the bedroom just long enough to snatch my phone and then descend the stairs, gripping the rail. I don't hear any crackling or snapping sounds, though the smell is still present. When I reach the bottom step, I fumble until I find the wall switch for the overhead fixture in the living room, which I have yet to use. The room floods with light and I scan it fast with my eyes. The odor is even stronger downstairs, but there's no evidence of a fire.

I dart into the kitchen next, where I'd left the light on earlier. Right away, I see that the dials for the burners and oven are in the "off" position. I lift my eyes to the smoke detector on the ceiling. The green light is on, indicating that the device is working. My heartbeat slows to a canter.

I step toward the oven and tug the door open. Inside, it's empty and not the least bit hot. So, no, I didn't slide in a casserole earlier and forget all about it.

Letting the oven door bang shut, I twist back around and take a deep breath. The smell is actually more like woodsmoke, the kind you sometimes pick up from standing near a fireplace even when there's nothing burning in the hearth.

I pause for a moment to think, and then head into the dining room, where I press my nose against the wall that borders the kitchen. Fireplaces are pretty common in old houses around here—the place Jamie was renting when I met him had one we used during fall and winter weekends—and though this house doesn't presently have a fireplace, there might have been one years ago that was later enclosed. If that's the case, the walls probably absorbed some of the smell over time. But there's nothing like that coming from the wall. In fact, I can barely detect the scent of smoke in this room.

I return to the kitchen, completely baffled but also unnerved. What if an electrical wire is smoldering somewhere, and it's only a matter of time before it bursts into flames? When I first moved to New York and was doing DIY projects in my apartment, my dad warned me not to leave oily rags around because under the right circumstances they can ignite on their own. But where could any oil rags be?

As if they're one step ahead of me, my eyes shift to the door to the basement, and my stomach drops. There's no way I want to go into a basement in the middle of the night, but I really need to check down there.

I unbolt the door, ease it open, and flick the switch on the wall, which activates a bare light bulb on a beam above the base of the steps. I start to descend but then reach behind me to one of the kitchen drawers and grab the flashlight that Clarissa pointed out during her tour.

Midway down the steps, I stop to survey as much as I can from my position. The space is unfinished with a poured cement floor, and it seems that the main things being stored down there are two badly scuffed leather trunks and an old refrigerator. A couple of raw wood shelves have been nailed to the far wall and lined with mason jars, but they all seem to be empty. Well, at least they're not filled with human body parts swimming in formaldehyde.

My pulse racing, I go down a few more steps, just enough to take in a full view of the basement. I flick on the flashlight and direct the beam into the corners that the light bulb doesn't reach. There's no sign of anything smoldering, and the only odor is the kind of musty one old cellars are known for.

I scurry up the stairs so fast I stumble and bang a shin hard against one of the steps. Cursing, I reach the top, slam the door shut, and shove the bolt back into position.

As I take a few steps into the kitchen again, I realize that the smell is almost gone now. What the hell? Could I possibly have imagined it in my worked-up state? No, it was strong enough to wake me, so clearly it's not only in my mind. The house must be giving off an old scent trapped in the walls, perhaps because of that one rainy morning.

I troop back upstairs, almost bleary-eyed with fatigue. But as soon as I step into the bedroom, I realize I'm bound to spend the rest of the night worried that somewhere below there are oily rags trying their damnedest to spontaneously combust or that an electrical fire is gaining ground in the walls of the kitchen. Wanting to be closer to an exit, I grab my phone, a pillow, and the cotton spread and return to the living room, tossing the bedding onto the couch. I switch off the overhead light but leave the light on in the dining room so I'm not in complete darkness. As I flop onto the couch, I notice that the smell is completely gone, like it was never here. But I know for sure it was.

Sunlight wakes me, poking in through the windows. I squeeze my eyes tight, hoping to drift off again, but as my brain registers the dull ache in my lower back, I remember that I'm on the couch—and the reason why.

My eyes shoot open, and I inhale deeply. There's no trace of any smoky smell.

Kicking off the bedspread, I struggle off the couch, and before I even turn on the coffee machine, I do a quick look around the three first-floor rooms, hoping to find a clue that I missed last night in my hyper state, but there's nothing.

I slide into one of the chairs at the dining table and do a search on my laptop, trying to determine what caused the smell and also how concerned I should be. I learn that electrical fires that originate in walls can take hours, even days, to advance, but the odor they give off is an acrid one, caused by the burn of the plastic coating on the wires. That's definitely not what I noticed. The only explanations I find for a trace of woodsmoke are charred log remnants in a fireplace or a wooden utensil accidentally left in an oven, neither of which fits.

Before fully giving up, I click on one more link for mystery smells, which ends up taking me to an online article called "Eight Signs Your House Might Be Haunted."

My god, I can't believe we're back to that. What am I supposed to do—call Ghostbusters and explain I now have three indicators of a poltergeist on the property? No, what I really need to focus on today is the Liam problem and how to handle it. I can't believe Sam never called.

But when I retrieve my phone from the coffee table, I'm surprised to see that I missed a text from him last night—sent just after eleven, when I was already asleep.

Sorry to be out of touch. Had to drive back to NY today to handle a work issue. Left messages for Drew. Still no word. Will let you know when I hear.

It's a relief to know that he hasn't dropped the ball, but I also feel an unwelcome twinge of disappointment that he's in New York, and no longer minutes away.

There's been an unexpected sense of security in having him close.

Thanks for letting me know, I write back. I have something incredibly important to talk to you about. Can we speak on the phone?

He might not even be checking messages this morning, but I hold my breath with the phone in my hand. A second later I see the three dancing dots, and then:

I'll be back in CT this afternoon. Why don't I stop by.

I respond saying Ava and I are having an early dinner and I have a few work calls scheduled, but mostly I'm around.

He sends a one-word reply: okay—without even a hint of a time frame. I hate how eager I feel to see him regardless of when it will be.

After a shower and breakfast—and hauling my bedding back upstairs—I settle in again at the dining room table. I'm in a holding pattern until I talk to Sam, and in the meantime, I just have to pray Liam isn't wise to my efforts.

My phone rings from its spot on the table, and I almost jump when I spot Tori's name on the screen, as if she's been eavesdropping on my thoughts.

"Kiki, how are you?" she asks.

"Getting by, thanks," I say. "How about you?"

"Like you, I'm sure, doing our best to come to terms with things," she says, then clears her throat. "Listen, I'm sorry about the other day. I should never have been so blunt with you. I just haven't been myself since this happened."

"Don't worry about it," I say, and leave it at that. I need to keep this as brief as possible because I can tell I'm not sounding very natural.

"So, what are you up to today?"

"A couple of client calls and then an early dinner with Ava at the club."

"You're still here, then?"

"Uh, yes, but I'm heading home soon, probably to-morrow," I lie. "I need to get back to the city."

"Well, let's stay in touch, okay?"

"For sure. Thanks for calling."

Did she sense the wariness in my voice? I hope her main takeaway will be that I'll be gone soon.

For the rest of the morning, I prep for two client Zoom sessions in the afternoon, finish the article I was struggling with—though the result seems less than scintillating—and finally pay a little attention to my social media accounts. Later I get through the first client call well enough, but the second—with an ar-rogant twenty-three-year-old male job seeker whose parents are paying for his sessions—goes off the rails almost immediately.

"It sounds like you're doing well lining up interviews, Keaton," I tell him after he's offered a brief rundown of his efforts. "But unfortunately they're not leading to any offers. Here's something that might help: try sitting toward the edge of your seat the next time you're being interviewed."

He scrunches up his face in distaste. "That sounds like something *girls* do."

"Really, everyone should," I say, fighting off the urge to scrunch up my own face. "Studies show that the biggest complaint interviewers have is that candidates don't show enough enthusiasm. Sitting toward the edge of your seat will make you seem eager."

By the time the session wraps up, the guy looks bored out of his mind, and I'm pretty sure my annoyance is obvious. Adding to my frustration is a cryptic text from Sam, saying something has come up and he's not sure when he'll be back from the city.

I'm grateful when it's finally time to dress for dinner with Ava. I strip off my shorts and Zoom-appropriate blouse and slip on one of the cotton dresses I packed. My mood instantly lifts. Before locking up the house, I circle the first floor for a few minutes, inhaling deeply, but all I pick up is the scent of freshly cut grass wafting in through the open windows I'm about to close. At least I can have dinner without worrying about it.

Though I went to the tennis and swim club a bunch of times with Jamie, I'm not a hundred percent sure how to get there from here, so once I'm in the car, I program the address into my phone and pop it into the dashboard mount. I realize with a pang that I'll be traveling the same route Jamie did when he rented this house.

I feel another pang almost thirty minutes later, when I cross the club parking lot toward the main building, a large white clapboard structure that manages to be elegant and understated at the same time. Jamie always said that his parents loved this place because of its relaxed vibe and lack of snootiness, and the fact that membership wasn't super exclusionary. That's partly why Jamie decided to continue to belong as an adult. During our two summers together, we enjoyed Saturday lunches here, followed by a swim in the pool or the lake. Jamie also came on his own to play tennis with Sam or Vic or another willing partner.

After giving my name at the entrance to the dining room, I'm led outside to the wraparound porch, where Ava is already seated at one of the wrought-iron tables in a French café–style chair. She's wearing a sleeveless, mango-colored top, and her hair grazes her shoulders, though she's clipped her side bangs off her face with a small barrette. She rises to greet me, offering a warm hug. My shoulders relax just from ten seconds in her presence.

"So wonderful to see you, Ava," I say.

"Same here. And Vic sends his best."

That's a relief to hear. I wouldn't want to think he was still upset with me or, worse, blamed me for Jamie's death.

Before settling into a chair across from her, I let my gaze follow the wide expanse of lawn as it slopes downward toward the colorful border gardens, then thickets of trees, and finally the edge of the small blue lake. Though the light is fading, I can make out the dock and the furled sails of the boats the club uses mostly for lessons.

"It's as lovely as I remember," I say. "Have you been coming here on your own—I mean without Vic?"

"Now and then. I'm not much of a country club person, as you know, but there are some Black families with memberships now, and partly I come to support them. But beyond that, I love how this porch—and the view from here—remind me of my grandparents' place."

"The farm in Virginia?"

"Yes, I adored visiting them, and they had amazing peach trees that I raided in the summer." With elbows on the table, she clasps her hands together and rests her chin on them, smiling wistfully.

"How nice the porch makes you think of them. Jamie loved this view, too."

Ava's smile fades. "I hope it's not hard for you to be here, Kiki. I wanted to cheer you up, but maybe this wasn't the best choice."

"No, no, this is fine—and besides, I'm dying for one of their Chicken Caesars."

Despite my assurances to Ava, it does feel strange to be here again. It seems both the same and weirdly unfamiliar, like I've been gone for years.

The waiter approaches, and we each order a glass of rosé and a Chicken Caesar salad.

"So, tell me about Boston," I say. "How was Vic's event?"

"He had a very good turnout and sold plenty of books—though between the two of us, I wasn't impressed with the author they recruited to interview him."

"Did he try to hog the limelight?"

Ava takes a sip of her wine, which has just arrived, and shakes her head. "Not that so much. His questions were just incredibly long-winded, and sometimes there were two questions packed into one. Vic lost his place a couple of times, which didn't seem to bother anyone in the audience, but I know it bothered *him*."

254 · KATE WHITE

"Did it concern you as well?" I ask softly.

"Oh, Kiki," Ava says and offers a wan smile, "thank you for reading between the lines. Yes, it did. I hated that Vic felt embarrassed, especially during such a special evening."

"Mature adult audiences are pretty forgiving, I've found."

"Right," she says.

"Are you worried about Vic's memory?" As the words spill from my mouth, I pray that the answer is a negative.

"Not at all," she says with a wry chuckle. "The man generally forgets *nothing*. But last week is still really eating at him. And though it was good to have Dan with us, he kept harping on the subject. I know he's been badly shaken by what happened and is trying to make sense of it, but all his questions only added to our stress."

I feel a glumness overtaking me. I, too, wanted our time together to be a brief respite from thoughts about Jamie's death, but neither of us can seem to escape those. Beyond that, I wish I could share everything I've learned with Ava, but I don't dare breathe a word yet.

Ava lays a hand on top of mine, clearly reading my

distress. "I've got an idea. Let's switch topics. I've got some hot gossip from our former workplace."

Ava is too discreet and respectful to trade in gossip that's anything close to hot, but she shares a couple of updates—a mansplainer we both disliked has been fired, and two women we admired have stepped into high-level jobs.

"How's *your* work going, by the way?" Ava asks, as the waiter arrives with our salads. "Are you finding it easy enough to do from here?"

"Yes, it's been fine," I lie. Without naming names, I describe some of the challenges my latest clients have been facing and skip any reference to my *own* challenges with a few of them. Ava has long been my go-to person when I'm in a professional slump, and I could use her wisdom, but I want to keep things as light as possible, which has already proved tricky.

As the waiter clears our plates, Ava asks if I have time for a decaf cappuccino.

"Definitely. But let me run to the restroom first."

Since I haven't been here in a year, I end up hiking to the ladies' locker room on the far side of the clubhouse, before recalling there's a much closer powder room off the front lobby. But I decide to use the one in the locker room as long as I'm here.

There are only two club members currently inside, both in capris and T-shirts, busy stuffing wet towels into tote bags. When I emerge from the stall a short time later, they've already departed, and the only person present is a locker room attendant I didn't notice a minute ago.

"Oh, hi," I say, and she returns my greeting with a smile. She's probably in her early thirties, with bright red hair, and not someone I remember seeing when I came to the club in the past.

"Does Blake still work here, by the way?" I ask as I'm drying my hands. I'm thinking of an engaging twentysomething woman I used to chat with whenever I changed after swimming.

"Yup, Blake's still here. But she's off today."

"Would you mind telling her that Kiki Reed said hi?"

As she promises to do that, I start to turn away and then pause. Maybe she can fill in a few blanks for me.

"Can I ask you one more question?" I say. "Were you working here when Jess Nolan was an attendant?"

"I wasn't, no," she says, her expression darkening. "But Blake was. She still talks about her."

"Were they friends?"

"Yeah. Blake said she was a really nice person, always sweet to everyone. She was going to school besides working here, and she still made time to volunteer at an animal shelter, that kind of thing. Blake was part of a group that helped raise money for a memorial they erected in Jess's honor."

"Such a sad story," I say. "And they think one of the fair workers did it?"

She gives a little shrug. "That's what I heard, but Blake said it might have been someone Jess knew—someone from here, even."

"Like from the area?"

"I mean from the *club*. Someone who worked here or was a member. She supposedly had plans to go to the fair with a guy the night she died."

"*Really?*" I say, feeling a chill. "Did the police look into that?"

"I assume so, but I guess they didn't have much to go on—because she apparently never told anyone his name. And people saw her alone there."

The attendant darts her eyes toward the door, suddenly looking flustered. "I really shouldn't be talking about this. Sorry."

"Please, don't be sorry," I say quickly. "I was the one who brought it up."

I trek back to the terrace, unsettled all over again by thoughts of Jess Nolan being assaulted and bludgeoned to death, the fear she must have felt, and the fact that the killer could be someone I've crossed paths with—who hasn't been apprehended and may never be.

Is that what it's going to be like in Jamie's case? Will I have to spend the rest of my life knowing that his killer is walking free in the world?

I stop in my tracks in the corridor. Whatever I do, I can't let things come to that.

21

Is everything okay?" Ava asks when I slip back into my chair. My face must betray the discomfort I feel.

"It's nothing to worry about," I say, and then glance behind us. Though there aren't many diners here tonight—perhaps because it's early in the week—I want to be certain no one can hear me. "But I just had a brief conversation with the locker room attendant about a female employee who was murdered, and it threw me a little."

"Someone from here was murdered? My goodness, when did this happen?"

"Four years ago. A girl named Jess Nolan."

"Oh, right, I know who you mean now," Ava says, nodding. "It was right before I moved to the area full-time, but Vic told me about her. She apparently was a lovely girl, and people were terribly distraught about it."

Two cappuccinos arrive, obviously ordered by Ava in my absence, and I wait for the waiter to move away before speaking again.

"The attendant said the girl supposedly had a date that night and it might have been with one of her co-workers from here—or even a member."

"A *member*?" Ava says. She'd started to take a sip of her drink but sets the cup back in the saucer with a clink. "This is the first I'm hearing of this."

"Could it be true?"

She lays a hand against a cheek, her brown eyes pensive. "Anything is possible, of course. Working in human resources for close to thirty years taught me that. But I'd be a little surprised if she'd had a date with a member. From what I've seen here—and you know how I tend to notice these things—there are clear boundaries, and people seem to respect them."

But what happens in private is a different matter.

Ava slowly lifts her cup again and finally takes a sip. The two of us had done a good job of shifting the mood in a more positive direction, but now I've cast another pall over the table.

As we're finishing our cappuccinos, Ava signals for the check, and a few minutes later we head down the steps of the clubhouse, arms linked. There are only eight or nine cars left in the parking lot besides our own.

"What a nice evening, Ava," I say. Despite those moments when the conversation turned dark, it was good to be in her company. "Thank you so much for treating me."

"My pleasure. It's been too long since we had a girls' night out."

"And don't forget, you promised to let me take *you* to dinner when you come to Manhattan this fall."

"Yes, but it will be later in the season than I thought. Vic has several book events in September, and though he'd been planning to travel alone, I've decided to join him, which means postponing my city visit."

"Okay, just let me know."

We hug goodbye. Ava ends up pulling out of the parking lot first, taking a left toward her home; I leave immediately after, turning right for New Burford.

Though the night is still warm, I decide against the AC and instead lower my window a few inches, letting the breeze whip my hair around. It's not even nine o'clock, but it's already fully dark out, yet another sign that summer will soon be gone. The summer I barely knew.

I hold my speed to fifty, or under. Living in the city, I don't drive very often, especially at night, and the road is not only poorly lit but ridiculously twisty. Mindful of deer, I also keep a close watch on the shoulders, especially when I'm shooting past cornfields, where the stalks are over six feet high right now. There are lights still burning in many of the houses I pass, but I have the two-lane road mostly to myself.

I haven't gone far when I notice how keyed up I still feel. Ava's last comment in the parking lot—about planning to accompany Vic on tour—has begun to gnaw at me. Maybe she's more concerned about him than she let on, and I should have pursued the topic further instead of letting the comment pass. Plus, I'm still so upset by what I know about Liam and Tori, and the fact that Sam never followed up with me. What the hell am I supposed to do with the information I've found?

My gaze flicks to the rearview mirror as two beams of light from another vehicle suddenly appear in it. It's almost comforting to share this stretch of nearly desolate road with someone. When, about a mile later, the road forks and I bear left onto Route 217, the other driver does likewise. We're obviously headed in the same direction, at least for now.

I reach Warren, one of the quieter towns in the area, where the sidewalks have already been rolled up for the night. Though I know my way from here, I keep an eye on the GPS just to be on the safe side. I take a right at the second traffic light in town, with only sixteen more minutes to go. And then I notice something else. Those two beams of light are still behind me.

I feel a prick of fear. Maybe I'm overreacting, but it seems more than coincidental that the car has traveled the same three roads that I have—unless the other driver's destination is New Burford too. Instinctively I roll up my window and look quickly at the phone screen, reminding myself there's a turn in another mile. Let's see what happens there, I decide.

Soon after, holding my breath, I flick up my turn signal and hang a right. And so does the other car. Jeez, *is* he actually following me?

My heart's thrumming now. I'm on a section of road lined mostly with fields, old barns, and silos, and there's not another vehicle in sight. I press down slightly on the gas pedal, picking up speed but not daring to go too fast.

With alarm, I notice the other driver speeds up, too. The vehicle is a dark sedan, I see now, not a truck or SUV, and it seems to be only inches behind mine. Tightening my grip on the wheel, I accelerate again— and so does he. Before long it feels like he's close to ramming my bumper. He's turned on his high beams, too, nearly blinding me. What the fuck is going on?

I keep accelerating, finally putting a tiny bit of distance between us. But my hands are trembling, making it hard to steer.

Squinting, I check the mirror again. A deer suddenly darts out from a field behind me and bolts across the road in my wake. I hear the other car brake to a screeching halt. I keep driving, letting out a gasp of relief when I see the high beams recede farther and farther behind me.

Soon, I spot the lights of New Burford studding the darkness ahead. I don't dare drive straight to the house on Ash Street, though. As soon as I reach the town line, I turn right into an open Sunoco station and quickly position the car so I have a good look at the road. A minute later, a black four-door shoots past. It might be the car that was behind me, but there's no way to be sure.

It doesn't seem wise to leave yet. I drive over to the far side of the lot, point the front end of the car toward the road again, and kill the engine. And then I just sit there, trying to get my breathing to return to normal and watching for black cars. I see a couple of them drive past, but nothing seems suspicious about them.

Finally, when I'm feeling fairly confident that I'm safe, I fire up the engine again and slowly ease out onto the road, making a right turn. I cover the short distance to the house quickly, checking the rearview mirror every few seconds. No one appears to be following me. I reach Ash Street and approach the house, but end up driving by it until I make sure the black car isn't in the vicinity. The only vehicles in sight turn out to be the ones parked in driveways for the night. A block farther along, I do a three-point turn, head back to the house, and pull into the driveway. The house on the right looks empty—I've had the impression since I've been here that the residents must be away—but there are lights on upstairs in the one to the left. After fishing the house key from my purse, I dash from the car, unlock the front door, and hurry inside.

I left several lamps on downstairs, so I can tell immediately nothing is awry, at least in the living room. I bolt the door behind me and proceed cautiously into the dining room and then the kitchen. No cold spots, no unexplained lights burning, no phantom smell. Returning to the living room, I peer out the front window into the street. It's still empty. I walk around the room, tugging all the muslin curtains closed.

I make a cup of chamomile tea and sit with it at the kitchen table, trying to calm myself. The house might not be up to any crazy poltergeist-like stunts right now, but my nerves are frayed from what happened on the road. It's possible the other driver was just some dick trying to scare me to death, but there's also the chance his plan was to run me off the road. He might have spotted me pulling my car out of the club parking lot, saw that I was female and alone.

What if the person was after me *specifically*? A memory suddenly slides to the front of my brain: my mentioning to Tori that I was having dinner with Ava at the club tonight. Did she tell Liam, who decided to follow me? His car is black, I remember. I should never have revealed my plans. By now they might have even found out where I'm staying.

I reach for my purse across the table and dig out my phone to check for messages. There's a text from my mom saying she hopes I'm doing better, and also one from Megan, asking if I'm free tonight for a phone call. I shoot her an apologetic response, saying I've been up to my eyeballs with work and promising to reach out soon. I miss hearing her voice, but I've been reluctant to call her after our last conversation. I know she meant well, but I don't want her discouraging me from what I need to do here.

There's still no word from Sam. I'm at a loss as to what my next move should be, especially since I only have a few days left on my rental. I have the option to extend but I hardly want to do that if things are at a standstill.

Out of habit, I also do a quick check of my inbox, and my stomach sinks as I notice an email from the father of the entitled and obnoxious young client I spoke to on Zoom earlier.

Keaton shared with me how poorly the session went today, he wrote. *It's obvious to me that the two of you aren't a good fit, and I suspect you agree. I know there are six more sessions to go on the contract, but I think it's only fair for you to release Keaton from this obligation and reimburse me for the outstanding sessions. Please get back to me as soon as possible.*

Though there's no one to hear, I let out a scream of frustration. This could mean the loss of close to two thousand dollars, money I already deposited in my bank account. I could certainly fight the father on this—we have a signed contract, after all—but if I do, I might end up needing to bring in a lawyer. And it would also increase the likelihood of the father bad-mouthing me with people in both his professional and social circles, or his bratty kid trashing me on social media.

And I've got no one to blame but myself. I didn't stay engaged during the second half of the session and I allowed the kid's obnoxiousness to get under my skin.

After checking all the windows and doors, I trudge upstairs, wash up in the bathroom, and slip into my pajamas. It's only when I pull back the bedspread that I realize I'm not going to feel comfortable sleeping up here tonight. The smoky smell might be gone, but now it's the driver I'm scared of. What if it *was* Liam, and despite my maneuvering, he managed to follow me all the way here?

I grab the bedspread and pillow and troop back downstairs. At least this way, I'll be able to hear if someone is snooping around the house. After making up the couch again, I flop down, pull the spread up to my waist, and close my eyes. Though my back will ache again in the morning, I know I'll feel safer here.

It takes a while, but somehow, miraculously, I finally drift off. When I stir, I sense in my gut that I've only been asleep for a few minutes.

This time it isn't a smell that's woken me. It's a sound. Something scuffling outside, near the stoop area.

Holding my breath, I squint, peering through the dimness toward the front of the room. It's possible it's only a skunk or raccoon out there, wildlife Clarissa mentioned I might hear at night. The porch light is on, but because I closed the curtains earlier, I can't see outside.

Suddenly a form appears behind the curtain on the window next to the door, the shape of a man's upper body. He's standing right there on the stoop.

22

I lay frozen on the couch, too scared to move. Can the person on the stoop see my outline through the curtain? Does he know I'm only a few yards away?

As freaked out as I am, I know I can't simply remain motionless, hoping he'll be sucked back into the night. I pluck my phone from the coffee table, slowly slide off the couch, and tiptoe across the room. As I near the door, the form shifts slightly, as if he's been startled by the movement.

"Who's there?" I call out, my voice breaking between the two words.

No response. But the body shifts again, now moving closer to the door.

"Who's there?" I call again, louder this time. I

tighten my grip on my phone, wondering whether to call 911.

"Kiki, it's me." *Sam.*

I exhale, feeling the tension loosen. I unbolt the door and swing it open. Sam is standing on the other side of the screen, illuminated by the glow of the porch light, and wearing nice jeans and a perfectly pressed cobalt-blue dress shirt, the sleeves rolled to his elbows.

"Did I wake you?" he asks quietly, eyeing my pajamas.

"No, I hadn't fallen asleep yet," I say, though it isn't quite true. "Were you just *standing* out there?"

"I'd been about to knock, but since I didn't see any activity, I thought you must be in bed. I was debating whether to leave you a note."

"Do you want to come in?"

"Sure," he says, stepping a few feet into the living room. "Sorry to be so late showing up. My research associate was having trouble with some data, and I ended up staying in New York longer than planned. Then I had to drive directly from the city to an event back here."

He's giving off a faint musky scent, obviously from a cologne he applied earlier. Has he been on a date? I wonder—I mean, there's the dress shirt, the sexy fragrance, the trimmed scruff and freshly washed hair. . . . I feel a pang at the thought. Maybe he's still involved with that violinist, and he drove up from the city with her. That could explain some of his recent unavailability.

Retreating into the room, I switch on the two table lamps and turn back around. "Do you want to sit down?" I ask.

"No, this won't take long, but it's good news, I think. After I didn't find anyone home at Drew's house on either Sunday or Monday, I left two phone messages for him and heard back today. I explained about the dog, and how we both feel Jamie wouldn't have abandoned him. I definitely had his attention."

I let out a small, hopeful gasp. "You think he'll go to the police?"

"I want to think so. He didn't come right out and agree with our theory, but I sensed he was taking it seriously."

"Good," I say, and I find myself smiling in gratitude. Sam followed through. Things might finally be in motion. Because I can't bear standing still.

"I have news, too," I say. "I went back to one of the houses on the list Jamie made, and it turns out that someone fitting his description had been there as well, making inquiries. So there's no question that alarm bells had gone off for him."

"Oh, man," Sam says, shaking his head.

"I know. It's more important than ever that Drew convince the police to keep investigating."

"Okay, I'll check back with him tomorrow," he says. "By the way, I hadn't intended to mention to Drew that you were staying in the New Burford house, but he kept pressing to know how you learned about the dog, so I ended up telling him the whole story. I hope that's okay. He didn't seem particularly fazed."

"Sure." I wouldn't have wanted Sam to be dishonest, but I just hope Drew doesn't think I chose the house out of some morbid fascination. And I have to pray he doesn't mention it to Liam. "Are you sure you don't want to sit down?"

Sam's been in the same spot ever since he entered the house, rooted in place as if he's been told there's a trip wire with an explosive device running between the two of us.

"No, I should get back," he says, sweeping a hand through his hair. "I just didn't want to leave you hanging."

Get back *where?* I wonder. To his cottage on his parents' property and whoever is awaiting him there? Well, I'm glad to have the hint because it might help burn off my infatuation once and for all.

"Thanks. I appreciate that."

His eyes dart toward the couch and the makeshift bed I assembled for myself. He cocks his chin in that direction.

"So you're just renting the first floor?" he says, a faint smile on his face.

The comment makes me chuckle. I'm not used to Sam being funny with me.

"No, I sprang for the full house. I—I just feel a little more comfortable downstairs."

"Why? And don't tell me because it's cooler on this floor. You've got all the windows nailed shut."

I lift my hands, palms up. "To be honest, a few weird things have happened lately."

"Weird in what way?" he says.

"I thought someone was following me in the car tonight on my way back from dinner with Ava. And there have also been some odd little disturbances in the house."

"Is there any chance someone got in here?"

"I always lock up at night and nothing's looked tampered with, but still . . ." I trail off. "Do you think Liam's figured out that I'm digging around?"

Sam lifts an eyebrow. "It's possible, but Drew didn't give any indication that either he or Liam is aware of that. Let me know if anything else happens, though, okay?"

"Of course, thanks."

Then, suddenly, Sam steps over the imaginary trip wire, moving in my direction. I look over my shoulder, curious if he's noticed something odd behind me, but when I spin back around, he's inches away and staring right at me. Reaching out a hand, he cups the back of my head and kisses me softly on the mouth. It sends a rush of desire right down to my toes.

"If only I'd met you first," he says, releasing me. His voice is so low it's almost a whisper.

And then he turns away, slips out through the door, and closes it tightly behind him.

As soon as he leaves and I've locked up again, I flop back onto the couch, pulling the spread over me. My mind is churning so fast, though, I know I won't be falling back asleep anytime soon. What was that kiss supposed to mean? Did Sam just feel a sudden rush of affection because of our unified goal in finding Jamie's killer? Or was he trying to say that there's an attraction on his side, too, that the awkwardness I've always sensed from him was due to his feelings for me?

Or what if "If only I'd met you first" was him telling me that any chance for us has come and gone?

I wake exhausted, and after taking a quick shower on autopilot, I sit down to a simple breakfast in the kitchen.

I'm starting a second mug of coffee, hoping to defog my brain, when my phone rings, and the screen flashes a number I don't recognize—one with a local area code.

"Katherine Reed," I answer, wondering if it could possibly be one of the police following up on their cell phone.

"Kiki, hello, it's Mel Weber," a woman's voice replies. "Drew Larsson's assistant."

I know exactly who she is—I've met her in passing on several occasions. In addition to helping Drew run his portrait painting business, she apparently organizes his personal life with Heather—their calendar, any events they host, even their vacations. I assume she helped plan the memorial for Jamie, too.

"Hello, Mel," I say, my senses on high alert. "How can I help you?"

"I'm calling on Drew's behalf. He'd like to speak to you, and he's hoping it can be sometime today."

My stomach tightens. "Did he say what about?"

"He didn't, no."

I suspect she's not totally in the dark, however. Jamie once remarked that Mel had an advanced degree in eavesdropping, so even if Drew hadn't come right out and told her, she might have a clue.

"What he did say," Mel adds, "is that he'd love you to come to the house. Heather will be there, too."

Okay, that makes all the difference in the world. If Heather's included and the meeting is held in their home, this get-together must be meant to be cordial. Obviously, Sam's call had an impact, and Drew wants to hear about the dog rescue directly from me and delve deeper into my suspicions.

"Yes, today is fine, whenever works. I look forward to seeing both of them."

"Let's say four o'clock, then. Do you need directions to the house?"

"No, that won't be necessary."

How sad that Mel's lost sight of how often I visited or assumes my relationship with Jamie is a distant memory to me. But the meeting is a very good sign, and I feel more upbeat than I have in days.

After we sign off, I pour a fresh cup of coffee and retreat to the dining room. I'm suddenly energized, eager to be at full throttle again and get back in sync with my work. The first thing I do is fire off an email to the disgruntled father saying that though I believe his son could benefit from my guidance, there's no point in the two of us working together if he isn't comfortable even trying my advice. I will release him from the contract except for the next two sessions—because it's too late for me to fill those time slots with other clients.

For the next hours, I work pretty much uninterrupted, my most productive day in over two weeks. If my meeting with Drew goes well, I think, maybe I'll finally feel up to drafting a letter to Ava's agent friend, and then send the proposal by the end of the week.

I'm so immersed in work that when I finally check my watch, I realize it's past the point when I should have started getting ready for the meeting. I quickly freshen up, apply makeup, and change into the freshest looking of the cotton dresses I brought from the city.

By three thirty I'm in the car, headed back to Sharon. I'm still feeling optimistic, but at the same time I'm a little nervous. If Drew seems on the fence about pushing the police to do more, I'm going to have to be as convincing as possible.

And then there's the question of Liam. There's no way I can even drop a hint about that today, let alone come right out and share what I've uncovered. Knowing Drew, he'd probably feel compelled to confront his nephew immediately, which would give Liam an opportunity to cover any tracks he hasn't taken care of so far. But it's going to be hard to sit on the information I have.

I end up parking directly across from the house, and after climbing out of the car, I take a few seconds to smooth my dress and hair. As I head up the front sidewalk, the windows on either side of the front door offer a look into the living and dining rooms, both of which appear to be empty. The house also seems incredibly quiet from the outside. It almost seems as if I've arrived at the wrong time or on the wrong day, but I know I heard Mel correctly. I press the bell.

No one responds at first, but just as I'm about to ring again, I hear footsteps echoing in the wide front hall, and the door opens. Mel's been sent to greet me. She's an attractive woman, probably close to fifty, with short, closely cropped black hair that accentuates her height—which must be close to six feet.

"Hello, Kiki," she says. Her tone is polite enough, but not what I'd call friendly.

"Mel, hi, nice to see you."

"Drew and Heather are in the back," she says, which probably means the family room off the kitchen. "Please follow me."

I trail behind her, flooded as I walk with memories of my times in the house. The decor is traditional but not fussy or dated, and many walls are lined with the striking landscapes Drew enjoys painting when he isn't doing commissioned portraits. Some are scenes from rural Litchfield County, and others depict Nordic farmhouses and fjords, inspired by trips he's taken to Norway over the years.

I feel a stab of sorrow recalling Jamie's hoped-for trip to Norway to see the northern lights and reconnect with his roots, a voyage he'll never get to take.

"Here we are," Mel says as we reach the kitchen, gesturing for me to enter the family room to the right. As I turn to thank her, I see that she's already retreating back toward the front of the house. Drew has obviously told her this is a private conversation, but her departure still sends a ripple of unease through me.

I step through the doorway and notice Drew and Heather on the crimson red sofa, sitting a few feet apart. Almost instantly I sense another presence in the room, and turning to my right, I'm shocked to discover Liam and Tori in two matching armchairs, their expressions blank.

Not good, I think. But I quickly assure myself that it makes total sense Drew would include them in a discussion about Jamie's death—they're family, and they were both at the party. What Drew has no way of knowing, of course, is that Liam might have reason to have killed Jamie. I nod hello at Tori and Liam, which draws no response, and then return my attention to Drew and Heather.

"Thank you for inviting me today," I say. "I've wanted the chance to tell you in person how sorry I am."

"Why don't you have a seat," Heather says. Though

there's no warmth in her voice, I assume it's because this must be as awkward for her as it is for me.

I perch on the edge of a small slipper chair, waiting for someone to open the conversation. Heather's in one of her typical boho chic looks today, soft flowy pants and a loose top, both in sage green, but there's a stern look on her face now, undercutting the vibe of her outfit. Something feels off.

I flick my glance between Drew and Heather, wondering whether I should try to break the ice. "As I started to say a minute ago, I am heartsick for your loss. I know—"

"Let me get right to the point," Drew says, cutting me off. "You left my nephew more or less at the altar, but that was between the two of you and there wasn't a damn thing I could do about it. But I *can* do something about what's going on right now."

My heart lurches. This is not going at all how I thought it would. But before I can defend myself, Drew suddenly shoots up from the couch, his eyes blazing.

"You have no right coming back to this area," he says, nearly bellowing. "No right to wreak even more havoc on me and my family. I won't stand for it, do you hear?"

23

Blood races up my torso, reddening my chest, then my neck and cheeks. Drew's words not only sting sharply, but they've opened the reserve of shame I've stored up from upending Jamie's life last March.

I need to get out of here. There's a door leading from the family room to the backyard, and if I exit that way, I could be gone in fifteen seconds. But I can't leave. I need to make them see the truth.

Drew is still standing but hasn't taken any steps toward me, which is a relief. With difficulty, I breathe deeply, trying to regain some composure.

"I'm sorry that's how you feel," I tell him, standing, too, so I'm more in control. "But I'm not trying to wreak havoc on any of you. All I want is for the police to just consider an alternate theory about Jamie's death."

"Because you can't bear the *guilt*?" Drew snarls and then rakes a hand through his faded blond hair. This time I feel tears fighting to free themselves from behind my eyes. I pinch the webbed piece of skin between my left thumb and forefinger, a trick I teach clients who fear they might bawl during a tough moment at work.

"No, because I know Jamie wouldn't have adopted a dog and then taken his own life. Didn't Sam talk to you?"

"Yes, but it was obvious he only called me because you put him up to it. And then you have the goddamned nerve to talk to my mother, upsetting her so much it took two caregivers to calm her down afterward."

So despite what she promised, the attendant ratted me out. My whole face is on fire now.

"That was a mistake and I'm terribly sorry about it, truly," I say. "I just wanted to speak to her about Jamie but hadn't realized how fragile she is."

Drew cocks his chin and locks a hand on each side of his waist. "And then you butt into Liam's business, harassing his tenant. What's your explanation for *that*?"

This means that Drew is aware Liam's a landlord. But surely he doesn't know the whole story. Maybe my best option is to drag it out into the open right now, so that we all have the same information.

"Yes, I spoke to his tenant," I say. "And I *do* have an explanation, a good one."

I turn and look straight at Liam this time. He's most likely come from his job, dressed in a short-sleeved burgundy button-down, black jeans, and tan work boots. He's staring hard at me, looking angry but wary at the same time. He must know I'm about to blow the lid off his secret empire.

I return my attention to Drew. "Before he died, Jamie discovered that Liam owns at least *nine* properties—I found a list of them that he put together. What's more, Jamie visited the same one I did, asking questions. He was clearly suspicious about how Liam could afford them all."

Now Liam shoots up from his seat, and as I turn to look at him, I can practically see the tension pulsing from his compact, muscular body.

"I don't owe you an explanation, Kiki," he barks, "but I'll give you one anyway. Eight years ago, Tori and I used our savings for a down payment on an investment property. The house appreciated quickly, and I refinanced the mortgage based on the new value. Then I took out a loan against the equity to purchase the next house, and so on and so on. And, by the way, this is the same thing I told Jamie when he raised the matter with me."

"When was this?" I ask, caught off guard by the

revelation. He's saying he gave Jamie an explanation, but I'm certainly not going to accept that at face value.

"We talked about it a few days before he died. I knew what he was implying and what you're implying, too—that I stole from our grandmother. I ended up showing him her statements so that he could see that nothing had been withdrawn from her account beyond what she's needed to live on."

Wait, have I had it all wrong the past couple of days? Or is Liam lying now, covering his ass in front of his uncle?

"And Drew's well aware of my investments," he adds, as if reading my mind.

I steal a glance at Drew. It's clear from his expression that none of this is a surprise. It looks like I *have* had it wrong, and I feel almost sick with embarrassment.

"Why hadn't Jamie known about the properties until this summer?" I ask. I can't let up until this all makes more sense to me.

"It wasn't some big dark secret. But you know as well as I do that Jamie could act like a bit of a know-it-all when it came to financial stuff, and he liked to drop advice on me whether I needed it or not, so I made a point of keeping certain things to myself. When Taylor was home for Memorial Day weekend and we were all here at the house, Jamie overheard him talking about the condos I own in Florida, and it obviously got his attention. If he'd only asked me directly, I could have saved him a lot of trouble."

I bite my lip, feeling utterly chagrined. "I apologize for misinterpreting the situation," I say. "I—I just wanted to turn over every stone."

Liam shakes his head in disgust. "Is that what you call it: turning over every stone? No, you convinced yourself that Jamie was murdered—contrary to the findings of both the local and state police—and you decided I had a motive for killing him."

I just stand there, unable to refute his points.

"Have you been to the cops with your theory?" he asks. "Should Tori and I be expecting a visit from them?"

"No, I haven't said anything about the real estate," I stammer. "I did tell them I thought Jamie's death wasn't a suicide, but that's the extent of it."

Liam shakes his head again, but his mouth is clamped shut now. I shoot a glance toward Tori, hoping for an ounce of sympathy, but she's staring off into the middle of the room, as if too disturbed to meet my eye.

"Are we done now?" Drew interjects. His volume is back to normal, but his tone is still hostile. "Have we satisfied your nosiness, or is there more in store?"

"I'm sorry," I mutter. "I just want to find the truth."

"As shattering as it is, we *know* the truth," he says.

"You need to pack your bags, vacate Jamie's house, and go back to where you belong. We're beside ourselves with grief, and your presence and reckless actions have made it even worse. Am I making myself clear?"

"Yes," I say, my voice not much more than a squeak.

"Good. Mel will see you out now."

I spin around to find Drew's assistant in the doorway. Maybe she's been hovering nearby all along.

"Please follow me, Kiki," Mel says calmly, as if she's a restaurant hostess showing me to my table. The next few moments are a blur. When I'm finally in the front seat of my rental car, I can barely recall leaving the house, making my way through those large, silent rooms. If Mel said anything else to me, I have no memory of it.

There are so many emotions flailing inside me right now, it's hard to sort them all. My burning cheeks tell me that for starters I'm ashamed—of deciding Liam was a murderer, of involving a sick elderly woman in the situation and leaving her in a state.

At the same time, I'm angry at myself. I was so eager for contact with the Larssons that I didn't take a step back and think about what the purpose of the meeting today was going to be.

But more than anything, I feel overwhelmed with despair. Liam didn't kill Jamie—which is largely a relief—but I know that *someone* did, and that person is still out there. And Drew has no interest in pressuring the cops to do more. I wish Sam had been more persuasive with him, and that he hadn't made it seem like all the doubts were coming from me.

I count slowly to ten, trying to calm myself enough to make it home, though when I stick the key in the ignition, my hand shakes a little. Just *drive*, I tell myself. I don't want to be anywhere near here for another moment.

The trip home is a blur, too, and once I reach the house, I stagger inside, open a couple of windows, and collapse onto the couch. As I lie there, finally feeling my pulse slow, I think through where things currently stand. It still seems pretty clear that the problem Jamie hinted about to Sam must have related to the list of properties. But according to Liam, the two of them addressed it shortly before the party. During the mudroom conversation I overheard between Jamie and Sam, Jamie told his friend he had something he wanted to circle back about, and that very well could have been it.

But if Liam didn't have a motive for murder, then who did?

My mind soon finds its way back to Percy. If I believe my own eyes rather than what she told me, Jamie was giving her the cold shoulder at the party and obviously couldn't have cared less about her. That must not have been pleasant. But once again I ask myself: Does a woman spurned after three or four dates choose *murder* as a form of payback?

I could go back to the police, I suppose, and remind them of her existence. But I've pleaded my case with them before without success, and it's hard to believe that this time I'd make a difference. Has the moment finally come to return to New York, to pack up my bags like Drew just ordered me to do? I have two more days, Thursday and Friday, on my contract for the house here, but perhaps I should cut it short. What's the point in staying if I can't do anything for Jamie?

I let my eyes close and as soon as I do, memories of him flash across my mind in quick succession. I see him smiling flirtatiously at me at the bike rack on the day we met, beaming the night we got engaged, and tearing up the morning I broke his heart.

I'm sorry, Jamie, I think. *I'm sorry I failed you yet again.*

24

At seven thirty that night I walk into town again, to the small bistro where I had a glass of wine the first night I arrived. I still have a couple of chicken breasts in the freezer, but I need to be out of the house, distracting myself. I'm still reeling from my confrontation with the Larssons and all its ramifications.

It's another very warm evening, almost sticky, but I ask for one of the sidewalk tables again, under the strings of fairy lights. The hostess seats me in a spot toward the very end, several tables away from other diners, so thankfully I'm not stuck listening to someone else's conversation.

As soon as the waiter appears at my table, I order a glass of wine and fettuccine Alfredo at the same time—because I don't want to linger at the restaurant. Just being out has helped calm me a little, but I haven't forgotten the car tailing mine and then nearly ramming my bumper. It probably wasn't Liam, I realize now—he and Drew had a different game plan for how to deal with me—but that leaves the question of who the driver was and whether he was after me specifically. I feel a need to watch my back.

The pasta arrives, and though it smells and tastes delicious, my appetite is nearly nonexistent. How could I have thought I'd enjoy a meal here with so much going wrong? Maybe I'll never be able to learn what happened to Jamie. His family will despise me forever. And Sam's kiss has roiled my emotions more than I thought possible.

I manage to eat about half the fettuccine before pushing the bowl aside. As I take a sip of pinot grigio, now far too warm, I catch a glimpse of someone walking in the direction of the restaurant and realize after a few seconds that it's Vic's agent, Dan. He spots me a split second later and lifts his hand in a wave.

"Kiki?" he calls out.

"Yes, it's me. Hi, Dan."

He approaches the table with a pleasant smile, carrying a small white plastic bag in one hand. He's dressed in khaki pants and a pink-and-white-checked button-down shirt, sleeves rolled to the elbows.

"How are you doing?" he asks, reaching me.

"Getting by," I say, forcing a smile. "I heard you were in the area, but I didn't expect to see you in New Burford."

"The pharmacy closest to Vic didn't have my allergy meds, so I had to stop by the one here. Mind if I sit for a moment?"

"Please," I say, surprised. "Want something to drink—or to eat?"

"Thanks, but I'm expected back at the house soon. I'd just love to chat for a few."

He slides into the chair across from mine and drops the drugstore bag on the table.

"How was your dinner with Vic last night?" I ask. "I ate at the club with Ava, and she said you two were headed out somewhere."

"We ended up scrapping that plan," he says. "Vic was exhausted from his Boston event and wanted to turn in early, so I grabbed a bite on my own in town. Listen, I mainly wanted to apologize to you for not expressing any sympathy to you that night. I only recently learned that you'd been engaged to Jamie. This whole thing must be devastating for you."

"Yes, very rough," I say quietly. "I appreciate you saying that."

There's no hint of the bossiness that had bugged me

that night. Maybe it was simply a manifestation of the stress he was under.

"Do you have family around here?" he asks. "Is that why you've come back?"

"No family in these parts. I just thought that being someplace Jamie loved might ease my grief a little."

"I get that," he says, offering a wan smile. "I didn't know Jamie well, but it's been harder than I expected."

"You and Vic found the body. That must have been incredibly difficult."

He nods. "And it still feels so unreal. My wife told me that when she heard the shot, she thought it was a firecracker, but I knew right away it was gunfire. I'd gone up to Vic's office, and I came tearing down the stairs, thinking someone at the party had shot someone else there."

I remember Dan on the steps now. He'd been looking for Vic upstairs, though it had turned out Vic was in the kitchen.

And earlier Dan had eaten dinner at the same table as Jamie. Is it possible he heard or saw something he doesn't even realize is significant? Since he's sitting across from me, I decide not to let the opportunity slip away.

"Was there anything about the night that seemed off to you?" I ask. "I mean, before you heard the gunfire?"

He grimaces. "You mean anything worrisome about Jamie's behavior?" I nod. "No, not in the least. Since my wife and I were staying over, we'd been there since midafternoon, and Jamie showed up for dinner on the early side. He seemed to be in good spirits. It's unbelievable how people can hide their pain."

He obviously hasn't questioned the purported cause of death.

"What was the mood at the table like? You sat with him, right?"

"Yeah. And everything was pleasant. Jamie had read an advance copy of Vic's book and so had my wife, and we shared some of the highlights with the others. There did seem to be a little issue with the woman he'd invited. She was clearly in a bad mood, and he pretty much ignored her—and then she left the table before dessert, never to return. But he hardly seemed upset by it."

"Anything else, Dan?" I say, a pleading slipping into my tone. "Anything that seemed strange to you?"

He shakes his head, his expression clouding even more. "Nothing, and trust me, I've gone over it again and again. I played doubles with Vic and Jamie a couple of times when I've visited, and though I wouldn't have been able to call him a friend, I really liked the guy. I just wish I'd noticed some warning signs that night—or had engaged with him more. Maybe it would have helped."

"Dan, there was no way you could have made a difference," I say, deciding at that moment that I had nothing to lose by telling the truth. "I'm almost positive that Jamie didn't kill himself."

Behind his glasses, his eyes widen in shock. "Are you telling me you think he was *murdered*?"

"Yes. I think someone shot him and staged it to look like a suicide."

"My god."

"But please don't relay any of this to Vic. There's no official cause of death yet, but Vic believes it was suicide and he doesn't understand why I can't accept that and move on."

He nods. "You have my word. But who could have possibly done it?"

"I've had no luck coming up with an answer to that. As you know, everyone liked Jamie."

"But you're assuming there was some kind of conflict that night?"

"What do you mean?" I say, confused by the question.

"That something happened between Jamie and another guest, and then the person decided to kill him?"

"No, I don't think there was any incident at the party—no one reported seeing something like that, and

I doubt it would have gone unnoticed. My gut tells me a guest came there planning to murder him. And though they would have done their best to act normal, they might have looked awkward around him or weirdly distant. That's why I asked if anything felt off to you."

Dan frowns. "I'm not discounting your theory—in fact I've had a tough time accepting that Jamie pulled the trigger. But if someone came planning to kill him, how would they know he'd be one of the last to leave, and that there wouldn't be other people getting into their cars at the same time?"

"Well, Jamie had gotten to be a pretty good pal of Vic's, so he was bound to stay toward the end."

He presses a hand against his jaw, obviously thinking this over. "Okay. But if the killer was another guest, where was their vehicle? Vic and I didn't see a car drive off when we ran outside."

"The killer would have left early, driven his or her car a short distance away, and then hiked back on foot," I say, articulating what I'd assumed was the MO if Liam had been the murderer.

"But if you're *planning* a murder, why make it so complicated? It seems like there would have been a simpler way and a better time to do it."

"So you think I have it all wrong?" I blurt out, with more than a twinge of frustration.

"No, I don't mean that. I'm saying the killer might have gone to the party without planning to do it."

It takes me a few seconds to get his point. "You mean it was a spur-of-the-moment thing?"

"Right. The killer would have known he was taking a chance but was too upset that night to care—or he felt his back was up against the wall and he had to act immediately."

I bite my lip and glance up at the string of lights above us. Dan's words are like the kind of wake-up call I try to give clients sometimes, challenging them to step back and see a situation from a different angle.

"Maybe the conflict that night was subtle, not some kind of big showdown," Dan adds. "And that's why no one noticed. It might have been just a brief exchange of words, but one that convinced the other person that Jamie was a real threat. Could he have been making a play for someone's partner that night?"

I scoff at the question. "That really doesn't seem like Jamie's style."

"You'd know better than I would." Dan glances at his watch. "I'd love to talk this out some more, but I'd better get back. Ava's making dinner."

"Of course."

He fishes a wallet from his back pocket and tugs out a business card. "I'm headed home tomorrow, but if I can help in any way, let me know," he says, handing it to me. "And again, I won't say anything to Vic."

"Thank you, Dan. And thanks for stopping to talk. You—you put some things in focus for me."

He takes off down the sidewalk, eventually jogging across the street to a parked car. Though I'd planned to have only one glass of wine, I order a second, feeling even more unsettled than when I arrived an hour ago. Dan's suggestion moves back and forth across my brain, like a tiger pacing in a cage.

I certainly hadn't ruled out a last-minute scenario, but mainly I've imagined something orchestrated, the killer arriving that night with well-laid plans to end Jamie's life.

Maybe the opposite is indeed true, that the murder *was* entirely unpremeditated. But what could have triggered it? Whenever I spotted Jamie, he was chatting casually with people, and I certainly didn't see him flirting with someone else's wife or girlfriend.

Of course, I only had eyes and ears on him periodically that night, and there were plenty of moments for the kind of brief exchange Dan alluded to.

I remember suddenly what Megan told me about suicide. The window of time between the decision to take one's life and the act of doing it might be as narrow as a few minutes.

Maybe the rule holds true for murder as well.

25

When I finally think to check the time, I'm shocked that it's close to nine o'clock. Despite my plan not to linger, I've done just that, too absorbed in my thoughts to see how late it was getting. I look around for the waiter and after catching his eye and getting the bill, I pay it and begin my walk home.

The main street in town is still busy, with cars cruising up and down and people clustered in front of the few bars and cafés, as well as the local ice cream shop. Most of those I see wear the happy grins of tourists who've squirreled away their vacation time until late August and are finally enjoying it. The mix also seems to include a fair share of weekenders—of which I used to be one.

When I'd broken things off with Jamie, I knew it meant there'd be no regular weekend plans for me this summer, that the most I could hope for was an occasional invitation from a friend or a last-minute trip on my own. As I told him the last time I saw him, I'd spent many of my recent Saturdays and Sundays hanging out on the rooftop garden of my apartment building, acting as if warm-weather weekends in the empty city held a certain magic for me. Which wasn't true at all. But when I get back to New York this week, at least September will be on the near horizon and I won't have to think as much about the summer that never was.

As soon as I turn onto McAlpin Street, the crowd thins, and before long it's only me and the shadow I cast under the glow of the streetlamps. I pick up my pace, turning around now and then to check behind me. The street is deserted.

My phone pings from my purse, startling me. I fish it out to see a text from Sam.

Everything okay?

What do you mean?

Your car's in the driveway but you aren't answering your door.

Walked into town for dinner. What's up?

I wanted to talk to you.

Ok, I'll be back in 5.

I'm on your stoop.

To my annoyance, my heart is thrumming at the thought of seeing him. That's another thing I'm going to do when I get back to New York. Drive Sam Morgan from my mind once and for all, even if it takes a visit to a hypnotist.

I turn onto Ash Street, and from half a block away I can see him sitting on the stoop, his long, lanky legs extended onto the sidewalk. It's been five months since I returned to a home where someone was waiting for me, and it feels ridiculously reassuring to know he's there and that I won't be looking over my shoulder as I unlock the door.

When I'm starting up the front walk, Sam rises and takes a few steps toward me. From the porch light I see he's in a weathered black T-shirt, shorts, and sandals, more casual than last night.

"I hope I'm not interrupting any of your plans," he says.

"No, I was headed home. Do you want to come in?"

"Yeah, if you don't mind."

I brush past him, unlock the door, and proceed into the house first, glancing around. So far at least, nothing seems weird. I open the door wider and usher Sam into the living room.

"Speaking of cars," I say, "where's yours?" I hadn't seen it outside.

"A few houses down on the block. I decided not to leave it directly in front of the house again."

"Why? You don't want to sully my reputation with the neighbors?"

He smiles faintly. "You never struck me as the kind of woman who cares what the neighbors think. It's other people I'm thinking of."

"Who do you mean?"

"Drew. I heard what an asshole he was to you."

"You did?" I exclaim. "Who told you?"

"Mel."

That's an even bigger surprise. "You talk to Mel?"

"She helped my parents on some charity projects long before she worked for the Larssons, so I've known her awhile. I called Drew late this afternoon to follow up with him, and she answered. After she told me he was out for the rest of the afternoon, she brought up that she'd overheard him berate you. She's a gossip, but I think she was also upset by how he treated you and wanted to vent."

We're standing only inches apart, and I can feel the warmth emanating from his body. Last night all I wanted was for him to step over the imaginary trip wire, but now that we're in such close proximity, I couldn't feel more awkward.

"Why don't we sit in the kitchen," I suggest, moving in that direction. "And then I'll fill you in. Do you want something to drink?"

"You don't have a cold beer by any chance, do you?" he asks, trailing behind me.

"No, sorry. Just white wine or sparkling water."

"Water's fine then."

I fill two glasses, set them on the table, and take a seat across from Sam, who's already flopped into a chair.

"The whole thing was horrible," I say. "When I was invited to the house, I convinced myself that he wanted to hear what I thought, but he lit into me the second I got there. And then Liam joined in. They seemed to know everything I've done, everywhere I've looked."

"That's exactly why I didn't leave my car out there. I wouldn't be surprised if they've been checking up on you, and I didn't want to give Drew any more fodder."

I shake my head. "I wouldn't have minded his fury if anything positive had come out of the experience, but it didn't. It seems clear that Liam's real-estate holdings are a dead end."

"You asked him about those?" Sam says, obviously surprised.

"They ended up giving me an opening." As tough as it is to rehash the encounter, I relate Liam's testy explanation for how he became a mini-real-estate mogul. "Does that make sense to you?" I ask when I'm finished. As an economics guru, Sam would certainly know.

He cocks his head, his expression pensive. "Yeah, that didn't occur to me right off the bat, but that trajectory is certainly possible in a good market, if he had enough for the first down payment. But do you think Drew might have been covering for Liam?"

I shake my head. "I doubt it. It seemed like Drew was fully in the loop, and he must have had enough access to Liz's bank statements to confirm that Liam hadn't made any inappropriate withdrawals. And if he had the slightest inkling Liam murdered Jamie, he would never hush it up, no matter what it meant for the family. He adored Jamie."

Sam nods and reaches for the glass with one hand, while the other rests on the faded oiled tablecloth. His hands are nicely shaped, with long, slim fingers, and I realize I was so busy trying *not* to look at Sam during my relationship with Jamie that this is the first time I've ever really *seen* them.

"Regardless," Sam says, "he's allowing his anger at you to get in the way of his judgment. And I feel guilty because I'm part of the reason you walked into a trap. When I spoke to Drew, I thought he seemed genuinely intrigued about the dog and what it might mean."

"He said he could tell you only called him because I talked you into it."

"He's lying," Sam says, his eyes flashing. "I told him I was as concerned as you were."

I exhale, happy to have my doubts about Sam quieted. "The bottom line is that he's not going to help us. We're back to square one and all by ourselves there."

"So, what's next?"

"Can I run something by you? Ever since I became convinced Jamie was murdered, I assumed someone must have gone to the party intending to kill him. But now I'm wondering if something occurred *at the party* that triggered the whole thing. When you were around Jamie, who was he talking to—and what was he discussing?"

Sam shrugs. "It was run-of-the-mill, I think. During the actual dinner, our table talked mostly about Vic's book, about the mass hysteria in Salem and how we've seen so many modern examples of it. There was a certain amount of awkwardness because of that fucking party-crasher, Percy, but she mostly sulked while the rest of us ignored her."

"What about before and after dinner? Did you hear or see him talking to anyone?"

He lifts his eyes up and to the left, clearly thinking. "He spoke to you in the study, of course. And right before that I overheard him chatting with a friend of Vic's, something about playing more tennis in August."

"I heard part of that. He was saying he was going to make pomodoro sauce and do some genealogy research." I'd missed everything after that, as a couple of people had pushed past me just then to get to the bar.

Sam nods. "Yeah, he told the guy he believed he had ancestors in Norway, but he wasn't sure how much his father had romanticized it. He'd just ordered one of those DNA tests from someplace like 23andMe, and he was thinking of going to Norway next year."

"Anything else?"

"Not really, and since I left before dessert, I know nothing about the last part of the evening."

"Maybe it's a stupid theory. As you said, nothing seemed out of the ordinary."

"Which brings me back to my previous question. What next?"

I offer a disconsolate shrug. "I don't know. I'm

heading back to New York soon, and I hope being farther from here will give me a fresh perspective. Maybe if I hold off for a while, let the dust settle, and then approach the police again, they'll do something more than direct me to victim services."

"When?"

"When do I plan to go to the cops again?"

"No, when are you going back?"

"In a couple of days."

He holds my gaze for a few seconds, pressing his lips together. I feel myself flush a little, remembering last night and the kiss he gave me before he stole away. The kiss from someone who said he'd wished we'd met sooner.

I look off for a few moments, flustered, and when I glance back, I see Sam checking his watch.

"Am I keeping you from anything?" I say.

"Quite the opposite. You've spared me from a dinner party my parents are hosting for four extremely pompous friends of theirs who love showing me how brilliant they are about stock futures."

"Still," I say, slowly rising from the table. "I should let you go."

He rises, too, and levels his gaze on me again.

"Is that what you want?"

I stare back. "What?"

"For me to go?"

I hold my breath for a few seconds and slowly exhale. "No. No, it isn't."

A second later he's kissing me, softly at first and then more deeply, my face cupped between his hands. I feel overwhelmed with longing but also disbelief. Is this really happening?

Sam presses his body against mine, and then our hands fly, exploring. Finally, he pulls away.

"What now?" he asks softly.

"Do you want to stay—I mean, for the night?"

"Yes. But . . ." He laughs lightly. "You're about to see what a nerdy professor I really am. I don't have any protection."

I smile awkwardly back at him. "Neither do I."

Inside I'm cringing, knowing that this is a chance for us, and I need to grab hold of it. If we say goodbye now, promising to meet another night, it's possible that night won't come to be.

"Wait," I blurt out. "Maybe in my toiletry bag. Give me a second."

I hurry upstairs, resisting the urge to break into a run. In the bathroom, I fumble through the bag and, miraculously, locate two condoms at the very bottom, purchased before I met Jamie but somehow not expired. I return downstairs, praying Sam won't have thought better of this in the meantime, but he smiles when I tell him we're all set.

Within seconds, it seems, we're in my bedroom, kissing passionately again. The sex is intense and electric, though it's hard to know if that's simply because we're a good match as lovers or because this is something I've craved for so many months.

Later, Sam slips his arm under me and strokes my forehead.

"I need to be honest with you about something," he says in the dark, and my stomach drops. Is he going to tell me he's seeing someone?

"Okay."

"I meant what I said last night, about wishing I'd met you first. I've thought that for a long time. Part of why I acted so foul after the breakup was because I was worried that I'd gotten drunk one night and sold my soul to the devil to make it happen."

"Thank you, Sam, for telling me that," I say, nearly giddy hearing the words.

Though sex has left me drowsy, it takes a while to fall asleep. As good as tonight was, guilt is gnawing away at the edge of my contentment. I'm lying next to Jamie's best friend, in a bed Jamie once slept in, no less. But at the same time, I can't help but be grateful. Because I know now that my feelings for Sam were always genuine, not simply a manifestation of my doubts about Jamie, and that those feelings have been reciprocated. However complicated this moment is, I don't regret what I've done.

I wake with a jolt, and it takes me a second to realize that the object between my head and the pillow is Sam's arm. I check the clock and see that it's a few minutes after three.

And then I realize what's roused me. It's the smell of woodsmoke drifting into the bedroom again. Unease ripples through me.

Once I've gently repositioned Sam's arm, I slip out of bed, quickly put on a T-shirt and my underwear, and pad quietly into the hallway. The odor is definitely there, not simply something that came back to me in a dream. I have to figure out what the hell is going on. I briefly consider waking Sam but decide against it— after all, I've dealt with weird things on my own on the nights I've been here alone.

Leaving him sleeping, I creep down the staircase for the second time this week. My disquiet grows with each step, but I keep going. I reach the bottom and grab a breath. It's dark, except for a faint glow coming from the kitchen. Because Sam was staying, I hadn't felt the need to leave more than a single light on downstairs, the one recessed above the kitchen sink.

Just like the other night, the smell is stronger down here. I tiptoe through the dining room and take a step into the kitchen.

To my shock, I see a huge jar candle on the kitchen table, with flames flickering from three different wicks. And closer to the wall, sitting in one of the chairs, is the figure of a woman. Even in the dimness of the room, I can make out the menacing grin on her face.

26

I gasp and reach toward the counter, gripping it with one hand.

"Who *are* you?"

But as she leans the tiniest bit closer, widening her grin, I see that it's Percy.

"What are you doing here?" I demand, my heart racing crazily.

"What am *I* doing here?" she says snidely. Her image is a little fuzzy in the candlelight, but I see that her hair's pulled back and she's wearing a black, long-sleeved shirt. "You can't be serious, right? I basically lived here before you came along."

"You lived—"

And then I get it. She means when Jamie was renting this place.

"You just can't stand to think about it, can you?" she says. "Me and your ex here together, playing house, having sex, enjoying the kind of crazy love you two never had."

No, it's not possible. She couldn't have been living here with Jamie.

"If you don't believe me," she says, as if reading my mind, "ask yourself why I have a key."

She lifts a key chain from the table with her right hand and wiggles it for my benefit. I shoot a glance toward the back door. I can see well enough to tell the lock hasn't been hacked off, that she hasn't broken in, at least from the back of the house. But I can't believe Jamie would have shared a key with her.

Instinctively my gaze shifts to the candle flickering on the table. This is where the smell is coming from, I realize. I've seen candles with a "woodsmoke" scent in small boutique shops.

"You've been in the house already this week, haven't you?" I say. She must have burned the candle in the kitchen the other night and snuck out when she heard me coming down the stairs. And it must have been her who turned on the light in the kitchen, who ran the AC in my bedroom. "Why?"

"Just having a little fun with you."

What the hell do I do? Sam, I suddenly remember. He's here in the house. But if I call out for him, I might trigger her to do something rash.

"Please, just tell me what you want, Percy."

She drops the key and taps her index finger against her lips a couple of times, a parody of someone deliberating what to say. At the same moment, a faint creak comes from above my head. Is it the bed moving? Footsteps? But Percy doesn't seem to notice.

"Well, for starters," she says, "an apology."

Humor her, I think. *Say whatever she wants and get her to leave.*

"Okay, sure, of course. For . . . ?"

"*For?* For showing up at the fucking party, that's what. At first, I didn't mind you were there. What difference did it make? But once I saw that you'd moved into Jamie's *house*, I realized that you must have had a whole game plan for that night."

"Percy, that's not true. I didn't have any kind of pl—"

"Of *course* you did." She's snarling now, like a guard dog on high alert. "You were there to strut your stuff in front of Jamie. You wanted him back, so you flirted with Vic and his other friends and made sure Jamie couldn't take his eyes off you. Miss Smarty-Pants in her little black party dress."

"No, I swear—"

"You wanted to fuck him that night, didn't you? Why don't you just admit it?"

She shakes her head in disgust and moves her hands, grabbing the edge of the table. And that's when I see it— something silver or stainless steel glinting on the table where her left hand was resting before. It's the blade of a butcher knife.

"Jamie and I were over," I say. I'm trying to keep my panic under wraps, but my voice betrays my desperation. "I'm sure *you* were the one he cared for."

Percy inches her chair back, scraping the legs across the wooden floor. Without further warning, she shoots up from the table, gripping the knife in her hand and pointing the blade in my direction. My knees go weak. Once again, I consider screaming for Sam, but what if that makes her lunge at me?

"You think any of that *matters* to me anymore?" she says. Now that she's standing, I see that the muscles of her face are tight with anger and her eyes are flicking back and forth in her head. "Jamie and I had something once, something special, but in the end, he didn't have the guts to go public with it, to let the world know about our love. And, besides, I got a glimpse of who he really was, and frankly, I didn't like what I saw."

"What do you mean who he was?" What the hell is she talking about?

"You think he was such a sweet, all-American boy, don't you? But he wasn't—and in the end he got what he deserved. Guys like him can't just be forgiven. They need to pay for their sins."

My stomach drops. Percy *killed* him. Rage floods through every inch of me.

"And women like you should get what they deserve too," she says next.

From the corner of my eye, I catch a movement in the living room. It's Sam's silhouette, shifting position in the barely lit space—but from what I can tell, he's not in Percy's line of sight.

"Percy, please put the knife down," I say a little louder, trying to warn Sam. "I get what you're saying, and I want to hear more."

Despite my caution, Sam doesn't freeze. There's a blur of motion as he advances toward the kitchen. I shake my head no, but that doesn't stop him, either. Noticing my gesture, Percy twists toward the entrance, and when she spots Sam, coming at her in just his boxers, she juts the knife in his direction.

I glance frantically around the room and spot the umbrella stand a few feet away, by the back door. I lunge toward it, grab one of the walking sticks stored there, and swing it at Percy.

There's a dull thud as it connects with her left arm, then she lets out a growl, both stunned and in pain. As she starts to turn in my direction, I aim again, whacking her in the head this time, so hard I hear a cracking sound. The knife slips from her hand, clattering to the wood floor, and seconds later, Percy falls, too. She lands in a heap, face up.

"Are you okay?" Sam asks, rushing toward me and grasping my arm.

"Yeah, just scared."

He chuckles grimly. "Damn, I had no idea you were that good with a light saber."

"Me either." I shake my head. "We need to call 911."

"But first, we should make sure she can't pull a fast one." He steps toward the fallen knife, kicking it away until it lands against the back door. Then he looks back at Percy. She seems to be conscious, but her eyes are closed and she's moaning in pain.

"Is there any rope in the house?"

"I think so."

After setting down the walking stick in a corner, I dash toward the storage closet. Inside I discover that what I thought was rope is only twine, but I grab it along with some duct tape and pass them to Sam, who's standing guard over Percy.

He works quickly, using the twine and the tape to bind her hands and feet. My eyes flick briefly to the kitchen counter and the wooden knife block. The largest slot is empty. It must have housed the knife she threatened me with.

As soon as Percy's mostly secured, I tell Sam that I'm going upstairs for my phone.

"Can you grab my clothes when you're there?" he asks. "I don't think the cops will appreciate seeing me in my underwear."

It suddenly occurs to me that I'm only half-dressed myself. After racing upstairs, I quickly wiggle into a pair of jeans and retrieve my phone. Then, pulling a breath, I tap the three digits.

"This is 911," the operator says as I approach the steps. "What is your emergency?"

I blurt out what's happened and also explain that I'm pretty sure the woman who broke into my rental home killed a man named Jamie Larsson two weeks ago.

After she promises to send a team and I sign off, I scurry back downstairs with Sam's clothes and sandals. Though my fear has subsided a little, my heart is still beating wildly.

"They said a car is being dispatched immediately," I tell him. He's leaning against the kitchen door frame with one eye on Percy, who's writhing a little on the floor. It's impossible to tell if she's in a lot of pain or just struggling to free herself.

"I don't think you did any serious damage," Sam says as he notices me taking her in. "But she might have a concussion."

"I don't care if she does," I exclaim. "She killed Jamie. She told me so."

"Yeah, I caught that part." He accepts his clothes and sandals from me but then gestures toward the dining room. "Why don't we wait in there? I can still keep an eye on her, but I'll be less tempted to strangle her."

While I drop into one of the chairs, he hurriedly dresses.

"So, tell me what happened earlier," he says. "I woke up because I heard you talking to someone, but how did *you* know she was down here?"

I explain about the candle smell and then fill him in on the parts of the exchange with Percy that he missed, as well as the other creepy incidents at the house that I now know she was responsible for.

"And she said Jamie gave her a *key*?" he says, finally sitting. "That makes no sense. Like I told you, he said they'd only gone out a few times."

"I know, but she seemed to know him better than that," I say. I'm still struggling to sort it all out in my mind. "And it now seems clear she was in a rage at the party, at a level that no one realized."

He reaches out a hand and lays it across mine. I feel my pulse begin to slow.

"God, Kiki, she was in a rage about you, too," he says. "She could have killed you."

"*Both* of us. Thank god you parked your car down the street and she had no idea anyone else was here." I glance down at my phone, which I've rested on the edge of the table. "Where *are* they?"

And then, as if it's answering me, the sound of a siren cuts through the night.

"Here we go," he says. He takes his hand back and sweeps it through his hair. For a moment I can still feel the warmth of his touch on my skin and then it's gone.

I struggle up and move quickly to the front window, with Sam right behind me, to see that an ambulance and a state police vehicle have pulled up to the front of the house.

"Okay, why don't you get the door," Sam says, "and I'll go check on her again." He reaches out and gives my arm a comforting squeeze. "And keep in mind, they're going to separate us before long. We're on our own from here."

"Right," I say.

I tell myself that there's no reason to be anxious, and that this is the moment I've been waiting for—to prove to everyone that Jamie didn't take his own life. All I have to do is explain the encounter with Percy and relay her chilling words about Jamie.

The siren is off now, and the sound of doors slamming and the clomp of footsteps comes from outside. There's so much to tell them, but there's one thing I have no intention of sharing: how Percy said Jamie wasn't the man I thought he was, and that he had sins he needed to be punished for.

I don't know what she meant, but it won't stop echoing in my mind.

27

I swing the door open. Two gray-uniformed state troopers—one male, one female—enter, followed by two EMS workers with a rolling stretcher, and then two more male troopers. The room starts to buzz like an overturned beehive. The woman appears to be in charge and introduces herself as Trooper First Class Gallagher. After Sam and I provide our names, I quickly recap what I told the 911 operator and Sam explains that the person who broke in and threatened me is tied up in the kitchen.

"Okay, please remain here for now," Trooper Gallagher directs us. Sam and I retreat to the far side of the living room as the rest of the group heads to the kitchen, minus one trooper who hangs back with us. Though I can't make out specific words from where

I'm standing, I'm aware of the ambulance crew and cops talking in short bursts to one another, and I hear crackling noise from a two-way radio. Next comes the click of metal and the sound of Percy moaning again. They must be moving her onto the gurney. I flash back to the look on her face as she sneered at me and the gleam of the blade she thrust in my direction.

Sam gives my hand a quick squeeze. "Hang in there," he whispers.

I squeeze back, grateful for the gesture. I'm starting to feel lightheaded, and my legs are a little wobbly, perhaps from the letdown of adrenaline that was surging through my body.

The trooper in the room with us, a clean-shaven guy not much older than thirty, seems to keep one eye on the kitchen and the other on Sam and me, but his face is otherwise expressionless.

Suddenly, both EMS workers emerge from the kitchen, rolling the gurney toward the front door, with three troopers alongside it. The body of one trooper blocks most of my view, but I catch a flash of bright red and realize that Percy's in a plastic head immobilizer. A second later I glimpse the lower half of her body, squirming beneath a sheet.

"She did it," she suddenly calls out. "She attacked me."

My heart jumps. That's all I need—for Percy to convince law enforcement that *she's* the victim.

After the troopers briefly confer with each other, one departs with Percy and the ambulance crew, and another returns to the kitchen. Trooper Gallagher and the oldest of the two remaining men stay in the living room. He asks Sam to take a seat on the couch, and Gallagher ushers me into the dining room. As soon as we're inside, she pulls the pocket doors closed behind us.

She's an attractive woman, tall and seemingly in great shape, with dark red hair secured in a tight bun and eyes the same color as the tie of her bright blue uniform. She motions for me to have a seat at the table and then lowers herself into a chair across from me. After taking down some basic information, she asks me to describe what happened.

I start with being woken by the smell, then heading downstairs to discover Percy in the kitchen, and from there I backtrack, describing the other weird incidents—because I want to be sure she understands how unhinged this woman is. I mention Jamie's death, the ongoing investigation, and Percy's involvement with Jamie. Then I return to tonight, how Percy threatened both Sam and me with a knife and how she said Jamie deserved to die.

Gallagher appears to listen carefully, asking me a

couple of questions now and then for clarification and taking notes with a ballpoint pen. From the kitchen I hear the intermittent scuff of the third trooper's shoes, and I sense he's taking photos or gathering evidence or both.

"Sounds like a harrowing night," Gallagher says when I finish.

"Yes, very."

"Just so I'm clear: How many times did you strike Percy West in all?"

"Uh, twice. The first time was on the arm and all it did was make her angrier. She stepped closer to Sam with the knife, so that's when I hit her in the head."

As I'm speaking, I assure myself that what I did was completely justified and in self-defense, but still, I've never intentionally injured anyone before, and it rattles me.

"And you sustained no injuries yourself?"

"Not unless you count being terrified."

Gallagher takes a minute to thumb through her notes, peering intently as she reads, and then glances back at me.

"You said you came downstairs at around three," she says. "You didn't wake Mr. Morgan?"

A warning bell sounds in my head—this might be a question I need to answer cautiously.

"No, because I thought it was just another weird occurrence in the house, which I wanted to figure out. I never imagined someone was actually downstairs."

She nods with her lips pursed, seeming to understand. But I know I can't take that for granted.

"And about how long were you alone with Ms. West before Mr. Morgan joined you?"

"Probably no more than ten minutes—though it felt like an eternity."

"And what is your relationship to each other?"

At that moment I'm suddenly struck with a sense of how the experience I've just described might appear to an outsider: In the middle of the night, two thirtysomething professional types summon the police to a house that neither of them owns, where a younger woman is lying dazed and hog-tied on the kitchen floor. There is no sign of forced entry. The only weapon is a knife from a wooden block on the kitchen counter. And there's a scented candle burning on the table. God, they could easily think it's a threesome gone horribly wrong.

I can't let the police doubt what transpired here, not only because it would be bad for Sam and me, but then they might not hold Percy responsible for Jamie's death.

"We've been friends for a few years," I say, "but things started to shift this week."

She nods again, her expression neutral. "Okay, I

think that does it for now. We'll need you to come by headquarters later today to give a formal statement." She slips a card from her pocket and indicates the address where I'll need to go.

"Thank you—and you'll speak to Detective Calistro?"

"Calistro?"

"About Jamie Larsson's death. How Percy West killed him."

"Yes, he'll be brought up to date."

She gives no indication that she appreciates the connection between the two cases, but I tell myself she's just acting professional—in other words, not giving anything away.

I almost groan with relief when she opens the pocket doors and I set eyes on Sam again, sitting alone on the couch. The trooper, obviously finished with the interview, is speaking quietly into a cell phone on the other side of the room. The other trooper, the one who'd been in the kitchen, seems to have left by now. As Sam hoists himself up from the couch, the trooper finishes his call and nods at Gallagher. They wish us both a good night and take their leave.

"You alive?" Sam asks as we meet in the middle of the living room. I notice light seeping in from around the edges of the curtains on the window behind him. It must be after five in the morning by now.

"Barely. How about you?"

"The same."

I duck into the kitchen and glance around. The knife is gone and so are the walking stick, the candle, the twine, the duct tape, and the key chain Percy dangled. I fill two glasses with orange juice and return to the living room with them.

Sam brings the glass to his lips and slugs back half the contents. "How do you think your interview went?" he says, after wiping his mouth with the back of his hand.

I shrug. "Okay, I guess. Yours?"

"Same."

"Do you think they're not totally buying our version of events tonight?" I ask.

"You mean do they really think some crazy shit went down here? Maybe. Cops get paid to be skeptical."

"Except in Jamie's case."

"Exactly," he says, darkly.

"But they *have* to look more closely now. They'll certainly check Percy's alibi for the second half of Saturday night. And won't they collect her DNA, and compare it to what was in the car?"

"I assume they have a right to do that, but since she actually dated Jamie, she could claim she'd been in the car on other occasions."

"God, you're right," I say, dismayed.

"But once Drew hears about this, he's going to take it seriously, and I'm sure he'll finally put some pressure on them."

I nod. "Let's hope. By the way, the trooper asked what my relationship to you was. Did you get the same question?"

"In so many words. I told them I was a friend and since some weird things had been happening to you lately, I spent the night."

I nod again. Our answers are probably similar enough to avoid any issue, but I can't help noting how they seem to be miles apart.

Sam drains the rest of his juice and then stares into the empty glass, like someone trying to read tea leaves at the bottom of a cup.

"How about coffee?" I ask. "I could make eggs, too."

"Thanks, but I should go."

Go? I think. Doesn't he feel a need to talk this through some more, or a desire to decompress together? I bite my tongue, though, rather than voice my chagrin.

He scrunches his mouth and I sense him reading my thoughts. "I promised my parents I'd have breakfast with them today to review some pressing things," he says. "But I'll call you later and check in."

"Okay."

"You going to be all right on your own?"

"Of course." It's beginning to seem as if everything from earlier tonight—kissing, falling into bed, making love—happened eons ago. Or only in my imagination.

Sam stares at me quizzically, obviously sensing his departure isn't sitting well, but after setting his glass on the coffee table, he pulls me into an embrace and kisses the top of my head.

"Things will work out," he murmurs, his lips still pressed lightly against my skin.

What things? I wonder, as I watch him trip down the front steps and jog across the lawn. Does he mean Percy being convicted for Jamie's death, or the situation between the two of us? Or both? I try to gauge my emotions, but they're impossible to interpret. I feel deflated, but I'm not sure if it's because I'm in the final stage of an adrenaline crash or because the man I just slept with dashed off mere hours after an intruder broke in and threatened my life.

I drift over to the couch and collapse onto it, dragging a chenille throw over me. At least I have the sad consolation of knowing once and for all that Jamie didn't take his own life. I can't bear picturing his last moments, but now that I've learned the truth, images fight their way into my brain. Jamie ignoring Percy at the party. Percy leaving in a rage. Then hurrying home, grabbing a gun that she'd gotten her hands on somehow, and returning to the field to lie in wait.

And it more or less confirms what Dan suggested. No one arrived at the party intent on killing Jamie; it was all decided on the spur of the moment.

There's still so much I don't understand, though. Percy claimed twice to me that her involvement with Jamie was more serious than anyone knew and that he hadn't wanted to "go public" with it. Could that possibly be true? She *did* have a key to the house.

What's eating at me most of all: What did she means when she talked about Jamie's "sins"? I can't help but wonder if there was a secret side to him that I never saw.

Exhaustion soon overtakes me, and I feel myself drift off.

28

I only manage to get another hour of sleep before sunlight forces my eyes open. After a hot shower and some scrambled eggs, I drive to the state police headquarters, about twenty minutes away, far more jittery than I'd like to be.

I'm interviewed by a burly, bearded trooper named Robert Rudnick, and after recounting my experience for a second time, I review and sign the written statement. He gives me no reason to think he doubts my version of events, but I'm still aware that the police might be reserving judgment.

"What about Percy West?" I inquire before rising. I've been worried ever since I woke up from my nap, wondering if she somehow managed to talk herself out of being arrested.

"Charges were filed against her already," the detective says. "They include burglary, aggravated assault, and unlawful possession of a weapon. There was enough evidence to show she had intent to commit a crime."

"Is she okay?" That's been worrying me, too, the idea that I might have injured her more seriously than I thought.

"She suffered a mild concussion but she's being released today from the ER—and as soon as that happens, she'll be taken into custody."

I exhale. "Thank you. Just one last question. Has someone been in touch with Detective Calistro, who's investigating Jamie Larsson's death?"

"Yes," he says without hesitation. "He's been looped in."

Finally, I think, as I hurry outside. *Finally, finally, finally.*

Crossing the parking lot, I scan the area. I'd half expected to see Sam dropping by while I was here, but there's no sign of him or his car. Once I'm in the driver's seat, I text Ava to say I have something important I need to tell her. I also leave a message for Clarissa, the rental manager, figuring I should bring her up to speed about what happened.

As soon as I return to the house, I plunge into work

at the dining room table. Though I'm still shaken and bleary-eyed, I manage to concentrate for a stretch, energized in part by caffeine but also by what last night means. Though I didn't love Jamie the way he deserved to be loved, and I upended his world, I came here and kept poking until the truth came out. No one's going to think anymore that he gave up on life. His killer will be sent to prison. And Drew is going to know that all my efforts were worth it.

At just before eleven, Ava calls.

"Oh, Kiki," she exclaims. "Sam just gave Vic the news. We can't believe what happened to you and what it means about Jamie."

"I know. It's good to know the truth, but it's also devastating."

"Sorry not to respond to your text immediately, but I only saw it when I went to call. Is there anything we can do for you?"

"I'm okay, thanks," I say, feeling better just from the sound of her voice.

"You must still be in shock, though. Would you like to stay at our place for a few days?"

"That's so kind of you, Ava, but I'll be fine. The police will be arresting Percy as soon as she's released from the ER, and they kept the key she used to get in."

"Won't you join us for dinner, at least?"

"Thanks for that, too," I say, "but I think it's best for me to stay in and chill tonight."

What I don't say, of course, is that I'm hoping to see Sam this evening. Surely he'll want to be together again.

"How about coffee tomorrow morning, then?"

"Absolutely."

She suggests ten o'clock at a café between her place and mine; before signing off, she urges me to get in touch if I feel at all stressed.

A few minutes later, I'm relieved to see a text from Sam, asking me to give him a call.

I do, but there's no answer. Fifteen minutes later I call again, and he fails to pick up this time too.

Then I make the kind of snap decision that's rare for me. After brushing my hair and swiping on blush and lipstick, I jump in the car and head to Sam's cottage on the outskirts of Salisbury. The breakfast with his parents is surely long over by now, and he's probably doing his best, like me, to process last night.

I've visited the cottage only twice in the past: the first time was last summer, when Jamie wanted to drop off a package for him. The second time, and the most excruciating one, was this past December. Sam had hosted a chili dinner for seven or eight people, including the violinist he was dating. By then my infatuation was ballooning at a terrifying rate, like the plant Audrey II in *Little Shop of Horrors*, and my efforts to stop it met with no success. I did my best not to look at him directly that night.

I remember the location of the cottage easily, and after about twenty minutes, I take a left onto the long private driveway of his parents' property. It's a spectacular piece of real estate, about sixty acres of rolling lawns, meadows, and woods, passed down over several generations, according to Jamie. I soon spot the main house. It's a large but tasteful clapboard structure with a beautiful stone terrace wrapping around the front. One day it will all be Sam's, though Jamie always said his friend felt more at home in his own small place.

Halfway down the gravel drive, I veer onto the short dirt road leading to the stone cottage, nestled in a cluster of fir trees. My pulse races at the sight of it.

Sam must be home. His car is sitting in the area that's been cleared for vehicles and his bike is leaning against the cottage. *Will he be okay with me stopping by unannounced?* I suddenly wonder, then remind myself that he shared my bed last night so he can hardly think it's too brazen.

I park my car and climb out. The air smells piney, and it seems slightly cooler here than in town, probably because of all the trees. When I visited before, I didn't dare let myself think how lovely it was, but it *is*.

As I approach the cottage, I notice classical music coming through one of the windows. Bach, I think. I'm about to knock on the door when I hear the scrape of a chair behind the house and realize he must be out back.

I drop my arm and proceed along the side of the cottage. Rounding the far corner, I finally see him, sitting in a wooden Adirondack chair on the small stone patio.

He's not alone, though. A woman is sitting across from him, resting her bare feet in his lap.

29

For a couple of seconds, I freeze, unsure what to do. Sam is facing away from me, so he doesn't spot me, but the woman definitely does, and even from a distance, I can see her squint in curiosity. I'm pretty sure it's not the violinist, though this woman is also a brunette. Maybe that's Sam's type.

Grabbing a breath, I spin around and retrace my steps, moving quickly but not *fleeing*. I have nothing to feel ashamed about, and there's no way I'm going to race to the car like I'm being pursued by zombies.

I feel dumb, though—for so many reasons. For showing up here without warning, for harboring a tiny belief that something more than sex was blossoming between Sam and me. And maybe even for misjudging Sam. Is the reserved, erudite, somewhat mysterious, often disheveled professor actually the playboy of the Western world?

"Kiki?"

It's Sam's voice calling from behind me. I'm so disconcerted, I hadn't even heard his footsteps. I stop and pivot until I'm facing him. He's changed shirts since I saw him last, and the sandals have been traded for black sneakers.

"Sorry," I say, and then regret the instinctive urge to apologize. "I didn't realize I was barging in on anything."

"Is there some new development?"

"No, but you asked me to give you a call, and when I couldn't reach you by phone, I decided to drop by."

He exhales a sigh. "I just called to see how you were—plus I wanted to find out if you'd given your statement to the cops yet."

"Fine, I guess, and yes. What about you?" I'm pretty sure my tone suggests that at the moment, I don't give a fuck what his answer is.

He narrows his dark brown eyes, perhaps surprised by the edge in my voice. But how could he not be aware of how this unexpected glimpse of another woman would make me feel?

"I'm okay," he says. "And yeah, I gave my statement, too."

"The guy I spoke to said they're in touch with the detective on Jamie's case. I'll text you if I hear anything."

I turn to close the distance to my car.

"Kiki, wait," he says.

Reluctantly, I face him again.

"I had these plans for a while and—"

"Please," I tell him, putting up my hand. "No need to explain."

He tries to say something else, but I don't give him a chance, just jump in my car and take off. As dumb as I feel for popping by, I'm now resigned to the facts. Yes, Sam was attracted to me, but it wasn't more than lust, and just because he'd slept with me didn't mean he was going to refrain from hooking up with someone else the next day. I need to get back to where I was in March—intent on bulldozing him from my thoughts once and for all.

As I return to Ash Street a short time later, I spot a woman pacing on the stoop of the house and realize it's Clarissa. Well, at least I'm not the only one in Litchfield County who likes to show up unannounced. Clearly, she's gotten wind of the nightmare on Ash Street, because otherwise she could have simply returned my call.

"Hey, Clarissa," I say, approaching her. She's in full

jersey again, a matching top and pants. "Did you get my message?"

"I did, Katherine," she says, her face pinched in concern. "I assume you were calling about the incident last night."

"Yes, did someone contact you about it?"

"One of the neighbors. Would it be okay if we spoke inside?"

I tell her of course and, after unlocking the front door, usher her in. The living room is warm and stuffy and smells vaguely like sweat, obviously from all the tense humans moving around in here last night. Clarissa perches on the edge of one of the armchairs, as if she wouldn't even think about getting comfortable. After taking a seat on the couch, I recap last night briefly.

"This woman snuck into the house other times as well," I add. "She was the one who blasted the AC that morning, trying to mess with my head."

"Goodness," Clarissa says, her eyes wide. "And this was someone Mr. Larsson was *dating*?"

"Yes, but he'd gotten wind of the fact that there was something off about her and was trying to put distance between them."

"How did she get in? I mean, will we need to get the locks replaced?"

"It's probably a good idea to replace them because

she actually had a key. She claimed Jamie gave it to her, though I find that hard to believe."

Clarissa scrunches her face, nervously fingering the small quartz pendant hanging from a chain around her neck. "Well, he certainly couldn't have had a copy of the key made—you need a special card for that." She frowns more deeply. "Wait a sec—Mr. Larsson reached out to me a few weeks ago saying he'd lost his house key and needed another. I never like hearing a renter say that, but it seemed like an honest mistake in his case, so I had another made right away."

"That explains it," I say. "She must have stolen the original key from him."

"And where is this woman now?" Clarissa asks.

I explain that Percy has been charged with several offenses and will be taken into police custody today. Clarissa nods slowly, digesting the information. Though some of the tension has drained from her face, she looks wary, like she thinks there might be more to the story than I'm letting on. She's right, but I'm in the dark, too. I still don't fully understand the meaning of all the references Percy made or what had really gone on between her and Jamie.

"I should get back home," she says, rising. "I'll check with the locksmith and arrange a time for him to come."

I tell her it's fine to have the work done after I'm gone, which will be in only two days' time, and then I walk her to the door. She probably can't wait to see the last of me.

Now what? I think, as soon as she's gone. I'd let myself believe that I'd be spending the next hours with Sam, that he was craving another night together just like I was, and that he'd also want to share the experience of finding closure now that the truth had surfaced.

I could call my mom, of course. But as eager as I am to report the latest to her, it's probably best to hold off until tomorrow, when I won't sound as fraught and emotional and she'll be less inclined to worry crazily.

What would really help, I finally admit to myself, is a conversation with Megan. It's been childish of me not to contact her over the past few days, but at the same time I haven't wanted her to plant even the smallest seed of doubt in my mind about what I've been doing. But the time for doubts has come and gone, and I'm dying to talk to her.

"*There* you are," Meg says happily after she picks up.

"You don't have a client now?" I ask. "I thought I might have to leave a message."

"My next one isn't for an hour. It's so good to hear

your voice, Kiki. I felt bad after our last conversation. I was trying to be helpful, but I know it sounded as if I wasn't honoring your opinion."

"And I'm sorry for not calling before this afternoon. It was silly of me. And beyond that, things got even crazier here over the last few days."

"What's happening?"

I take her through everything—my investigation of Liam's properties, the confrontation at Drew's house, the creepy moments inside the house, and the nightmare experience with Percy last night. As I wrap up, I confess that Sam and I went to bed together.

"Wow, I don't even know where to begin," she says. "For starters, are you *okay*?"

I sigh. "I'm still pretty rattled, but at least I finally know what really happened."

"Your instincts were so right. But why would this woman kill Jamie? What could he have possibly done to her?"

"Those are questions I should probably be asking *you*. She claims she had a relationship with him, that they'd been having sex, but he wanted to keep it under wraps for the time being. According to Sam, though, Jamie had only seen her a few times, and they definitely hadn't slept together. How much rage can you generate over the course of a few dates?"

There's a pause, and I sense Megan processing on the other end of the line.

"It sounds like she might be suffering from erotomania," she says finally. "Are you familiar with the term?"

"I've heard it, but I'm not sure what it means. Is it some kind of sexual obsession?"

"That's what you might think from the name, but erotomania is actually a form of paranoid delusion. Men sometimes experience it but the condition mainly affects women. The person suffering from it is convinced that another individual—often someone of higher social status, even a celebrity—is in love with them, despite clear evidence to the contrary."

"But when I saw her out in the world, interacting with a customer at the garden center, she seemed perfectly normal."

"In other regards, these people *are* normal. They might have good jobs and even high self-esteem."

"They're just deluded about this other person?"

"Right, and their delusion has probably been triggered by some previous stress or trauma in their lives. And no matter what the object of their desire does to discourage or rebuff them, they come up with reasons to explain that behavior. It sounds like this Percy woman convinced herself that any rejection on Jamie's part was simply due to him needing to keep the relationship a secret."

I let out a long sigh as the puzzle pieces start creating something whole in my mind.

"But if she was obsessed with Jamie and wanted him so much, why would she kill him?"

"That's not unheard of in extreme cases. One expert describes the stages of the syndrome as 'hope, resentment, and grudge.' The patient starts off convinced it's a real relationship, then starts to feel humiliated by the rejection, and ends up hating the person and possibly turning abusive. Though I've only read about men with the condition becoming murderers, I would imagine women have, too."

My stomach twists. "Why come after me, though? She seemed so furious that I'd showed up at the party, but practically in the same breath she claimed she didn't want Jamie anymore."

"It's possible she was trying to convince herself that she was the one who broke things off with Jamie, but part of her might have still hoped to be with him. And she needed to punish you for becoming an obstacle to that."

"Wow, if this is the case, it explains so much."

I'm tempted to ask her about the ominous things Percy said about Jamie—him not being the man I thought he was and needing to pay for his sins—but I'm not ready to go there yet.

I glance at the time on my phone. "I should let you prepare for your next client. But I'll be back in the city in two days, and I'll call you then."

"Can't wait to see you." She chuckles a little. "And maybe we can talk about Sam then."

"Oh yeah. As long as you promise to explain how I can finally purge him from my thoughts."

As I end the call, I feel some of my tension dissolve. Not only have I smoothed things out with Megan, but I have possible answers to most of the questions that have been ricocheting around my head.

Feeling less morose now, I put together a dinner salad with some of the last items in the fridge, and after deciding that having a meal in the kitchen might remind me too much of Percy, I carry my plate to the living room and eat off the coffee table. Just two more nights to go.

Should I return tomorrow instead? I suddenly ask myself. Though I wouldn't get my money back for forfeiting a night, there are plenty of reasons to bail: I've accomplished all I hoped to do, I'm almost out of food, and there's no chance of spending any more time with Sam.

One major hitch: I have two client sessions booked

for tomorrow afternoon, so I'd have to leave super early to be back in time for them, which would mean skipping my final get-together with Ava, and that's a deal breaker for me.

Besides, there's one more thing I've decided I have to do before I leave Litchfield County. Something that will bring me the last piece of closure I need.

30

As I step onto the patio of the café the next morning, I catch a glimpse of Ava already seated at a wooden table for two. To my surprise, Vic is standing beside her.

"Kiki, over here," he calls out, not realizing I've spotted them. "Don't worry, I promise to let you two catch up," he says as I reach the table. "But I had to go out myself this morning, and that gave me a chance to say hi."

"It's good to see you, Vic," I tell him. As he embraces me, I realize this hug is much less awkward than the last two he gave me, which is a relief.

"First, let me say how glad I am that you and Sam are okay," Vic says, releasing me. "And second, let me apologize for ever doubting your efforts to get to the bottom of this."

"Oh, don't worry about it, Vic. This has been a crushing time for all of us."

He does look less stressed than when I last saw him, as if the revelations about Jamie's death have brought him some peace.

"Well, that's really all I had to say," he says. "Now, why don't I let you two lovely ladies enjoy your time together."

Ava turns her cheek for him to kiss, wishes him a warm goodbye, and then directs her attention on me.

"I'm sure you still feel pretty shaken," she says.

"I do, but last night I had a conversation with my friend Meg that provided a lot of insight."

The waitress arrives to take our order and after she departs, I recap what Megan told me about erotomania and the delusions that might have been going on in Percy's mind.

Ava shakes her head. "I didn't like her from the moment I set eyes on her that night. There was just something so unpleasant, even hostile, about the woman."

"I know. Not that I'd ever blame Jamie for what happened, but I'm still having a hard time understanding how he was drawn to her to begin with, even if she did misrepresent herself."

"A lot of us make stupid choices on the rebound,"

she says, lifting a shoulder. "I know I certainly did over the years. I remember Vic saying that after Jamie broke up with that girlfriend who moved to Hong Kong—and before he met you—he went through a period of dating women who just seemed too young or too silly or all wrong in some other way."

The comment perplexes me.

"Really? I know he was only dating casually then, but I never heard him categorize it that way."

Our cappuccinos and croissants arrive, and after taking a sip of my coffee, I smile sheepishly at Ava. "Speaking of rebound dating, I probably should address the elephant in the room. You must be wondering what Sam was doing at my house in the middle of the night."

She smiles back. "I'd be lying to say I wasn't, and I'm all ears if you want to talk. But I would also understand if you wanted to keep it private."

I tell her that for a brief period I thought something was blossoming between us, but there's no there there after all.

"I have to admit, it hurts," I add. "But I'm headed back to New York tomorrow and I intend to put it behind me."

"Tomorrow? Oh, Kiki, I'll miss you."

"Same here, Ava. As horrible as this has been, I've loved getting to see so much of you."

"What are your plans for your last night?"

"Packing."

"No, no, Kiki, you shouldn't be alone tonight. Why don't you come with Vic and me to the Foxton County Fair. We're not big on carnival rides—I get dizzy even looking at them—but it's so much fun just to wander around the fairgrounds."

I'm two seconds away from declining her invitation. I'm not up for a big night, especially given the fair's associations with the young woman who died there four years ago. But on the other hand, it would be good for me to be out in public, people-watching and eating funnel cake for dinner instead of wandering the house in a funk, picturing those pretty bare feet in Sam's lap.

"I'd love that, actually," I say. "I tried to get Jamie to go last year but he wanted no part of it."

"Good, I'll text you the details later."

After we finish our drinks and croissants, we accompany each other to the parking lot and hug goodbye. I'm glad we'll be seeing each other again tonight.

I'm just about to start the car when my phone rings, and I'm shocked to see Tori's name on the screen. Though I guess the call shouldn't be a surprise—she's clearly heard the news about Percy.

"Kiki," she says after I answer. "We were so upset to learn what happened at your house. Are you okay?"

"Yes, doing better today, thanks."

"I'm so glad. I also want to apologize for the meeting at Drew's. Everyone came on very strong with you. And in hindsight, I see you were just looking for the truth."

I'm gratified to hear this from her. "As I said the other day, I'm sorry, too—for jumping to conclusions about Liam. But I've been sure for a while that Jamie was murdered, and I've been trying to figure out who was responsible."

"Had you suspected Percy before the other night?"

"At times, yes," I tell her. "But mainly I'd come to see that something must have happened at the party to make one of the guests feel angry with Jamie or threatened by him. I just didn't know who or what it was until Percy showed how upset she was about being rebuffed." I sigh. "I'm relieved that I can finally go home now."

"You're leaving today?"

"No, I'm planning to go to the Foxton Fair tonight. Then I'll head out first thing tomorrow morning."

"I wish you the best of luck. And so do Liam and Drew."

I wish her the best as well and, after signing off, check my watch. My client Zooms are at two and three, and though I want time to prepare, there's that one loose end I need to tie up before I pack. I've decided to drop by the animal shelter and check on Maverick.

The drive takes me close to a half hour. The shelter, I realize, is nearer to Jamie's old rental than to the house on Ash Street. According to Gillian Parr, he'd done volunteer work at the shelter, and that must have been why he decided to adopt a dog from there, even though there might have been a closer place.

The long brick and wood building is industrial-looking, but flowers have been planted all around the facade, giving it a more inviting feel. Even with my windows rolled up, I can hear the howls of dogs. The noise dies down moments after I open the car door, but as I approach the building, a single bark is soon followed by an entire chorus, like the barking chain from *101 Dalmatians*, one dog setting off another. The workers here must need earplugs.

The small, plain lobby is nearly empty when I enter, just a young male clerk behind the counter and a female pet owner across from him, holding a soft-sided carrying case. Through the black mesh at the end, I can make out the face of a skittish-looking tabby cat.

"And should I brush her teeth?" the woman asks, grimacing.

"Not right away," the clerk says. "Give her a few

days to settle in at her new home. After that, try letting her lick a little cat toothpaste off your finger for a few weeks before you attempt any brushing. That will get her familiar with the concept."

"Right, right," the woman says without confidence. As soon as she departs, I step toward the counter and ask if Gillian is in.

"She is," he tells me. "Who should I say is asking?"

I give my name and the clerk places a call to Gillian, then says she'll be with me shortly. *Please*, I think, *let her have good news about Maverick*. A couple of minutes later, Gillian enters the lobby from a door on the right. She has a small straw purse over her shoulder, as if she's on her way out.

"Kiki, hi," she says, smiling. "Nice to see you again."

"Good to see you as well. I'm here to check on Maverick. I didn't apply to adopt him myself—unfortunately I'm not able to take on a pet at this stage of my life—but I wanted to be sure he's okay."

"That's so thoughtful of you—and I've got excellent news. Someone's already applied to take him. The adoption should be approved any minute."

"What a relief," I exclaim, almost giddy. "I was worried about the little guy." I smile at her. "Well, that's all, I guess. Thanks for letting me know."

"Why don't I walk out with you, I was just leaving for an appointment."

She steps ahead of me to push the door open, then motions for me to precede her.

"How are you doing?" she says softly as we head toward the parking lot. "Not long after we talked, I saw Jamie's obituary, and I also read a news item saying his death was a possible suicide. I can only imagine how difficult this must be for you."

"I'm doing a little better, thanks—in part because there's been a new development. A woman broke into the house on Ash Street the night before last and confronted me with a knife. I'm fine, but it emerged that she murdered Jamie. That his death *wasn't* suicide."

Gillian stops in her tracks. "My god, how chilling."

"I know, it's horrific in a whole other way."

She shakes her head. "You just don't think of things like that happening in this area—it's so peaceful in these parts—but I guess no place is immune. A young woman who volunteered with us was murdered four years ago this month."

My breath catches. "You don't mean Jess Nolan, do you?"

Gillian nods.

"I was told she volunteered at an animal shelter," I say, "but I didn't know it was this one."

"Yes, we were all devastated. And so, in fact, was Jamie."

My jaw nearly hits the ground. "What do you mean?"

"I think I mentioned that Jamie helped us put together a new financial plan. Jess was volunteering here at the time, and they got to know each other. He was kind of a mentor to her—I think she had a little crush on him, actually."

I feel a weird ripple of unease. "Oh," I manage. "And yes, what a sad story. Well, I'd better dash. And thanks again for finding a home for Maverick."

From there I almost sprint to my car, feeling my discomfort swell. Jamie told Sam that he'd had no idea who Jess Nolan was. Why would he deceive his best friend?

I assure myself there has to be some kind of explanation, that Sam might even be remembering incorrectly.

My phone rings as I'm unlocking the front door of the house, and when I check the screen, I'm surprised to see Sam's name. I gave him an easy way out yesterday afternoon, and I assumed he'd take it. Another surprise: I find myself letting it ring. He's probably calling out of politeness to make sure I'm doing okay, but why torture myself with the sound of his voice? I'm sure I'll have to talk to him again over the next weeks as more information about Percy surfaces, but I don't feel up to it right now.

A half minute later, a ping indicates he's left a voice message. My curiosity gets the better of me and I tap the forward arrow to listen.

"Hey, Kiki," he says, sounding rushed. "Call me as soon as you can. It's urgent."

With my heart skipping, I immediately return the call. Has Percy been released, and he's calling to warn me she's at large? Or did the police decide that some crazy love triangle had in fact gone down on Ash Street, and this is going to blow back on Sam and me?

"Where are you?" he asks, not bothering with a "Hello."

"At the house. What's going on?"

"I've got some news from Drew—but you're not going to like it. According to the cops, there's no way Percy could have killed Jamie."

"*W-What?*" I say, the word nearly stuck in my throat. "Why do they think that?"

"She has a rock-solid alibi."

"But how could they know that already?"

"They apparently looked into her right after the party—since they'd been told she'd left in a huff. I guess they were doing more than we gave them credit for."

Percy is clearly dishonest and unwell, so I'm not buying anything yet. "Where was she, supposedly?"

"She went directly from the party to the Boat House in Salisbury, where she sat at the bar for close to two hours, having a burger and a couple of beers, and talking to the bartender. They've got her credit card receipt and CCTV footage of her coming and going."

I drop into one of the kitchen chairs, stunned and distressed, and force my mind back to the early morning attack by Percy.

"But Percy said Jamie got what he deserved," I protest. "That he paid for his sins."

There's a short pause before Sam speaks.

"But she never came right out and claimed she murdered him, did she?" he says, his tone even. "Even though we heard it as a confession, it may be that she simply resented Jamie for whatever grief she thinks he caused her and didn't sweat the fact that he died."

God, he's probably right.

"Where do you think Drew's head is at now?" I ask. "Even if Percy isn't responsible, can he be made to understand that Jamie didn't take his own life?"

Another pause.

"I hate to say it, but I'm not hopeful at this point," Sam admits. "And there's apparently more bad news on the horizon. Vic heard that the police are finally going to release their findings in the next day or two, and the ruling will be suicide."

I let out a groan, feeling all the relief from the past hours seep from my body. I'm back to square one again, wondering who the hell the killer is. And I don't have a single idea.

"And what do *you* think, Sam?"

He groans as well. "I keep coming back to the dog, like you do, Kiki. That the Jamie I knew wouldn't have abandoned a rescue animal. But at the same time, I just can't be sure."

"I better go," I say, eager to have this call over and done with. "Thanks for alerting me."

"Of course. I'll let you know if I hear anything else."

"Wait, one more thing," I say, suddenly remembering my conversation with Gillian. You said the other day that Jamie didn't know Jess Nolan, but I don't think that's true."

"What do you mean?"

"I went by the shelter to check if they'd found a home for Maverick, and one of the people in charge mentioned that Jess and Jamie volunteered there at the same time and they were friendly."

"Maybe I misunderstood him—because he had no reason not to tell me he knew her."

"Okay," I say, mollified.

The call over, I make a cup of tea and pace the house with the mug in my hand, letting Sam's news about Percy and the imminent ruling sink in—along with those unsettling words of his: *I just can't be sure.*

Is it possible that I've been going down the wrong path ever since Maverick appeared in the driveway? Maybe no one wandered those amber-hued rooms intending to take Jamie's life, or decided to do it on the spur of the moment. Maybe Jamie took his life because of me—or for some other reason I'll never know.

I shake my head. No, I don't believe that. Something had to have happened with Jamie at the party, just like Dan said, something that triggered fury at him or a fear of what he might do. It could have even appeared small and inconsequential to everyone there, except the killer. I have less than a day left here, but I have to figure out the answer—no matter how hard it tries to squirm from my grasp.

Four Years Ago

It wasn't until the next day, around lunchtime, that he realized he'd fucked up.

After he got back from dumping the stuff in Massachusetts, he stayed close to the house, doing yard work all morning and reassuring himself he had nothing to worry about. Though he wasn't exactly relaxed—how could he be?—he wasn't freaked out, either. The local news outlets he'd checked online were treating it like the fucking crime of the century, but from what he could tell, the cops didn't have any idea who'd done it or even where to look.

They weren't going to find any clues, either. The girl and him had made their plans in person, not by text. He'd barely been on the fairgrounds, and there were no CCTV cameras hooked up there—he'd noticed that as soon as he'd arrived. If anyone *had* spotted him, the brim of his baseball cap had been low enough on his face so that his features hadn't been visible.

And in the end, he hadn't even had sex with her. He'd thought about it, but by the time he got her pants down, blood was everywhere, and he couldn't stand the thought of it.

When he went back into the house to fix a sandwich, he realized he was reeking of sweat, so he stripped down and turned on the shower. He let the water get super hot, figuring a second scalding shower within twenty-four hours wasn't a bad idea.

He felt the sting from the spray the second he stepped into the tub. The problem, he could tell, was on the far side of his right arm, high up. He stepped back from the spray and used his left hand to twist the bicep around. There was some kind of scratch there, maybe five or six inches long.

At first he assumed that he'd scraped himself doing yard work, but then, with his gut starting to churn, he realized it was from last night. Everything had happened so fast that he must not have noticed it at the time.

Cursing, he stepped back under the spray and quickly lathered himself with the bar of soap, going over the injury a few times, even though it hurt like a bitch. He climbed out and dried off as fast as he could, being careful to avoid his arm. The last thing he needed was someone noticing blood on a towel, even if the blood was his.

Dropping the towel to the floor, he stepped over to the sink and examined the back of his arm in the mirror. The scratch was ugly and bright red, and easily seven inches long. She'd clearly gotten him with those fucking nails of hers.

He'd watched enough *CSI* to know what it meant. It meant his skin was under her fingernails.

For now, at least, he was okay. He'd never been arrested, which meant his DNA wasn't in the fucking system. But if they ended up connecting him to her and took a swab, or they went through his trash, looking for soda cans or pizza crusts, they'd put it together. And he'd be toast.

31

I don't finish the tea, feeling too wired to drink it, let alone sit quietly with my thoughts. After replying to a batch of emails that have gone unanswered for several days, I do my best to power through my back-to-back client Zooms. They're not quite a bust, but it's hard to imagine either client concluding that I've inspired them to bold new heights in their jobs.

At least I have the fair to look forward to. Ava had texted earlier to meet her at the ticket booths at six, when the fair opens for the night. But just after I finish packing and changing into jeans and a T-shirt, another text from her arrives, saying apologetically that she has to cancel. Vic's come down with a terrible stomach bug, and not only does he need to stay home, but she doesn't want to leave him on his own.

After texting back that I understand and wish him a speedy recovery, I wonder if it's all for the best, that maybe what I really need is a quiet night at home. I spend the next hour doing some busywork for my job and then open my iPad to read. But within minutes I'm nearly jumping out of my skin, hating the idea of being cooped up in this house tonight, with nothing for company other than all the new questions I have about Jamie's death. Plus, there's hardly any food left. In a split second, I decide to head to the fair on my own.

I stuff the contents of my purse into a cross-body bag, grab a cotton sweater, and lock up the house. By the time I pull into the fair's parking lot, there must be close to a hundred cars on-site already. I find a place far down the lot, park, and follow several families making their way to the ticket booth.

Once I reach the gate area, I can tell by the number of people ahead of me that I've got a good ten-minute wait to buy a ticket, but I don't mind. It's nice to see people so excited and little kids jumping up and down in place, desperate to finally be inside. I always loved these kinds of fairs when I was young and went each summer with my parents. As I'd told Ava, Jamie had shrugged off my suggestion to go to this one last August, which had surprised me. After all, he was the kind of guy who loved anything that guaranteed an old-fashioned kind of fun, even clichéd touristy activities—like heading to the top of the Empire State Building or taking the Circle Line cruise around Manhattan.

"Wait, you really don't want to go?" I remember asking.

"Nope," he'd replied. "Do you mind?"

"Of course not, but it's not like you. You don't even want to win me a giant giraffe?"

"I do," he'd said, finally smiling. "But okay—true confession time. When I was about ten, I went with my parents and a bunch of family friends and *their* kids, and I ate a ton of crap—one of those giant turkey legs and then donuts and a big grape Slurpee—and then I got on the Tilt-A-Whirl and threw up right on the ride. I don't think they could use my compartment or car or whatever you call it for the rest of the night. And then after hours they probably had to have someone clean it wearing a hazmat suit."

I'd laughed out loud as he told me the story and let him off the hook. And then the next day he gave me a stuffed giraffe he'd bought at FAO Schwarz.

Finally, I advance to the ticket booth and pay my fee, then pass through the gate. All of a sudden, I'm a girl again, walking along a carnival midway with my hand in my dad's. I feel like I've been beamed back, *Outlander* style, partly because of all the flashing colored lights and the clanging, whirring, chugging sounds of the rides, but mainly because of the smells—the sharp aromas of corn dogs and fried pickles and the cloying scent of caramel apples and endless mounds of cotton candy.

I've had almost nothing to eat since the croissant with Ava this morning, so the first place I head is the food stands. I'd promised myself a funnel cake but for now I opt for a bag of chicken tenders and a Coke. There aren't many places to sit—the idea here seems to be to eat while you walk—but after roaming a bit, I find an empty plastic table for four not far from the carousel and plop down with my meal.

I devour my food absentmindedly, taking in the scene around me. Most of the attendees I can see from my perch are parents with young kids, headed left toward the rides, though there are also a few couples as well as some antsy-looking young teens and the occasional pack of guys in their twenties and thirties. A few of them seem restless, even sullen, like they're looking for more than a county fair is supposed to deliver.

And then, as if a switch has been flipped, I'm thinking of Jess Nolan and remembering the photo I saw of her—her sweet, pretty face and long, light brown hair. Her tragic story has been inserting itself into my life for days, and I guess it's impossible to be in this place without having her conjured up. The fair is obviously dismantled after its run each season, but it must have looked pretty much the same four years ago.

I consider the theory the locker room attendant shared with me in a near whisper, that Jess had been murdered by a club employee or member rather than a stranger. If that's the case, why hadn't they been spotted together at the fair? Had her so-called date been nervous about being seen with her for some reason, insisting they stay only a short time? Maybe the guy was married? If that was the case, why invite her here at all? Perhaps he thought it would sound fun and harmless to her, and then immediately after they met at the fairgrounds, he'd suggested they slip away.

As I've already considered, it's possible that her date was someone I crossed paths with at the club before, even someone I knew casually. Based on what Gillian Parr said, Jamie was Jess's pal and mentor, maybe even her crush. Could she have confided in him about who she was seeing? Had Jamie had an idea who the murderer might be?

And then a horrible thought slithers into my mind like a snake. What if her date that night had been *Jamie?*

As my heart races, snippets from memory bombard me: Jamie knowing Jess but not admitting it to Sam and never mentioning it to me. Percy saying Jamie craved forgiveness. Jamie being uncharacteristically dead set against attending the fair.

Had *Jamie* killed Jess? Then had Percy somehow stumbled upon the truth? Is that what he needed to be forgiven for?

Stop, I command myself. It's utterly insane of me to be thinking this. Because there's no way that Jamie could have tried to rape a woman and then bashed her head in. I hate myself for having given that horrible idea even thirty seconds of mental airtime.

After wadding up the chicken tender bag, I toss it into a nearby trash can and quickly push off from the picnic table. I need to move around and flush my mind of these thoughts. I make my way along a row of game stands, where people are tossing rings, shooting darts, throwing bean bags at fake milk bottles, or bunched around watching others do one of those things. I pass the bumper-car rink, more game and food concession stands, and finally reach a cluster of microbrewery booths.

After a brief wait in line at one of them, I order a small blond beer. I don't even like beer all that much, but I need something to hold, something to do besides think.

With the cup in my hand, I wander until I find

370 · KATE WHITE

another empty plastic table and settle in one of the chairs around it. I take a few sips, concentrating at first on the bitter taste of the beer and the foam on my lips. Eventually I let the scene around me come back into focus. The fair is overflowing with people now, probably in part because of the pleasant weather and the fact that this is one of the last nights it's open.

I sweep my eyes over the immediate area. I'm at the far end of the fairgrounds now, close to the fence. The dusk has dissolved into twilight, but there's enough light cast from the rides and concession stands to see into the distance. Beyond the fence is an overgrown field, and beyond that a thick, wooded area.

As goose bumps race up my arms, I realize I'm staring at the same woods where Jess Nolan was killed, woods far more extensive than I'd pictured in my mind. Thinking of Jess again triggers another pang of guilt. I can't believe that minutes ago I let myself ponder, even briefly, that Jamie might have been her attacker. No matter what thoughts tortured him at times—thoughts that he never betrayed to either me or Sam—I know he was a good, moral person.

And beyond that, even if he *had* done it, under the influence of drugs or because he'd temporarily lost his mind or for some other staggeringly unfathomable reason, he certainly wouldn't have returned to the area weekend after weekend, visiting the tennis and swim club and renting a home in a nearby town. Only a psychopath would have the stomach for behavior like that.

Plus, it would have been dangerous to come back here. He would have worried that someone might catch a glimpse of him and remember seeing him at the fair. It's still an open investigation, after all. The police could very well have a DNA sample from the crime scene, and he would have felt exposed, wondering if the cops might one day tie it to him.

Out of nowhere, it seems, a thought begins to paw at my mind, and though I try to grab hold of it, it wiggles away.

I tell myself once again to *stop*, that Jess's death is a terrible thing that had nothing to do with Jamie. I push off from the table, toss the half-full cup of beer in a trash bin, and wander toward the fence. It's an endless series of slatted metal sections, linked together by chains. I follow along the side of it for a while, with the beer booths behind me and pens of livestock off to my right, smelling of hay and manure. The crowd is thinner in this area, though there are two security guards not all that far from me, chatting and probably keeping an eye out for anyone trying to sneak into the grounds.

Up ahead, I notice that the chain has been unfastened between two of the fence sections, perhaps to allow in the farm trucks that deliver the animals. I step close to that break in the fence and stare out at the woods, the woods where Jess Nolan died. I have to get a better look, I realize, so I can stop seeing her in my mind, wondering about her and what happened that night. I drag one of the metal sections over a few inches, and after squeezing between that and the next one, I start across the field.

"Hey," someone yells from behind me. Turning, I see it's one of the security guards.

"I have an emergency," I call back. "I need to leave now."

He certainly can't prevent me from exiting, right? And though it won't be possible for me to get back into the fair from here, I don't need to. I want to go home soon, and I can find my way back to my car just by walking along the perimeter of the grounds.

I keep moving toward the woods, picking up my speed a little. The field grass pricks at the skin on my ankles, and all at once a swarm of mosquitoes is buzzing around my face, too many to swat away. As I close in on the wooded area, the noise of the fair recedes, even though I'm not that far away. I finally reach the very edge of the trees and peer into the pitch-black spaces between the massive trunks.

Jess, who did you come here with? I ask myself.

The woods are dark and foreboding, like woods in a fairy tale like *Snow White*, and it's hard to believe she would have snuck back here with a stranger, someone she'd met only moments before. No, she must've been with someone she knew. Now that I've seen this place, I couldn't be more certain.

I'm about to turn around and trek to the parking lot when I notice a white gleam coming from farther inside the woods. Could it be the memorial, the one that Jess's friend at the club mentioned? It seems almost ghoulish to have erected it here in the woods, though I've seen many memorials for people on highways, in the exact spot where they were killed in an accident.

I venture slowly toward it, doing my best not to stumble. I can feel rocks underfoot, as well as tree roots and fallen branches. For a few seconds I lose sight of the white glow, and then suddenly there it is again. I point myself in that direction and keep moving, grateful I wore sneakers tonight.

As I finally approach the source of the light, I see that it's not a memorial at all, but a heap of stones, probably remnants of a very old farm fence. It's shining because beams from the half moon have found their way to it through the tree branches.

I shudder. It's time to get the hell out of here. As I start to pivot, I hear the crack of twigs behind me, as if something heavy has broken them. I spin around with my heart hammering. My eyes have adjusted a little to the dark, but I don't see a thing. Maybe it was a fox or a possum, creeping through the brush behind me.

And though I've probably frightened it off by my presence, I don't want to go back that way now. Narrowing my eyes, I peer through the trees on my right. From this angle I can see the low lights of the parking lot, and they don't even look that far, I assure myself.

I hear another sound behind me, and my heart slams into my rib cage. Because this sound is even louder, surely made by a person, not an animal. And if I had any doubt, I can even hear him panting now.

I start to run, crashing through brush and the trees. *Faster*, I plead with myself. *Faster, faster.* When my foot snags on a root, I start to pitch forward but catch myself in the nick of time.

And suddenly there's a rush of wind, and the person grabs hold of me. He throws me hard to the ground, landing on top of me, his body a dead weight. I try to scream, but there's not enough air in my lungs.

I'm going to die, I realize, right here in these dark, awful woods. I'm going to die right where Jess Nolan did.

The weight on me suddenly eases a little, and I wonder if I have an opportunity. I kick, then try to squirm out from underneath, but he grabs the back of my shirt and hauls himself farther up on me, driving one side of my face into the ground. Out of the corner of my free eye, I see a large hand near my head, a hand with a rock in it.

"*Please*," I try to beg, but my voice is no more than a desperate whisper.

And then comes the sound of more twigs snapping and another rush of air. Someone else is here, right behind us. I hear a loud crack—a crack of bone, I think—and the body on top of me goes limp, squishing me even more into the ground. Next, someone is yanking him off me. When I'm half free, I scrabble out from under him and flip onto my back.

It takes a minute to see, but then I make out the person above me. It's a woman. *Tori.* She's holding a rock, too, but her stance isn't threatening. It was she who hit the person and dragged him off me.

"Hurry," she shouts at me.

I struggle to my feet.

"What's happening?" I gasp, trying to catch my breath. Glancing back, I see that it's Liam sprawled on the ground, writhing in pain. Liam was planning to kill me? "Why did he do that, Tori? Is it because of the houses, what I found out?"

She's close enough that even with so little light, I can see the blankness on her face.

"No," she says. "Now *go.*"

"I know he killed Jamie," I say. That has to be the reason he came after me. I lurch farther away from Liam but steal another look. His body has gone limp again, but the rock is still loosely in his hand—a rock that must be like the one used to kill Jess Nolan. I glance back at Tori. "And he killed Jess, too, didn't he?"

Because why else is he here in the very same woods? Tori says nothing, but I read acknowledgment in her haunted eyes.

"Run," Tori shouts, shaking her head. "Just fucking run."

This time I do. I scramble through the woods, and then tear through the field, checking behind me again and again to make sure Liam isn't in pursuit. There's no sign of either him or Tori.

As soon as I reach the parking lot, where I'm surrounded by people heading to their cars, I rifle through my purse for my phone and call 911.

"Someone attacked me at the Foxton Fair," I say. "He tried to kill me. He killed a man named Jamie Larsson. And he killed a girl named Jess Nolan four years ago."

32

A state police vehicle shows up in a matter of minutes, followed by two others. I bolt out of my car, which I've locked myself into, and blurt out my story to two male troopers. As they usher me into the back seat of one of the vehicles, radios crackle, police call out to one another, and then several of them take off for the woods. People coming from the fair start to form a crowd, their curiosity in overdrive.

"No, please, I don't need a doctor," I insist when one of the troopers suggests escorting me to an ER. I assume my face is badly scraped, but it doesn't feel like there's any serious damage. One of the troopers takes pictures of my face with his phone, just for the record, and another pops his head into the back seat to say that a detective will be arriving shortly to take my full statement.

As I wait in the stuffy back seat, my mind churns so hard it hurts. Liam killed Jess Nolan. Though he didn't spend a lot of time at the club, he was a member, and he must have crossed paths with her there at some point. He's obviously a sexual predator, maybe even a psychopath, and there might be even more victims. From what I remember, he sometimes deals with clients over the border in Massachusetts and New York.

And Liam killed Jamie, too. I could tell by the look in Tori's eyes. But *why*? It seems Jamie somehow determined the truth, and Liam must have figured out that he knew. Had Jamie perhaps remembered a detail Jess had told him? But why would he kill Jamie the night of the party, when there were so many other less risky opportunities to do it? Had Jamie said something that night that had tipped him off?

And then, as if out of nowhere, an answer slams into my brain, almost fully formed: the DNA test.

According to Sam, Jamie had announced at the party that he'd just ordered one, and it seems likely he would have sent off a swab in the coming days or weeks. Tori had been in the study when he was telling Vic's friend, and she clearly overheard him and mentioned it to Liam—perhaps even innocently. He would have guessed the police had his DNA from the crime scene, but given his lack of a criminal record or obvious connection to

Jess, they had no one to link it to. He must have read, though, just like I have, that the police often use genetic genealogy databases to look for DNA matches.

Even though he never would have submitted his own DNA to one of those sites, he would have realized he'd be in danger if a relative did. Because there would be enough similarities to identify the suspect as part of that family pool.

Where is Liam now? I wonder desperately. Did he somehow manage to escape? And what about Tori?

After what seems like ages, a detective arrives, and I share everything that's happened and also what's just occurred to me about the DNA. He asks plenty of questions, and I'm grateful that he seems to take me seriously. Eventually he has a medic from the fairgrounds check out my face, then tells me that I'm free to go, though I will need to come by tomorrow to sign an official statement.

"Will I be safe tonight?" I ask. The cops assure me that both Liam and Tori have been taken into custody.

By the time I stagger to my car, after declining a ride from the police, it's close to ten, the fair gates have closed, and the only remaining vehicles belong to law enforcement. My hands tremble as I maneuver out of the parking lot, and I keep my speed to a max of thirty most of the way back.

As soon as I'm in the house, I fish my phone from my purse, desperate to talk to someone. I know I should call Megan or Ava or my mother, but I tap Sam's number instead. Yes, I need to get him out of my mind, but he deserves to know the truth before anyone else.

Surprisingly he answers on the first ring, and with halting words, I share the outlines of the story.

"Oh god, Kiki," he says. I hear clanging behind him and also strands of conversation, as if he might be in a restaurant. I expect him to tell me that he can't talk long, but instead he says, "Give me twenty minutes and I'll be there."

After we disconnect, I pour a glass of water and wander over to the small mirror hanging on the kitchen wall. The entire left side of my face is puffy, and criss-crossed with abrasions from having my head ground into dirt and roots. I take a long sip of water and then tap my cheek gently with my fingertips. It's really painful to the touch.

Without warning, I start to cry quietly. Before long I'm racked with sobs, and tears stream down my cheeks, making the abrasions sting. It's not simply about me and what happened tonight. I'm thinking about Jamie and the horrible reason for his death. And Jess Nolan, too.

By the time I hear Sam's car pull into the driveway,

the sobs have subsided. I grab a couple of tissues from a box on the counter and dab at my eyes before opening the front door to him.

"Hey," Sam says, pulling me into a hug as soon as he enters. I wish it wasn't so ridiculously comforting to feel those arms around me.

We separate and he leads me to the couch. He's in a long-sleeved collared shirt and dress pants, like he's been out to dinner. As we sit down and he gets a better look at my face, he reels back in surprise.

"Whoa," he says. "Shouldn't they have sent you to an ER?"

I shake my head. "It looks much worse than it is."

"Can I do anything, Kiki?"

"Just bear with me if I start on another crying jag."

"Of course." To my surprise, he takes one of my hands in his and strokes it gently. "Tonight must have been so terrifying."

"It's not just that. It's knowing that Jamie died for no other reason than mentioning his summer plans at a fucking dinner party."

"When did you piece everything together?"

"Only when I was sitting in the back of the police car after I was attacked. But ever since you and I talked about how uneventful the party seemed, without any drama that could explain Jamie's murder, I'd been wondering if the truth was apparent in of one those ordinary moments, hiding in plain sight."

"So, Jamie's murder really *was* a spur-of-the-moment thing," Sam says. "Liam was probably worried from the start that his DNA had gotten on Jess, but he might have relaxed a little as time went on. And then, boom, he finds out that Jamie ordered the genealogy kit."

"And he knew he had to act before Jamie had a chance to send in a sample."

"Could Liam really have been implicated from Jamie's own DNA sample?"

"Yes, from what I've read, many police departments rely on genealogy sites to get matches or near matches. It would have taken time, but once Jamie's DNA was in the system, there would have been some kind of an alert. His DNA wouldn't have been a direct match, of course, but the police would be able to identify him as a relative of the killer, and they'd soon find their way to Liam. Their next step would be to try to get *his* DNA—from something like a cardboard cup he tossed in a garbage can."

Sam shakes his head in disgust. "I remember Liam driving off from the field just as I was getting into my car. He clearly went home, got an illegal gun he kept, stashed his car someplace, and approached Jamie in the field, saying he wanted to discuss something with him privately. And then they both got into Jamie's car."

As an image of that moment flashes before my eyes, I taste bile rising in my throat.

"But how did he fake the gun residue on Jamie's hand?" I ask.

"I don't know, but the cops will surely take another look at it. Here's something else I want to know: Was Tori aware all this time that her husband killed Jess Nolan?"

"Unless she's totally screwed up herself, and I don't think she is, it's hard to believe she knew the full picture. Maybe he told her at some point that he had a reason to avoid a DNA test without ever explaining why."

"Whatever it was, she was willing to let Jamie die because of it."

I shrug, not convinced that's the case. "It could be that after she overheard Jamie, she simply wanted to *alert* Liam, without imagining what extremes he would go to. I remember how she held her hands over her ears when the car horn wouldn't stop. Like she couldn't stand it."

I pause for a couple of beats, still trying to understand how everything played out.

"Once Liam acted, though, she must have thought she had no choice but to protect him," I add. "She's been checking in with me ever since I arrived, asking what I've been up to. She also tried to make me think

Jamie was devastated by my presence at the party, implying that's why he killed himself. And I'm sure that was conveyed to the police by her as well."

"But in the end," Sam says, "it seems she was only willing to go so far for Liam. She wouldn't let him kill you."

"Right," I say, nodding. "At least I can be grateful for *that*."

"How did he know where you'd be?"

"Tori called me earlier today—supposedly to apologize—and I told her I was going to the fair. They must have followed me there and seen I was on my own. I don't think this was the first time Liam tracked my whereabouts. It was probably him who followed me in my car that night, trying to intimidate me and get me to leave town. Tonight, though, he had more in mind than intimidation."

"But wait—if you didn't figure it all out until you were in the police car tonight, why did he see you as such a threat?"

I lean back in the chair biting my lip. "I've been wondering that. When Tori called, I still thought Percy was the killer and I mentioned that I'd become convinced that something had happened at the party that led to Jamie's death. Once it was clear Percy had an alibi, Liam must have realized I'd be back looking for suspects, asking questions about the party, and circling closer to the truth. The irony is that you'd mentioned the 23andMe test the other day, but I didn't put two and two together then."

"But Liam was obviously convinced, based on how determined you've been, that you'd get there at some point."

"I can't be sure, but I do know I wouldn't have quit."

Still holding my hand, Sam flops back on the couch and lets out a ragged sigh. "It's staggering—all of it."

"I know. And it's going to shatter Drew," I say, and without warning, my eyes well again with tears.

"Do you have any wine left?" Sam asks. "I could pour you a glass."

"What I could really use is some chamomile tea. Do you want some too?"

"Isn't that the stuff that tastes like boiled weeds? Sure, why not."

He follows me into the kitchen, and after filling the kettle, I join him at the table. It's odd to have him here—considering what happened yesterday, I didn't expect to ever be sitting across from him again. While we wait for the water to boil, I tell him more details about the night as they occur to me, piecing it all together as I do.

The kettle clicks and though I start to jump up, Sam

insists on making the tea himself. He returns to the table with a mug for each of us.

"Does it surprise you?" he asks quietly.

"What part?"

"That Liam was capable of this?"

"Yes, it's shocking—not only that he murdered his own cousin, but what he did to Jess. It's like something a psychopath would do."

"Did you ever see any hints of that with him?"

"Never, but from everything I've ever read, homicidal psychopaths can appear normal. I mean, didn't Ted Bundy have a girlfriend while he was murdering women? And some have wives and kids."

"It's just—"

I pull back in my chair. "Wait, what are you saying, Sam? You don't think Liam killed the two of them?"

"I can accept that he killed Jamie—that's obviously why he came after you, because he was worried you'd figure it out. But there are some parts that just don't add up. Jess was this sweet young girl and it's hard to imagine her having any interest in a guy like Liam. Besides that, I almost never saw him at the club, even before Jess died, so how would they even have met? And the whole idea of Tori covering for him doesn't sit right with me. She'd have to be some kind of monster to do that."

Though my first instinct is to protest, I take a deep breath and digest what he's saying.

"It *does* seem improbable," I admit. "But if he killed Jamie, it had to be because of the DNA test and the fact that it would link him to the other murder. What other explanation could there be?"

Sam nods his head lightly, clearly deliberating.

"Not to bore you with economics, but in my line of work, if the data you gather rejects your hypothesis, you need to assume that either the hypothesis is wrong or the data is wrong."

I scrunch my face, letting his words sink in. "Are you saying my hypothesis—that Liam's the killer—isn't entirely supported by the available data? So I need a new hypoth—"

And then at that moment, the hypothesis shifts in my brain, making me gasp. "What if Liam didn't kill Jess, but *Taylor* did? He taught sailing at the club, so he would definitely have crossed paths with her. And—and that could be why he moved away four years ago."

"Yeah," Sam says, nodding slowly. "That makes a lot more sense. He must have confessed in a panic to his parents at some point, or they figured it out. Though the kid had a reputation as a fuckup, Jamie always said Liam and Tori were fiercely devoted to him. If this is what happened, they obviously decided to keep quiet and just ship him off to Florida, praying he'd never do it again."

"And that explains why Tori would cover it up—she was protecting her son, not her husband."

At that moment, I understand so much more about her—the glumness and air of disappointment, the look in her eyes that always suggested a fear that the other shoe was about to drop. "Should we say anything to the police?"

"Yeah, you should mention Taylor when you give your statement tomorrow, but I bet they're halfway to figuring it out. Tori helped you get away, so she might have even come clean."

I bring my hands to my face and press them against my eyes, being careful not to touch my throbbing cheek. The muscles in my lower back ache, too, probably from the way I landed when Liam tackled me.

"You okay?" Sam asks.

"Yeah, but fried. I probably should try to get some sleep."

"What if I stay?"

I lower my hands and meet his eyes. I take a minute to think, but from the start I'm pretty sure of my response. As hard as it is to say no, I shake my head.

"Thank you, Sam," I say. "I appreciate the offer, but I think I'm going to pass."

"I wouldn't have to share a bed with you," he says. "I could sleep on the couch and just keep an eye out. I hate the idea of you being alone tonight."

"That's very thoughtful of you, but I'll be okay here."

He cocks his head and studies me with one eye squinted. "Is it because of Jamie? I know how guilty I feel on that front, so I'm sure you must, too."

"Yes, I do. Though I think I could come to terms with that in time. The bigger problem is that you're clearly seeing someone, and I can't just ignore that fact."

He nods. "Look, Kiki, I know our timing has been lousy so far, but I want to make this work between us. Yes, I've been seeing someone, but it's very casual, and I just need a little time to straighten things out with her."

And while I was waiting for him to straighten things out, would I be hoping for the phone to ring, like I've been doing constantly over the past days, wondering where he was and who he was with and when he'd finally surface? I've begun to worry that being with Sam could mean lots of frustration in the short run, and real heartache down the road.

"Sam, I wish it could work out with us, too," I say. "I feel even more strongly about you than I did months ago. But I now see that some of the very things that attracted me to you could spell doom for the two of us. I love that, for a guy who spends a lot of time with numbers, you're kind of a free spirit. You don't like being pinned down. But I need something more stable in my life right now, especially after everything that's happened."

He looks off, pressing his lovely fingers lightly against his mouth, and then glances back at me. "I have to respect how you feel, Kiki. But I think you might have the wrong read on me, and I wish I could change your mind."

I manage a small smile. "Maybe we can talk about it some more after a little time has passed."

Once we've said our goodbyes and Sam leaves, I double-check all the locks and head upstairs. Fortunately, I'm so utterly exhausted, I fall asleep instantly.

33

I arrive back in New York the next day at around noon. After dropping off my suitcase and tote bags at my apartment, I return the rental car, buy groceries, and take a stroll along the East River. I need the exercise—I'd gotten next to none in Connecticut—but I also thought that a walk would help me feel grounded in the city again. And it does. After days of endless fields and barns and silos, it's good to gaze across at the Queens skyline and watch tugboats pull barges along the sparkling gray river.

When I'd called Megan on the drive home, she offered to fix me dinner, but I asked if she'd mind coming to my apartment tonight instead, explaining that I'd feel better in my own little cocoon. Which is true, but I also wanted to make sure it was just the two of us. I like

Colin, her live-in boyfriend, a lot, but I'm not up for a group conversation.

Besides, there's something I need to ask Megan alone, without anyone else in the room. Something about Jamie.

She arrives at my place at six thirty on the dot. I'd given her a partial update from the car, but as soon as I've poured us each a glass of wine and she has her legs tucked beneath her on the couch, I fill in the remaining gaps.

"Will you have to go back up there anytime soon?" she asks, looking concerned. "I mean, because of the case?"

"I gave the police an official statement before I left today. Then I guess it all depends on whether Tori and Liam plead not guilty and the case goes to trial. But surely if that happens, it won't be for at least a year. As for Taylor, when I brought him up today, the cops didn't look surprised, so they might have already figured it all out. I guess if the DNA definitely points to him, he would be taken into custody in Florida and extradited to Connecticut."

"Wow, so there's still a lot up in the air."

I nod, then excuse myself and fetch the rotisserie chicken I bought earlier and set it on the table next to a simple green salad, a baguette, and a large, decadent wedge of Brie. Since it seems we've talked about nothing other than me lately, I beg Megan over dinner for details about her own life these days. She shares some news about her parents and sister and also tells me about a trip to Costa Rica she and Colin are planning for November. But soon she's circling back to me.

"You must be so proud of yourself, Kiki," she says. "You ignored the doubters, me included, and worked like hell to make sure the truth eventually came out."

"Thanks for saying that, Meg—though there's one moment in all this that I'd prefer to forget."

"Explain, please."

"You're the only person I'd ever dare admit this to. There was a very brief period last night when I was thinking about Jess Nolan and how her story kept coming up again and again, and I actually wondered if Jamie might have been the one who murdered her."

She doesn't overreact—that wouldn't be Megan— but I see her eyes widen a little. "Okay, tell me why you think your mind went there."

I rest my elbows on the table and my chin in my hands, staring out the window.

"I found out that he knew Jess Nolan through some volunteer work he did. I'm never going to know whether they were just friendly or actually dated, but he told Sam that he'd never met her, and he definitely never mentioned her to me. Plus, Percy West had told me Jamie was looking for forgiveness and that he needed to pay for his sins. That added to my concerns."

She cocks her head. "Kiki, over the past days, you've had a lot of weird and conflicting information coming at you, and you had to sort through it all. No wonder that idea popped into your head."

"Fine, I'll let myself off the hook with your permission, but I'm still wondering if there was some side of Jamie I never saw. *Did* he need to be forgiven for something? There were times during our relationship when Jamie seemed preoccupied or worried, but claimed to be fine, and I wondered if he was troubled by things I didn't know about."

"Let's unpack this one detail at a time," she says after several beats. "First, Jamie not coming clean about knowing the murdered girl. Since we're sure he *didn't* kill her, he obviously had some other reason for not admitting it to Sam. He might have been embarrassed to tell Sam he dated someone as young as Jess—and someone who worked at the club, where it was probably a no-no."

"Okay."

"As for Percy, as I told you, she seems to be suffering from some kind of disorder. She probably said those things about Jamie to get a rise out of you, make you think less of him."

"Really?"

"Yes. I wouldn't take anything she said seriously. Even if Jamie *had* done something for which he needed forgiveness, he certainly wouldn't have told her after a couple of dates." She takes a quick bite of salad and then sets her fork back on her plate. "And finally, *all* of us have sides of ourselves we never reveal to others, even the people we care about most."

"But in Jamie's case, what could it have been?"

"Well, he lost both his parents when he was relatively young, and he probably felt heartbroken about it but didn't want to burden anyone. And I know this might be surprising, but he might have found it tough always turning on that charm people expected from him—family, friends, and clients alike."

"Right," I say, nodding. "And, who knows, maybe he even sensed my ambivalence, but didn't dare raise the topic."

"Yeah, that's possible, too," Megan says, smiling wanly. "The bottom line is that we can never completely know our romantic partners, and we just have to accept that. It's one of the mysteries that comes with living—and one of the risks that comes with loving someone."

"Thanks," I say.

What she's also saying is that dwelling on it is a futile task, and I need to let it go.

We clear the dishes and I carry a bowl of clementines out to the living room along with some chocolate chip cookies and a bottle of sparkling water.

"So, do you want to tell me about Sam now?" Megan asks.

"Why don't we table that for the moment," I say. "Talking about him just makes me think about him more, and I'm pretty sure it's over and done with."

We split a clementine and devour a few cookies, and then it's time to hug goodbye. I thank her profusely for being here tonight. After she leaves, I pour myself a fresh glass of sparkling water and plop onto the couch with my feet on the coffee table.

Despite how weary and sad I am, Megan's comment—that I should be proud of myself—echoes in my head. I guess I *am* proud. I stuck with my mission, and I didn't let Drew or anyone else intimidate me.

And for the first time I have the sense that the kind of confidence I had in my midtwenties, before R assaulted me, is fully within reach. Yes, I'd regained some self-possession when I finally moved out of HR—the field I fled to in a state of panic—but trying on a new career and then starting my own business have often been super stressful. I've second-guessed myself plenty of times, like I did on a couple of those Zooms in New Burford.

The time has come to silence my doubts and take some bigger risks. Over the next days and weeks, I'm going to regain my focus during Zoom sessions and sign as many new clients as possible. I also want to follow a few leads I have for more corporate training work. And I'm going to email the book proposal to the agent I met at Ava's.

On the personal front, I decide, I'm going to finally fix up my apartment as well as schedule a trip to Phoenix to see my mom. Maybe I'll even summon the nerve to download a dating app and try it out.

As I consider whether I can keep my eyes open through a TV show, my phone rings, and to my surprise, Sam's name is on the screen. I honestly didn't think I'd hear from him this soon, if at all.

"Hope it's not too late," he says when I answer.

"No, no, I'm still up."

"You got back okay?"

"Yeah, thanks. And I just had a nice catch-up with a girlfriend."

"I wanted to fill you in on a few details I heard—all from Vic, who spoke to Drew. The guy is shattered, just as we'd expected, but he's also angry as hell and wants justice for Jamie. It's early days, of course, but it sounds like Tori might take some kind of plea deal, that she's not covering for either Liam or Taylor anymore—

and yes, it's looking like it must have been Taylor who killed Jess."

"We were right, then."

"Here's something else: Taylor has already moved once since he's been in Florida and there's a rumor that he might have gotten in trouble with the law in Fort Myers, the first place he lived."

I shiver. "God, that's awful to contemplate."

"It seems his mother is only willing to go so far to protect him."

"I appreciate the update, Sam. But there's still one big unanswered question. How was Liam able to fake the suicide so effectively?"

"Vic pointed out that Liam was in the military years ago and knows about guns. And apparently you can fake gunpowder residue with ash so maybe that's what he did. He was a smoker, right?"

"Yeah. Poor Jamie, he must have let Liam into the car thinking there was just some minor matter to discuss."

"I know. I can't imagine what he thought in that brief moment when he saw the gun. . . . Just one more thing you'll want to know. Percy is out on bail, but she's still facing charges."

I sigh. "Hopefully she'll get some psychological help, too."

"Maybe. I'll let you know if I hear anything else."

"Are you still in Connecticut?"

"Yeah, for now."

"Well, enjoy."

I feel a pang, thinking of what it would be like to be with him there, in that lovely cottage, waking to the smell of pine trees and the sound of birds.

"Before I let you go," Sam says, "there's someone who wants to say hi to you."

"Are you with Vic and Ava?" I ask, confused. He hadn't indicated anyone else was present.

"No, it's not them."

A couple of moments of silence follow, and the next thing I hear is a snuffing sound. Either it's a pig rooting for truffles or a dog sniffing the phone.

"Wait, is that a dog?"

"Yeah."

"You have a dog now?"

"Not *any* dog. Maverick."

I can't believe what I'm hearing, and I nearly start to cry. "Oh, Sam, that's so wonderful."

"I knew you'd learned he'd been adopted, but I didn't want to tell you it was me until it was a sure thing."

"Were you afraid it wouldn't go through for some reason?"

"A little." He chuckles lightly. "I figured there was a chance I might be disqualified for being a 'free spirit.'"

I can't help but laugh out loud. "Well, I'm glad it all worked out in the end."

"Anyway, I'm coming back to New York on Monday. What if I brought him over to say hi?"

I hesitate. I'd told myself I needed to get Sam out of my head once and for all, and yet I can't pass up the chance to see Maverick again.

"Okay," I finally say.

"Five o clock?"

"Sure."

"You see what I'm trying to show you, right?"

"That you're more of a dog lover than I ever knew?"

"No, that I'm easier to pin down than you think."

I smile to myself. "See you then."

After hanging up, I lean back against the couch and gaze out the window across the room. There are now long, gorgeous swaths of pink, red, and yellow in the sky, left by the setting sun. I feel an unexpected sense of contentment from being back in my apartment with some plans for the fall.

What about Sam, though?

Even thinking about him leads to a twinge of guilt. If Jamie were alive, I'd never pursue things. But he's not here and so I wouldn't be causing him any pain if Sam and I become a couple. And as I told Sam, I feel I could get beyond my guilt in time.

But would I be able to count on him in the long run?

Megan said earlier that love is about risk, and risk is what I preach to clients all the time—and I hope to take more of them myself. But I also warn clients that there are smart risks and dumb ones, and it's essential to know the difference. I insist they need to ask themselves what benefit might result from a decision, and also what harm.

So I guess that's what I need to do with Sam Morgan—figure out if he'd be a totally dumb risk for me to take on.

Or, maybe, a smarter one than I think.

Acknowledgments

I'd like to offer a huge thank you to everyone who generously allowed me to interview them as part of my background research for *The Last Time She Saw Him*. Part of the fun of writing fiction is making things up, but when it matters, I want to get the facts right, and these wonderful sources helped make sure of that: Susan Brune, Brune Law; Barbara Butcher, consultant for forensic and medicolegal investigations and author of *What the Dead Know*; Paul Paganelli, MD; Joyce Hanshaw, retired captain from the Hunterdon County (New Jersey) Prosecutor's Office; Trooper First Class Sarah Salerno, Connecticut State Police; Liz Bentley, executive coach and author of the upcoming *Escape the Complacency Trap*; Eliot Kaplan, career coach; James White; Cheryl Brown; Betsy Fitzgerald; Richard Furlaud; and Elias Isaac.

Thank you, as well, to my awesome editor, Emily Griffin, who, per usual, was such an enormous help on the book and also an absolute pleasure to work with. In addition, I'm incredibly grateful to the entire team I'm involved with at Harper, including Amy Baker, Lisa Erickson, Heather Drucker, Robin Bilardello, and Stacey Fischkelta.

A huge thank you, as well, to my agent, Kathy Schneider, of the Jane Rotrosen Agency. You are an amazing advisor, editor, listener, brainstormer, and cheerleader, all of which means so much to me. I'm very, very glad ours paths finally intertwined in this way.

And then there's my own personal team: website editor Laura Nicolassy Cocivera; social media manager Imani Seymour; and website tech director and designer Bill Cunningham. I'm so lucky to have you.

Finally, to my readers: Thank you for all your terrific support over the years. Man, I'm so grateful to you. This is my eighteenth suspense novel, and some of you have been with me from the very beginning, from that very first Bailey Weggins mystery (and yes, she'll be back). If you have the chance, I'd love to hear from you on Facebook or Instagram or both. And it would be a real rush for me to meet you in person one day. Just check my website, katewhite.com, for where my book tour will take me.

About the Author

Kate White is the *New York Times* bestselling author of ten stand-alone psychological thrillers, including *Between Two Strangers*, *The Second Husband*, and *The Fiancée*, as well as eight Bailey Weggins mysteries, including *Such a Perfect Wife*, which was nominated for an International Thriller Writers Award. The former editor in chief of *Cosmopolitan* magazine, Kate is also the editor of *The Mystery Writers of America Cookbook*. She has been published in over thirty countries worldwide. To learn more about Kate, visit her website: www.katewhite.com.